1200

NO
MAN
IN
THE
HOUSE

NO MAN IN THE HOUSE

CECIL FOSTER

ONE WORLD

**BALLANTINE
BOOKS
NEW YORK**

A One World Book
Published by Ballantine Books

Library of Congress Cataloging-in-Publication Data
Foster, Cecil.
    No man in the house / Cecil Foster.
    —1st American ed.   p.   cm.
    "A One World Book"—T.p. verso
    ISBN: 0-345-38067-3
    I. Title.
PR9199.3.F572N6   1992
813'.54—dc20   92–53189
                                                   CIP

Design by Holly Johnson

Manufactured in the United States of America

First American Edition: October 1992

10 9 8 7 6 5 4 3 2 1

Dedicated to
Munyonzwe and Michello

NO
MAN
IN
THE
HOUSE

It was early morning. Sweat was already running down my back and over my face, cold and sticky, causing the heavy khaki shirt to cling to my back. As we stood in rows at the back of the school, the boys around me were wiping their faces or fanning themselves with white handkerchiefs. Despite repeated warnings from Mr. Allen, our class teacher, I did not have a 'kerchief. I could not afford one. I had noticed how the men fixing the tar roads under the hot midday sun kept the perspiration out of their eyes; I not only admired but wished to emulate them. In the little village of Lodge Road, these were the only people that worked all year, with the possible exception of the domestic servants. Not only did they have work between the harvests of sugar cane but they were employed by the government, which apart from guaranteeing a pay cheque every Friday, made them pensionable in their old age and provided them with privileges when they wanted to borrow money from the Vestry. Their small modest houses were painted every Christmas and had furniture in the front for visitors to sit on, particularly when members of Pastor Allsop's church held prayer meetings at them. Their children slept in beds, not on rags on the floor like my two brothers and me. Picturing the men in my mind, I dragged an index finger across my brow and, with one smooth action, snapped the finger against the others, sending the oily perspiration scattering into the dry dusty earth of the schoolyard, just like the men patching the hot tar roads.

Quietly, I shuffled my bare feet in the dust, taking care not to hurt my blind toe but hoping to ease its throbbing pain.

"What happen that you wiggling so, like some worm?" Oliver Mayers, next to me, whispered under his breath. Oliver was the oldest of the forty-three boys in Class One C and was my best friend. None of the boys would pick on me when Ollie was around, for not only was he the best fighter but he also knew more of the village gossip than we did. We were too young to stand under the street lamp at nights and listen to the men talking. But Ollie was old enough and he filled us in on the details, enjoying his superior position.

"You don't know how bad this big toe cutting my arse today, Ollie boy," I answered, resting for a moment from the constant shuffling. "It's giving me licks like fire, man. Pure licks."

"Not as hot as what Toppin will give you if he catches you hoppin' 'bout like some rabbit with its foot broken," Oliver answered. "You better try and keep yourself quiet. Better still, why don't you ask Mr. Allen to excuse you and go to the toilet and cool off the foot with some pipe water? I do that myself when I got a bad foot that's hurting all the time."

Grandmother had told me the toe was as blind as a mouse, for it was impossible to stop me from crashing the lame and exposed limb into some object every time I moved. For either the toe was blind or I was, Grandmother had reasoned.

Already this morning I had banged the unfortunate toe against a stone half-buried in the track across the grass pasture. The pain had forced me to hop all the way to school, and even as I stood in the assembly line before the day's prayers, it continued to ache.

As usual, my two brothers and I had left home late and had to rush to make it to school on time. Ambling along slowly, we heard the school bell ringing in the distance as if confirming we had not learned anything from the painful floggings Mr. Toppin dished out every morning to the late arrivals. The sound of the bell was a signal for us to break into a run—that and the presence of Everick Waite. This good-for-nothing man, Grandmother said, was our sworn enemy, and he liked to hide in the grass with a pile of stones, no doubt meant for us. Grandmother gave him the name Brutus for obvious reasons; it stuck and spread throughout the village, shaming him and putting us in mortal fear of his straight aim with a stone. As Grandmother would tell us, drinking and harassing people were the only things Brutus did well and we should always be on the lookout for him. In truth, we knew that Everick Waite turned against us after our Aunt Pretty spat at him from the safety of a crowd when he tried to get too friendly with her; he had sworn that he would eventually get even. Everyone in the village had talked about Pretty's rebuke and how Everick Waite promised to come in the middle of the night to drive us out of the little shack that cast a blight on his sister's bigger house next door. We pretended not to know this side of the story, but nonetheless we remained in constant fear of the bully who seemed to get no greater pleasure than when he was armed with stones.

Clang! Clang! Clang! The sound echoed down Water Street, greeting us as we turned the corner from the unpaved plantation cart road onto the main highway. Every morning at nine o'clock, the head boy would stand on the high cement steps in front of the school. As usual, he was smartly dressed in the prescribed school uniform—a navy blue cotton shirt and khaki pants, a big neat part in his hair—as he vigorously rang the bell for three fleeting minutes. Clang! Clang! Clang! It pealed out rhythmically, spreading the message around the village while the ringer sweated under the warm tropical sun.

Mr. Toppin had sent us home the day before with a stern warning. He expected every one of us to be early for the ceremony initiating the new principal. He wanted all of us well dressed, wearing our uniforms. I didn't have a navy blue cotton shirt, so I had to wear my faded khaki shirt and run the risk of being singled out. On top of that, neither I nor my brothers possessed the handkerchief that was as mandatory as the school uniform and which had to be produced for inspection every morning. For those reasons, we didn't want any confrontation with Mr. Toppin.

"I don't want any of you running in here at the last minute, shirt tail flapping behind, like some bunch of vagabonds," the out-going headmaster had warned the assembled school before the evening prayers and dismissal. "Otherwise, I'd have to use my strap for the last."

Mr. Toppin had said repeatedly that the heavy leather strap in his desk drawer—which he never hesitated to use—was the only thing that kept all of us out of Dodd's, the government reform school for young delinquents. Every one of the seven hundred and thirty boys on the school register had been flogged by him more than once. There was a reason for these beatings, he said. "This is a duty that every parent should give me thanks for," he was fond of saying. "At least I save them from having to spend their money running down to the police station in Oistins every week, or looking for lawyer money." Not that he liked wasting his strength on hard-backed young men, but he had to try to keep us out of trouble, away from Dodd's and a life of crime. It was well known across the island of Barbados that the villages around Christ Church Boys' Elementary had provided more than their fair share of inmates for Dodd's and Glendairy, the prison for the adults who graduated from the reform school. Mr. Toppin's job was to ensure that few of us followed their example. His attitude was that people like us would always need someone in authority, who knew better, to constantly point us in the right direction. That was why he would not be part of this independence foolishness sweeping the island. Because he could not support the government in rushing head-long into such madness, he had no choice but to resign from the civil service so he could speak out in opposition forcefully, if he so desired, at a later date.

Now we were restlessly and anxiously waiting in line.

"Tell me though, Ollie, what you think about the new headmaster we getting now?" I asked. "You hear anything?"

"You mean Bradshaw?"

"Yeah, I think that's his name. What you think 'bout him?"

"I don't have to think nothing," Ollie answered sternly. "What I know is that he does beat real, real bad, too. I hear he does keep a big leather strap soaking in a bucket of water in the office just waiting to let loose the dog on some poor body."

That frightened all of the boys within hearing distance. What Oliver was telling us was cause for worry. True, we were happy to see Mr. Toppin leave, but deep in our hearts we were beginning to have second thoughts. If Ollie was right, this new headmaster could be worse; none of us would admit it, but we had grown accustomed to Mr. Toppin and were sad he was leaving. We dreaded the unknown.

"Well, I don't know about the rest of you," Grantley said, joining the conversation. "But if he ever raises a hand at me, I'll tell my father. And you know my father, he don't make no sport when he gets ready. He can be real ignorant."

Grantley was standing behind us with Carl at his side. The four of us lived only houses apart and we often played together. We had moved through the infants' school together and were now stranded in the stream reserved for all slow learners. In another five years we would be out on the streets, if we were lucky enough to survive in school for that long. Soon, we would go through the formality of sitting through the Common Entrance Examination to find out if we deserved a scholarship and free education at any of the island's posh grammar schools. This would be the biggest test of our lives, one that could dramatically change our futures if we were successful. Nevertheless, although we knew the day was coming and that we should start preparing for it, we weren't bothered about the exam or our prospects.

Nobody, including ourselves, gave us any chance of passing the examination. The teachers didn't even try to do more than teach us how to read and to do a few simple arithmetic sums—certainly not enough to pass the examination. More attention was given to the students in the A and B streams, who would have a chance of passing the examination. We were tolerated as the group from which came the future cane cutters, fishermen, masons, carpenters, and, if we were lucky, road crew men. Most of the days we spent in the school kitchen garden, growing vegetables and learning to fork and fertilize the ground. Twice a week, we would march into the trades room to learn to measure, saw, and plane wood, or to make and glue together pieces of furniture. Occasionally the headmaster, accompanied by his strap, made unannounced visits to the room, not to help the teacher educate us but to keep us in line.

"Remember the last time Toppin hit me and I went home and told me mother?" Grantley recalled. "She said she didn't like it one bit, that she didn't send me and my little brother to school for some headmaster that doesn't even know anything 'bout us to wale up our skin. She then tells my father that he should do something 'bout all this ill-treatment we receiving and my father said the next time he will. I hear him say so with my own ears and all of you know how ignorant my father can get. Remember the time he beat up that policeman and he had to go to court and pay money?"

"What you think your father could do if the new headmaster hit you?" Ollie sneered. Like most of us, he didn't have a father to protect him.

"Lick in his ass, nuh!" Grantley shot back, raising his voice slightly. "You think my father's frightened or something? I ain't like the rest of you, not like Howard here who ain't got no father to defend him so that anybody can pick on him and his two brothers."

They looked at me and I had that feeling of embarrassment again.

"I ain't the one to talk 'bout," I respond sternly. "My Grandmother did tell me only yesterday evening that my mother and father in England will soon send for me and my two brothers. She got another letter from them yesterday. So I don't have to worry about no new headmaster 'cause I hear in England you can't go around beating up the people's children. Not unless you want a piece o' jail."

"What England you talking about?" Grantley jeered. "I'm getting real tired hearing you talk all the time about soon going here and the next place and then I don't see you go nowhere."

"Don't mind that," I shot back bitterly. My one defense was under attack and I couldn't allow that to happen. Going to England was my solution to all that ailed, hurt, and frightened me. In my heart, I knew it was only a matter of time before I escaped from the island; I knew that everyone else in the class was jealous because they would never get the opportunity to live in England.

"And besides, my mother done tell me England ain't no big thing anymore," Grantley said. "You ain't see that even Mr. Ward's big daughter come back here from England to live? And them is white people that could get in England real easy. England ain't no big thing anymore and nobody really wants to go up there. It ain't like it's in America."

I was stumped. That was the talk of the village. Why had Miss Ward come back to the island? A woman who had all the privileges, connections, and money to be successful in England had given up on the mother country. We turned to look at the big great house on the hill among the trees. The white house with the red top, the early morning sun shimmering off it, overlooked the surrounding villages and Christ Church Boys' Elementary School. According to Ollie, even her father, the most powerful politician in Christ Church, if not Barbados, couldn't understand what his daughter was doing.

"You're an idiot, man," I said. "You don't know anything."

"Do I hear somebody talking down this line here?" Mr. Allen was suddenly moving between us and slapping the side of the board rule in the palm of his hand. He was a tall slim man with a short scraggly beard. In our books, Mr. Allen was a softie, not to be feared, as he didn't like to beat and we knew we could get away with a lot. He was young and friendly, not like the older teachers, not like Mr. Burton and Mr. Hopkins, or Mr. Downes, or Mr. Timson, who were always walking around with a strap or a piece of dried bamboo. We liked Mr. Allen. If a boy came to school and didn't have any lunch, or his parents couldn't afford to give him a new exercise book or a pencil, Mr. Allen would get him one.

"Remember, I don't want to hear one whisper when you go into the hall," Mr. Allen said, raising his voice. He made a quick turn at the front of our class to review us. "I won't hesitate to use this ruler here or to pack off this whole class to the headmaster for a good flogging. So don't push me this bright morning."

The class to our right was making its way into school and then it would be our turn. My toe wasn't much better. It would probably throb for the entire day, particularly if I had to stand for a long time. But I had more than the toe to worry about, namely the things Ollie and Grantley had said.

2

It was dark inside the building; my eyes never adjusted readily to the shock after the bright sunlight, and usually I would have cloudy sight for most of the day. As I tried to adjust my eyes, I saw the Queen, with her crown of jewels and looking no more than a teenager, sitting proudly on a chair, hands folded across her chest, looking down on us from the framed picture. She was the only one who seemed to be smiling. No matter where I stood in the hall, she appeared to be looking at me. Sometimes in the middle of the Lord's prayer, I would open my eyes and see her staring, as if encouraging me to flout the regulations that said prayers had to be spoken with clasped hands and closed eyes. In a separate picture, her husband Philip, the Duke of Edinburgh, an older man with a sharp nose, was standing holding the silver top of a sword swinging from a holster at his side. There was less of a smile on his face, or maybe it was his long pointed nose that made him look too serious. Either way, his smile looked forced.

All around me, I could feel change. During the long vacation and especially in the three weeks that we had been back at school, the older boys had been teasing us, telling us that life would be getting tougher, that we would be getting a new headmaster. They said that every new headmaster had to establish his authority and the surest and quickest way was for him to be ruthless with the students—and the teachers as well, if necessary.

These thoughts raced through my head as I leaned against one of the green painted wooden poles that ran from the roof to the floor of the main school.

Sitting on the platform were Reverend Weekes, the regional education officer, Mr. Toppin, and a host of white government officials, some of whom we had not seen before. Also present were two members for the House of Assembly, Mr. Ward and Leslie Jones.

In the center of the platform at the table under the pictures of the Royal couple sat a short black man in a British army blazer, the only black man among the brown skin and white faces. He looked out of place, and he appeared to be feeling the uneasiness, saying little to anyone, but simply surveying the crowd below him as if he were seeking a recognizable face in the audience.

I guessed that this stranger was to be our new headmaster. According to the older boys, the new man would be black, for he had gone to Christ Church Boys' and had lived in the area as a boy. His name was Bradshaw, and the rumor was that he was a strict disciplinarian, a soldier from the Second World War. Still, the man sitting there, slightly apart from the others, didn't look like a headmaster to me.

As usual, I was frightened by what was happening. In fact, I spent most of my time frightened by one thing or another. Standing there in the hot building with so many bodies crammed together, the fan overhead moving in slow motion and providing no relief from the stuffiness, I could feel the sweat pouring out of me. Having to stand for almost an hour, dead still, not talking, was pure torture, especially with an aching toe. Frequently, there would be a loud crash. Then a momentary interruption as three or four of the bigger students lifted the wilted, exhausted body and took it outside to get some fresh air. Once or twice it happened to me; my eyes went black and my knees wobbled.

I hated this building, and every morning while standing by the pole I would think of giving it a good shake, to see if it would collapse, the same way Samson in the Bible had destroyed the temple in anger. That was one way of ending the torture and everything else. But unlike Samson, I wasn't quite that strong and not ready to die in the rubble.

On a day like this, precedence fell to the regional education officer, a tall white man who drove a big noisy eight-cylinder Ford Zephyr. He was an Englishman who had come out to the colonies some time ago and had been appointed as a type of superintendent by a former governor, a personal friend from England. His job was to visit the schools in the Southern District of the island and to make sure they were following the teaching curriculum that was sent out from England every September. Over the years, he had built up a permanent tan on his face, arms, and legs. Even after his friend the governor had been recalled and knighted for his services long ago, he didn't see the need to return home to England, although he never hesitated to tell us how much he missed the theater and cultural life of London. He also enjoyed lecturing us on the pride of public school students in Britain, children we were supposed to emulate.

The Officer—none of us knew his name—was standing at the center of the table with Mr. Toppin to his right and the short black man to his left. He cleared his throat, and we promptly settled into a heavy silence, not even shuffling our feet anymore. Mr. Toppin smiled broadly; we were not letting him down. This was the kind of quiet he liked, where he could hear a pin drop at the farthest part of the room or distinctly make out who was coughing. Beads of sweat were on his forehead. Dressed in his white shirt and black tie, he looked young, too young for retirement.

The Officer took off his white cork hat and placed it on the table in front of him.

"My dear students," he began in a broad strident English accent; each word was carefully and slowly enunciated. "We are here this morning to, shall we say, have a changing of the guard. We have here a man who has served with great honor and distinction in the armed forces of Britain, our beloved mother country. He is the kind of person with that type of selflessness that our beloved Sir Winston Churchill himself talked about. You should be honored to have him as your new headmaster and, I say, we should all welcome him with loud applause."

The Officer looked at the new headmaster and started clapping. Immediately, the invited guests joined in and slowly the rest of the school followed. All eyes were focused on the short black man, who, although smiling, again looked out of place. Slowly the clapping subsided, but the smile on the black man's face lingered, almost deviously. The Officer continued to talk, telling us how we should safeguard the legacy that Mr. Toppin was leaving us, that we should make sure that the ever-growing demand on the ministry's budget was not misplaced, and that we should all strive to be good British subjects, willing to defend the Empire and the Commonwealth and the Christian principles they stood for.

"Here, here!" Mr. Ward stood in the center of the stage and applauded. "What you say couldn't be more correct in these troubled and confusing times, sir, when people who should know better, who call themselves political leaders, keep putting a lot of strange ideas in people's heads." We all applauded, too. The new headmaster continued to smile benignly.

The Officer's voice wafted over the gathering and after a while I had trouble following what he was saying. Between comprehending the strange accent and trying to understand the big words, I was soon lost and my mind drifted back to the past summer holidays.

The usual game playing and summer fun had been painfully interrupted by the death of Duhdah, my mother's father. Unfortunately, my brothers and I hadn't had the chance to spend the usual four weeks of the vacation with our mother's family. This had been a grave disappointment, for we always looked forward to spending time away from Lodge Road and to returning with bags full of guavas, soursops, Bajan cherries, sweet tamarinds, and a quarter or so in our pockets. Sweet tamarinds that didn't edge the teeth were a rarity on the island,

and the boys of the village always went easy on us until our supplies of the fruit ran out. In addition, my mother's parents lived just outside Bridgetown, and to get there we had to pass through the city by bus. The ride was worth it and something we could brag about later.

This year we had no bargaining clout. As a rule, Grandmother never gave us pocket money. She argued that we were never in need of anything but the basic plate of food she provided once a day, and the clothes on our backs. Often both were in short supply, and our pants had to be patched and darned several times over. Sometimes patches were sewn on older patches. In any case, she was a huckster, going from house to house selling mangoes and oranges, nuts and sweets, the kind of things we would spend the pocket money on anyway. She felt it was wiser that we pay her the money and keep the few coppers—as she called all money that wasn't in paper—within the family.

It was different with Duhdah, for he was the kindest and friendliest person I had ever met. I would sit for hours on his carpenter's workbench while he built the side of a house or repaired the wheel of a donkey cart or half-soled a shoe. He liked to regale me with funny stories of when he was a boy and couldn't go to certain areas of the island because he wasn't white; and about my mother, whom I couldn't remember, except for the larger-than-life images building in my mind and the framed black-and-white pictures of her in Grandmother's house. I thirsted for information about her. Was she gentle and loving or did she like to beat bad like some mothers? Enthusiastically, I asked him every and any type of question, trying to fill in the holes left by our absent parents. He would laugh pleasantly at the queries and keep me entertained and informed.

But eventually, he always noticed the forlorn look on my face from missing my mother and father and would bribe me out of my sorrow with a sweetened carbonated drink. "Come with me, boy, and let's go over there to Mrs. Hammond's shop and buy a cold drink," he would say, giving the signal for me to jump from the carpenter's bench in preparation for the short walk to the shop. He would tell me how wonderful life would be when I got to England, and of the nice Englishmen he had worked for in Bridgetown. He said the English were the fairest people on the earth; they could always be taken at their word and that was why God had blessed them with so many territories and islands.

But Duhdah wasn't always in such a mood, and I wondered sometimes if his feelings about England were genuine or if he was saying these things just to make me feel better. Sometimes he got angry with my mother for leaving and forgetting us.

He would pause and escape into his thoughts, planing a piece of board with a heavy, clumsy-looking wooden instrument, the type Joseph always seemed to be using in Bible pictures.

"Young children like you and your two brothers need a mother to look after them, to take care of them. You and your brothers are only children, and every child should be with his mother," he said, the veins in his neck and arms bulging as he strained to push the plane across the piece of wood. "It's okay if the father runs 'long 'bout his business. But things different with a mother. You's the youngest one, a little dot that ain't lost your mother's features yet, and you need care and attention. I mean, you only got to just look at all these cuts on your two feet, like you served in the Boer War or something, to see what I'm saying. No little boy should have all them cuts and sores. But the Lord knows what he's doing and he always promises to look after the little children if nobody else will, so I left you in his safe hands. I can only pray for that when the night comes."

When he talked like that I felt uneasy, mostly because it reminded me of the strain between the two sides of our family. Grandmother always claimed that my mother was no good and that she had trapped my father by saddling him with three children, then chasing him to London when he tried to escape. For their part, my mother's family would wonder aloud about what mum saw in our father in the first place.

My brothers and I always felt that we were caught in the middle. Fortunately, Duhdah never got caught up in the intra-family rows and never made us choose which side we should come down on. But we knew that our mother's and father's families didn't trust each other.

"Things will change," he said repeatedly. "Things will be different when the people on this island wake up and realize that they don't have to go anywhere to make a life for themselves. Barbados is where they were born and where they should die. We are of a proud African heritage, good enough to rule ourselves." And just as quickly, he would snap out of his mood, probably seeing the confusion it was creating for me.

The last time I saw Duhdah was near the end of the last school term. I had come home from school and found him sitting in Grandmother's best Morris chair. When I came through the door, he jokingly teased me for not coming home properly dressed, but with my shirt tail flying about. "Your father would never do that. He was a real style Doutes, a real saga boy. He really liked his clothes and wouldn't walk the streets unless he was well dressed. You ain't nothing like him, yuh."

Grandmother smiled and I hastily started tucking the shirt tail into my pants. They laughed loudly and he reached out and grabbed me. We hugged.

"What did you do at school today? You learn anything?"

"No."

"No," he echoed, feigning astonishment at such an answer. "Why you warming up the people's school bench if you ain't learning nothing when the day come? Don't you know you gotta start opening up your brain if you want to learn something?"

"I didn't mean that," I said, trying to clarify the answer. "I mean that . . . that I didn't learn anything new. That we did some sums and things like that, that's all."

"Sometimes I wish Howard learned school work as well as he learns the songs on the radio," Grandmother said. "He only gotta hear somebody singing a song one time and he done catch on to the words. Just so."

"That's true?" Duhdah said, still refusing to get serious. "You is a singer and dancer, boy? Well, in that case you better show me what you can do."

"No," I said shyly.

"Come on, Howard, you can sing 'Jean and Dinah,' " Grandmother said. "What them words is now? You sing them all the time. 'Jean and Dinah, Rosetta and Clementina. 'Round the corner posing, dah dah dah.' " She improvised the ending with the final words of the popular calypso, " 'Working for the Yankee dollar.' "

"Nah," I said, getting down off Duhdah's lap and rising to the bait. "You don't sing it like that."

"Well, you know, I ain't another Mighty Sparrow, the Calypso king of the world, like you. So you show me how," she said.

With that I started singing, softly at first and terribly off key, my hands covering my mouth, and finally racing through the last words. That was good enough for Duhdah.

"Boy, you is a real good singer. The best I ever heard in all my born days. Like I gotta put you in a band or something. Now let me see the dancing."

"You gotta get music to dance," I protested half-heart-edly.

Grandmother took down the tambourine that sat on the shelf in the corner and began to slap it with the palm of her hand. I started to wriggle, my hands swinging at the sides, doing the twist, the new dance I had copied from the boys at school.

"That's real good, boy. Now let me see you limbo, let me

see how far down you can go," he encouraged, casting an approving glance in Grandmother's direction. Eventually, I couldn't bend any further without hurting my back or toppling over, so I gave up and came around to stand in front of him. Grandfather fished into his pocket and gave me a coin.

"Go outside and play now. Me and Grandmother got some business we want to talk about alone. I'll see you before I go."

I kissed him and went into the back yard and through the broken gate in the paling, fingering the coin in my pocket.

Several weeks later, Grandmother took the three pairs of black pants that my brothers and I wore to Sunday school and ordered us to take the black shoes from under the bed and polish them. We didn't know why, but we suspected something was wrong from the whispers and hushed discussion. Grandmother had spent most of the early morning talking to our neighbors.

The news must have been dreadful for they shook their heads sadly and pondered some untold implications. It was only when Grandmother told us not to return to school after lunch the next day that we knew the reason. Duhdah had died, and we were going to the funeral. The night of the funeral, I gave my bed a good soaking, more than the usual, so much so that piss soaked my brothers, going through to the floor beneath us. It took almost all day in the sun to dry the bags and heavy cloth.

Reverend Weekes had finished blessing the school, the departing headmaster, and the new one. The education officer called on Mr. Toppin to say a few final words and then introduced Mr. Bradshaw to us. Nobody in the room stirred, perhaps because most of us were thoroughly dehydrated and ready to drop.

Finally, the officer called on Mr. Bradshaw to take charge by dismissing the school from the morning assembly.

"But of course we will have to give one of our finest renditions of our sweet and precious anthem, a song that is such an inspiration of loyalty and devotion for all of us so fortunate to be British subjects. A song that truly kept our soldiers going in the darkest days on the fronts of both the First and Second World Wars, as I am sure Mr. Bradshaw, our new headmaster, knows so much about. Mr. Burton, will you please lead us with the anthem."

Mr. Burton, the short bespectacled music teacher, had a wry sense of humor that was not on display at this solemn occasion. Before the announcement, it had been widely anticipated that as deputy headmaster, Mr. Burton would succeed Mr. Toppin. According to the village gossip and from what Ollie had heard under the street lamp, there was no doubt how disappointed Mr. Burton felt. He faced us and raised his hands. In one of them was a tuning fork, which he banged against the table and placed to his ear. We waited for his signal.

"Doh," he sang in a deep sonorous voice. "Doh. Doh. Doh." With each note he raised the pitch until he got it right. The education officer, Mr. Toppin, Mr. Bradshaw, Reverend Weekes, the parliamentarians and everyone, except Mr. Burton, turned from us and made an about-face to look at the Union Jack hanging limply from a short pole over the platform.

We burst into the anthem, our voices sounding like one, as Mr. Burton waved his hand slowly in time. I belted out my own rendition of "God Save Our Gracious Queen." Then we filed into our separate classes for another day of waiting, until Phillips, the head boy, rang the bell at three o'clock to end another school day.

In the months ahead, the pretentious show of unity on this day would evaporate, like the rains from a brief tropical shower on the parched earth. The country, and my own smaller world, was about to be turned upside down. None of us knew it at the time, but Mr. Bradshaw, and others like him, were to change things forever.

3

"Howard, get up and bring me that bottle of kerosene oil there in the kitchen," Grandmother called to me angrily from the back yard. "Alma didn't remember to put any oil in the blasted lamp this evening. Now the damn thing is sooting up like it's burning the wick and soon going out."

Alma was my youngest aunt, Grandmother's last daughter after Pretty; she was about fifteen years old. Her main daily duty was to refill the lamp with oil and to light it if darkness fell before Grandmother got home. This chore was entrusted to Alma because Pretty was usually at work until all of us had gone to sleep, and Grandmother didn't trust any of us with her precious lamp. But of late, Alma had other things on her mind and had been neglecting her duties. As soon as darkness fell, she would send me inside the house so she could bathe in the large galvanized tub in a corner of the yard. And after dressing and powdering her face, she would rush out of the house to be with those her age. Often she was gone before Grandmother got home to find me alone in the house and in darkness. Alma would be in such a hurry she would often not only ignore the lamp but also the dishes and pots from the evening meal. She was supposed to wash them and bring them into the house from the back yard where we ate. Most nights, even though she was tired, Grandmother ended up washing the dishes too, for she couldn't stomach the idea of leaving them overnight in the back yard, where they could attract ants, stray dogs, and rats.

Frequently, Grandmother grumbled that she didn't like the way Alma was turning out; she kept saying that she might have to put her hand to her again just to teach her one last lesson. But apart from talking, there wasn't much she could do. Mavis Thorpe, our next-door neighbor with whom Grandmother frequently talked over the paling, would tell her not to worry her head too much, that Alma was getting to be a young woman and would soon be taking her own ship out to sea.

"No amount of beating can change a young person's mind when set on a particular course," she advised Grandmother. "So it ain't no use bothering your head." All the same, Grandmother continued to worry, especially when she came home and found the lamp not well attended to.

"I don't know what to say 'bout that girl," Grandmother said, marching into the house and standing on the tips of her toes to reach for the tall imperial-looking glass lamp. It was impressive and majestic, sitting on the shelf in the corner above the table. "She's turning doltish or something. All night she's out there licking her mouth with people that ain't no good for her, that will only lead her astray. I just hope she don't bring home any trouble, 'cause the Lord knows I already got more than I can handle."

"More of what, Grandmother?" I asked.

"Trouble," she shouted. Placing the lamp on the floor, Grandmother knelt beside it and with the hem of her dress tried to unscrew the heated brassy-looking top with the burned wick. "That's what I'm talking 'bout, trouble. I just hope that Alma knows what she's doing."

"But what kind of trouble you talking 'bout?" I put the half-empty gallon bottle with the kerosene and an old rusting funnel with a broken handle beside her. Grandmother reached for them, letting the top with the wick hang over the side of the lamp.

"You don't worry 'bout that," she snapped. "They still got things in this world that you ain't ready to learn 'bout yet."

Alma had left school two years ago and still hadn't found a job, a fact that Grandmother never let her forget. Alma's argument was that work was difficult to find anywhere on the island and that none of the girls her age in the village were working anyway. This had no effect on Grandmother, and it didn't stop her from reminding Alma that when she was her age she had been working as a domestic servant for three years. It was a good way for any young girl to keep herself out of trouble.

"Here, Howard, hold this bottle for me while I clean off the lamp and put it back on the shelf." Grandmother handed the bottle to me again. Maybe it was because of the oil running down the sides, but the bottle slipped through my hands and fell to the floor. The foaming oil gushed out. I stared at it in bewilderment and dismay.

"Lord, looka this thing!" Grandmother cried. She snatched up the bottle to prevent more of the contents from spilling. "You see why I can't let any of you near my lamp!"

For the rest of the night, the house smelled of kerosene. For days, a large circle was imprinted on the floor where the oil had spilled. Grandmother would not let me or Alma forget why it was there.

"Lord, there goes Ma again," Grandmother said, turning away from the table and sniffing the air. "She and them bad-smelling cigars she does smoke. I think God did plan to make her a man in the first place but he made a mistake."

"But God don't make mistakes, Grandmother," I corrected. "You said so yourself."

"Boy, what's wrong with you? Why is it you always gotta examine in so much detail everything people say? You always taking what people say and examining every word inside out like you's some lawyer. You got to learn people say things one way and mean something else."

Ma was the oldest woman in Lodge Road and she lived alone in a little house on her acre of land near the rock quarry at the edge of the village. Her house was the last before the cane fields; this location away from everyone else and Ma's fondness for wearing only long white dresses lent an air of eccentricity to her doings, setting her apart from every other woman in the district.

"Where does Ma get them cigars to smoke from?" I asked.

"From Babsie Bourne's shop, when she's down there drinking the grog every night with the men and arguing stupidness about independence. I mean, she's old enough to be my mother, but if you'd only see her throwing back the liquors and carrying on in the shop with the rum drinkers, you'd think she was a young lamb. Lord knows I've never seen another woman like Ma."

The acrid smell of the cigar was getting stronger and we could hear the unsteady sounds of Ma dragging the cane behind her, or pausing to lean against it as the alcohol caused her to sway.

Everyone had heard the stories about Ma, of how she could hold her own drinking, smoking, and swearing with any man. As a younger woman, she had been known to come home late on Friday nights and toss out of the house the men she lived with from time to time. This was in an era when men routinely stamped their authority on the home by getting into drunken stupors on weekends and beating their wives. Ma did the beating in her house, and the drinking too. And she also raised two daughters, who Grandmother said turned out to be nothing like their mother, but who had become respectable married women and were living in town. Ma never had any use for the men who married her daughters, either.

Even in her advanced age, Ma was still capable of defending herself. When drunk, everything failed her but her memory. The next day, sober, she was capable of exacting painful revenge on whoever offended her. She was the only person in the village to own a gun and sometimes late at night she would stagger outside, line up an empty can and blast away. The fact that she rarely missed her targets reminded everyone how dangerous Ma could be if offended.

"Listen to her going down the road in that sad and sorry state," Grandmother said, lowering her voice conspiratorially, as if she expected Ma to stop in front of the house and listen. If she did, Grandmother certainly wouldn't want Ma to hear what she was saying.

"The only good thing is that when you hear her coming down the road in front of this house, you don't need a clock to know it's just past nine o'clock," Grandmother said. "That woman won't set a foot outside that rum shop until Babsie Bourne closes his doors at nine o'clock."

The dragging of the cane continued, disappearing into the distance. Only the smell of the cigar lingered.

"I don't know why them two brothers of yours don't find their way home at this hour of the night," Grandmother complained, opening the window at the front of the house and nervously peering into the darkness. "I keep telling them it ain't safe for two little boys their age to be out so late on a night like this."

Usually on evenings when we were alone at home, which was most nights of the week, Grandmother would tell me funny stories about the old days when she was young, growing up when life was so much sweeter and my father wasn't born yet, far less living in England. Even the food tasted better in those days, she said. Nothing like what we were eating, for the food was now so tasteless that it seemed like God had cursed the land. It was a time when a young boy or girl could begin their working life by going to one of the white homes down by Top Rock and getting a job as a maid or a gardener. The mistress or master of the house would lend one enough money to set up a home and to buy some clothes. That ensured job security and gave the young people a start in life.

Most nights, Grandmother had me read the Bible, the King James version with the soft silky pages with red edges; I had to lick my fingers and turn those pages with extra care.

She liked the Psalms of David, Proverbs, and the Book of Revelations. She would sit listening with her eyes closed, but taking in every sentence and, without as much as checking the page, correcting me each time I stumbled over a word or a name. Every so often she would stop me to explain the significance of a passage or, as she would say, to put it in its proper context for my enlightenment. Then she would tell me to read the explanation in the margin, written in red in small italics and in modern English. There wasn't anything in the Bible she didn't know, so I never had reason to doubt. But all the same she made me read the notes as well. Occasionally, she would leave me reading in the house while she cleaned up the back yard.

"We should put some oil in the lamp, before you mash up your eyes reading like that and gotta wear foolish glasses," she said at the first sign of the light turning a yellowish color. To her, glasses, like all things associated with doctors and medicine, were unnatural and should be used only sparingly, if at all. She could tell us the names of scores of people who had died as soon as they visited a doctor or had an operation. This only went to show that the doctors on the island, even if they were trained in England, didn't know what they were doing. In the first place, if they were any good they would have remained in England and made more money. She couldn't understand why people would keep running to them for a few cuts or scrapes.

In place of modern medicine, she swore by the curative power of prayers supplemented by the usual dose of bush-tea, a potent but bad-tasting concoction made by boiling several different bushes, herbs, and roots. A bottle of brownish black bush-tea was always on hand in our home. So was the usual bottle of castor oil, or package of Epsom salts, so that we could always receive a good cleaning out. The key to brewing a potent pot of bush-tea was to have the right number of vines and roots, and Grandmother would spend many hours searching the pasture for them. "You only got to watch what the cows eat," Grandmother would explain. "If they don't poison the cows, then they're good for humans."

Switching from my eyes to feet, she said, "Take a look at that blind toe you got there. That would've healed long ago if you'd let me put some alcohol on it straight away the night you stubbed it. Now you're paying the price."

"But the alcohol would burn too much," I pointed out.

"That's only because it's killing the germs before they set in the flesh. The burning's good." I doubted that.

Our conversation on medicine was suddenly, rudely interrupted when, from out of the darkness, stones started raining down on our roof. The first one hit with a resounding ring that startled the two of us. The stone must have hit the front part of the roof and then skipped over to the back before rolling down the side. It landed in the back yard with a crash, sounding as if it had dropped on the unwashed pots and pans. Then there were more. From inside, it sounded like the stones were coming from every corner. We looked at each other, momentarily stricken with fright.

My first thought was that someone had set a steel donkey on us, to stone the house until we were forced to flee from it and have to sleep in the open. In a bid to keep me at home nights, Grandmother and Mavis Thorpe had frightened me with stories of how wicked people like witches would work to cast spells on poor people so that something called a steel donkey would seek them out on nights and stone them. There was no way of escaping the nightly stonings.

"Murder! Blue murder!" Grandmother screamed at the top of her voice. I was speechless, too frightened. "Looka these wicked people pelting my house this night and I ain't do them nothing. Nothing at all."

The stoning continued. I sat looking at the roof.

"I know it's you, Brutus Waite. I know it's you," she shouted, going to the window facing the road, but wisely not opening it. "I know it's you, Brutus, you vagabond you, pelting poor defenseless people. First thing tomorrow, I going down to the police station and lay a complaint against you."

Suddenly, there was a loud bang as a stone landed near the window where she was standing. The window rattled from the impact and the iron latch came loose from the fastener. Grandmother jumped back and screamed for help again. I was confused. Why didn't the neighbors help, and how did Grandmother know with such certainty it was Brutus? Just as quickly, the stoning finished and we sat at the table, watching each other.

"You see what I mean when I say that we gotta put these wicked people in God's hand. Now you tell me. What did I do to Brutus Waite that he gotta pelt our house when the night comes? All that stoning'll only bore more holes in the roof for the rain to fall through. And I didn't do nothing to him, not one thing. I saw him this morning with his hands full o' rocks ready to pelt the three of you on the way to school. And I had to speak to him and to ask him why in God's name he don't go and look for work. Now he had to come and pelt my house tonight just because all his friends started laughing when I had to talk to him. But God is my defender and my judge. I leave him in God's hands."

Just then there was the sound of someone beating on the side of the house. There was shaking on the door, rattling the latches, as if he wanted to shake them loose. We could hear him laughing and swearing, but in my fright I couldn't make out what he was saying. What was more frightening, I was sitting by the door, and if it had opened, I would have been the first one to be reached. Grandmother was now certain beyond a doubt the voice was Brutus's.

The confirmation also emboldened her. She took up a tin cup and filled it with water from the bucket that was on the table. With a loud splattering noise, she threw the water through the flaps of the door.

"Take that!" she shouted. We could hear the footsteps retreating.

"I'm only too sorry that it ain't some seven-day piss instead of just plain water," she said.

The answer was another stone on the side of the house. Grandmother got up and made sure the flaps were firmly secured with two pieces of wood lodged at the bottom to prevent the louvers from being opened from the outside.

"Go 'head, Howard, you go to bed. Go ahead and spread the two bags and go to sleep. I'm going to lower the light." Just the same, she peeked through the wet flaps into the darkness. Squinting her eyes, she said, "I think he's gone now, but I'm going to lay a complaint with the police tomorrow. I wish them children would come home. They're out there in the dark with only God watching them, protecting them from that vagabond Brutus."

"I ain't ready to sleep yet. I think I'll wait here till they come home," I begged. I was too frightened to abandon myself to sleep.

"Okay. Why don't you come and lay down at the foot of the bed if you're so frightened then? I hope you washed your feet clean this evening before you come in the house."

Her mind obviously wasn't on me now, but on Chester and Alvin and the possible dangers they confronted. "They're only little boys," she said, sounding as if she were pleading with Brutus not to harm them. And almost as quickly, she was angry, probably with my brothers for being out so late but perhaps also with herself for being so defenseless.

"I know what I'll do with them," she said, climbing into the bed. "I'll ask the headmaster of your school to take the three of you under his control. That's what I'll do. I'm going to place all three of you in Bradshaw's hands, you mark my word, if they don't stop staying out so late at night, so that anybody can pelt them."

I was shocked. That would be the ultimate in humiliation if Grandmother, in turning to Mr. Bradshaw, had to admit that the three of us were so unruly and had gotten so badly out of hand that a woman like she could no longer control us. I had to find a way to warn Chester and Alvin. No way did I want to be placed under Mr. Bradshaw's care!

"Come and see if you can't get to sleep," Grandmother

said, " 'cause it doesn't make any sense staying up and worrying our heads over them two boys out there in that darkness."

No sooner had I climbed into the grass bed, and Grandmother had pulled the cloth blind that separated the bedroom from the rest of the house, than we heard footsteps again and someone trying to open the door.

"Ma. You up? Open the door." It was Alma, and I was relieved.

Grandmother swung out of bed and I followed behind her. Alma and my two brothers came in.

"Any of you see that good-for-nothing vagabond Brutus Waite out there?" Grandmother asked as they filed through the door unaware of the terror we had just experienced. "You know he gave this house one good pelting tonight? Ask Howard here. We were sitting there, talking and reading the Bible. We just finished filling the lamp with oil, because somebody forget sheself this evening, when all kinds of rocks started landing on the poor house. But I know who it was and I shouted out and let him know that I know it was him. You sure none of you didn't see Brutus out there?"

"No. We ain't see nobody," Alma said.

"All of you come home together?"

"Yeah," Alma said. "I saw Chester and Alvin standing underneath the light with the rest of the boys, so I tell them to come home with me. They didn't want to come at first, but when they saw Pretty passing in the car, they come along."

She was hoping Grandmother would approve of her sense of responsibility and that this would be enough to forgive her for her earlier dereliction of duty.

"Good. 'Cause he might've seen the three of you coming home one by one and tried to do something to you. I was just hoping that Henry would bring Pretty home in the car."

Grandmother went back into the bedroom. Alma followed her and started changing into her nightgown. Chester took the rank-smelling bundle of bedclothes and started to spread them on the floor, beginning with a first layer of brown heavy crocus bags while Alvin, my oldest brother, looked on. It was Chester's job to make up the bed, the same way it was mine to take out the bedding in the morning. The latter responsibility fell to me automatically as I was the one that soaked the bed every night, requiring the sunning to make them dry. Then before going to school, I would get the white soap powder, water, and a piece of the white top bush that grew at the sides of the streets, and scrub the piss spot on the floor. This way, Grandmother said, the flooring wouldn't rot. In the middle of the night, we, the three boys, were supposed to go into the back yard and relieve ourselves. Chester and Alvin would, but I slept so soundly that I could never tell when I had to go. The women used the enamel topsy under the bed, and in the morning Alma took it out and threw the piss in a corner where it wouldn't smell so strong.

"You and Chester better start behaving yourselves and start listening to Grandmother," I whispered to Alvin. "If not, she's going to put the two of you in the headmaster's hands and you know what that means."

"What kind of foolishness you telling me?" he asked sternly. Alvin always seemed to be in a bad mood when he had to go to bed. I think he blamed me for the three of us not having a bed of our own. "I hope that you went outside and peed already so that you don't soak me and Chester tonight, that's what you should worry about."

I didn't answer. Alvin had delivered a low blow. I would have nothing more to say to him and he would get whatever was coming to him, even if he embarrassed us by proving to be so uncontrollable that Grandmother had to make him a charge of the new headmaster. In the morning, I'd try talking to Chester.

"You ready now so I can turn down the lamp?" Grandmother shouted from her bedroom. "Say your prayers and go to sleep."

"Yes," Chester said. I changed into one of Alma's cast-off dresses, and Chester and Alvin into the pants and shirts that were too old and patched for them to wear outside anymore. We got into bed in the semi-darkness. In minutes, I could hear they were asleep. Chester, Alvin, Alma, and Grandmother. I wanted to pee. Outside crickets and night creatures were making noise. Brutus was also waiting. So I decided to wait until Pretty came home before dashing outside and relieving myself. But I fell asleep waiting. Sure enough, the next morning I had pissed the bags.

I never found out if Grandmother laid the complaint with the police.

4

The telltale signs from the previous night's stoning were evident in the back yard and around the house. Several of the stones rested on the roof; others had fallen to the ground near the steps to the back, and one had actually knocked the blackened skillet off the four large stones that formed the fireplace. The force from that stone had left a big dent in the side of the skillet, as well as a more ominous-looking hole.

But even if we were to dismiss the stoning as a cowardly act done under the cover of darkness, the bright morning light brought its own problems. As usual, Grandmother was up at the crack of dawn and, even before any of us had stirred, was out in the yard feeding the chickens and turkeys that helped supplement our food and income. Every night, the six to eight turkeys slept on the branches of the big cherry tree that grew beside the kitchen. The only white turkey slept on the roots of the tree because its weight no longer allowed it to take the heights. This was Grandmother's prize. The other fowls slept in the nests under the house or in a corner in the yard, beyond the paling between the sheep pen and outhouse, where they also laid their eggs and hatched the chickens.

Grandmother liked to rise as the turkeys were stirring and would be out in the back yard feeding them scratched grain—a mixture of broken corn and oats—that I bought in big brown bags at one of the shops in the village. Occasionally, when she was in a good mood, we awoke to hear her singing a church song, calling out to the neighbors and joining them in offering praises and thanks to the Lord for allowing them to see another morning. All the while, she circled the birds in the yard, stopping only to grab the ones she believed to be pregnant, giving them the finger test to confirm her suspicions. Before the fowl realized what was happening, she would insert the little finger of her right hand into the fowl's bottom and feel for the egg. Then she would release the chicken, squawking and fluttering, to join the rest of the stock eating the grain.

This morning Grandmother was furious. She wasn't talking to anyone and the silence was eerie. The unusually loud banging of the grain cup against the house not only awoke us but was the first hint that something was wrong. At first, I thought it was anger left over from the previous night, but it was far worse than that. The biggest turkey, the one that was providing the most eggs, the very one Grandmother was making plans to sell to the supermarket in Oistins at Christmas, was gone. Few people in the village could understand how much we were losing with that turkey gone, and Grandmother wasn't in a mood to keep all of the hurt to herself.

"Here, chick-chick-chick," Grandmother was calling loudly in the back yard. She was still pounding the tin cup with the corn against the house, so hard that she must have left some dents in the decaying wood. Until now, banging the cup against the house, or even shaking it in her hand, was a strategy that never failed to get the attention of the chickens and turkeys. Every morning, at the first sound of the can, they would come running from behind the paling where they would be pecking grass, or from under the house if they were hatching chickens. But they always answered the call to be fed. Then there was the ritualistic pecking, but this time there was a difference.

Grandmother wasn't calling out to the neighbors and there wasn't the predictable fluttering of the fowls trying to escape Grandmother's clutches. It was an ominous silence. Alvin and Chester shifted beside me, changing sides. I could feel the cold wetness of the soaked nightgown and the bedding that my two brothers were trying to avoid. Grandmother went through the paling door, shaking the can, followed by some of the poultry, looking for the missing bird. The turkey showed no sign of appearing. Grandmother returned inside the yard and sat on the big smooth stone by the fire hearth, the chickens and turkeys gathering around her.

"Somebody gone and thief me biggest turkey, a turkey that I worked so hard to raise all these months. You think that is fair?" she asked rhetorically.

"As true as there is a living God above, this can't be fair a-tall, a-tall, a-tall. I don't know what I do to these bad-minded people around here. I mean, we living peacefully here in this little one-roof shack, minding our own business when the day come, not troubling a single soul, and this nigger man Brutus Waite had to up and start stoning me house just like that, without any rhyme nor reason, and then to the back of it all, he gone and steal my best turkey, too. I can't understand why when you don't do people anything, they don't leave you alone."

"What happened now, Ma?" Pretty asked, coming from behind the cloth screen that divided the three of us from the three women. She was still dressed in a long white, sleeveless nightgown and she was rubbing her eyes with the back of her hand. All of us were now awake and I was busy trying to separate the pieces of dry bedding from the wet ones.

"It is that good-for-nuthing nigger man, Brutus Waite, that I talking 'bout," she answered, her voice rising for the neighbors to hear. "First he up and stone the house last night and now he up and steal our big white turkey. I ain't know what we've done him or what he wants from us. But I done put him in the hands of the Lord. I'll give him a good praying-for. Evil'll follow him all the days of his life. He can never ever prosper in this world. That is what'll happen, as sure as I standing here this bright morning."

Brutus's sister, Mavis Thorpe, our next-door neighbor, opened her side door and looked into our back yard.

"Mrs. Howell? Good morning," she said sarcastically. When Grandmother didn't answer, she continued, while pretending to be civil. "Mrs. Howell," the voice still calm, "but how you could be taking my brother's name in vain so bright and early this morning? What'd he do to you? You answer me that," she demanded.

"What he do me? What he do me?" Grandmother repeated. "Well, I beg yuh pardon but he ain't *do* me nothing personally. 'Cause he can't touch me. But he only just pelted the old house in the dead o' the night like he is some duppie, you know, a walking dead, that can't find no resting place, and then this morning he only just stole my best turkey. That's all he's done me, since you asked."

"But, Mrs. Howell," she interjected, "how can you say them things? Them is bad things to say about anybody, unless you see the people doing what you said they did with your own two eyes." She was warming up and we could tell that a good cuss-out was in the offing. The five of us gathered in the doorway peering into the back yard to witness the fight. Alvin, Chester, and Alma cowered behind the half-opened door, while I stretched out the chore of separating the bedding and taking off my soaked nightgown.

"I don't got to see anybody with my own eyes; anybody can tell the work of the devil, when they see it. There are certain ways of a thief and a vagabond." Grandmother went through the motions of what a thief would do. It was all so straightforward to her.

"But what makes you think it's my brother Everick? That's what I'm asking you and you can't tell me. What makes you think it was him?" Mavis continued to ask. Grandmother, obviously thinking her argument would have convinced any impartial jury, said nothing. Mavis continued: "Well, let me tell you something, Mistress Howell, we ain't got no thieves in this family, you hear me? We's all confirmed Christians, in the Church of England. If you want to see a real thief, look inside yuh own house. Look at Pretty and Alma that does be walking 'bout the road when the night comes, thieving the young men's money or selling themselves."

"Well, looka this thing. Bright and early this morning, Miss Malicious'll tell me my fortune," Grandmother shot back. "She'll tell me where I was born and who's my mother and father. Well, let me tell you something, Mrs. Thorpe, you don't go spreading no nasty rumors 'bout me two daughters like that. I won't have it. Not when it's you that does got all the men breaking down your door when the night comes, so much so I can't count them on my fingers and toes. And to think your poor husband is away working his ass off in America and bringing you back all that money and nice clothes—you ungrateful and unfaithful bitch."

"Look who's talking. All I'm going to ask you, Mrs. Howell, is where your husband is? Answer that. Never mind 'bout mine, he's coming back from America soon and I'll tell him what you say, too. The same husband that left you to live with another woman in New York, and he don't give you one blind cent. So much that you got to live in that house that does leak whenever God sends his good rain to grow the plants. And every Sunday morning you got to wear the same dingy white dress to your church. I can still say with pride that I am Mistress Thorpe, I still have the ring and can wear it proud. Not like you. So you should mind your own business, and make sure that Pretty and Alma grow up like two young ladies and that they stop doing some o' the things they doing a'ready."

"What you know 'bout me, Miz Thorpe?" Pretty said, joining in and seeking to defend her honor. She pushed open the door and stepped into the bright morning light. Grandmother looked at her. "What news you got on me, tell me right now, this very minute and let me deal with you. I walk the road with my head held high, minding my own business, not troubling a soul. So you tell me what you got on me."

"Look who's talking," Mavis exclaimed. "The black princess, the one with the man from town with the motorcar."

"You's too jealous and bad minded," Pretty said. "Just because I don't take on your brother Brutus when he comes talking up to me. The next time I'll not only spit on him but I'll hawk up some good green cold and splatter it all over his face if he don't leave me alone, you tell him that for me."

The voices from this early morning cuss-out were ringing through the village when Ismay, another of Brutus's sisters, came over to help defend her younger brother. She joined Mavis in a blistering attack on us, the heat of which caused Grandmother and Pretty to retreat, and for me to remain seated inside the house with the wet bedding in a bundle.

Grandmother always felt she could hold her own against Mavis, but not against Ismay, whom Grandmother had long described as a woman with no shame. In previous encounters with more formidable opponents, Ismay had been known to utterly disarm them with language that Grandmother claimed never to have heard before in all her born days—words capable of turning her hair white, and which even the most disreputable women shied away from using. Ismay had a proclivity for bringing the conversation as quickly as possible down to basic bodily functions, such as talking demeaningly about the sizes of various parts of the body, who had holes in their bloomers, and what the men in the village were bragging about. She could always be counted on to be the star attraction of a genuinely nasty village cuss-out; she also had a habit of throwing her skirt over her head to prove to all within viewing distance that her underwear was in fact clean and had no holes.

"Who you calling a fucking thief?" Ismay yelled. As usual, we heard the high-pitched voice before we saw her. "Don't make me turn up the heat on you right now. 'Cause when I'm done, you won't know which God yuh fucking well serving."

By this time, Brutus had shown up armed with two big stones.

"Miz Howell, why don't you step outside that paling so I can see yuh good?" he shouted. "I just get outta my bed and heard you spreading all kind of nastiness 'bout me, so I come to defend meself. Why yuh don't step outside the paling? You know, just there by the sheep pen, behind the paling door so I can get clear aim. I'll let these rocks here do the talking for me. Then you'll have something to tell the police."

"No, Everick, don't get yourself in no trouble with these people," Mavis said. She had come out of the house and was running around her enraged brother trying to knock the rocks from his hands. "They got little children in the house and you don't want to hurt them when they ain't done nothing to nobody."

"I don't give one damn this morning," Brutus continued.

"Leave the man alone," Ismay shouted, pulling at Mavis's hand. Brutus was trying to get away from Mavis, who was trying to escape from Ismay. "Miz Howell and her tribe deserve whatever they fucking well get."

"No. No," Mavis was pleading, "you'll only bring yuhself real trouble."

Grandmother and Pretty seized the moment of indecision in the enemy's camp to escape to the partial safety of the house, closing the door behind them. We sat on the wooden bench and listened to Brutus screaming and swearing what he would do to all of us if we would only come out. Grandmother and Pretty had stopped answering him. Still, Brutus's voice continued to terrorize us, entombed and imprisoned in the leaky house.

At this point, Grandmother double-checked the iron latches on the door and placed the long knife in her lap.

"I feel like breaking down that door and going after them," Brutus continued. "That is what I feel like doing, now that I got the devil in me and my blood's hot, cause I ain't done nothing for her to accuse me of stealing a turkey and stoning the house."

With that said, the back door reverberated under the impact of a stone. Another landed on the boards beside the door, causing one of them to break. Then came silence as we waited for the next development. Nothing happened. Brutus's voice had faded into the distance and we could hear Mavis calling Theo, her son, who was three months older than me, and the others for their morning tea. Ismay must have gone home. After several more minutes, Grandmother opened the back door and peeped out. The coast was clear, the cuss-out over. The turkey was gone forever, but the fear and a deep realization that we were quite vulnerable lingered on. Most of all, Alvin, Chester, and I knew that, once again, we would be late for school. Hurriedly, I placed the bedding on the pile of rocks in the yard that was used for bleaching clothes. Chester and Alvin got into their school clothes and waited for Grandmother to get the wood fire going for our breakfast. We all sat on the big rock in silence watching Grandmother.

"Now you three boys see that for yourself," Grandmother said, talking slowly and calmly when she had finished sharing the boiled cocoa. "This is a bright morning with the people all around here looking on to see that nigger man pelt this poor house again. Did any of you see anybody in this village try to help us? Now you know why I don't want you walking 'bout in the dark at night. Some of the same neighbors go to the said same church as us, we is brothers and sisters in the Lord, we drink from the same communion cup, but nobody, nobody"—she added for emphasis—"would lift their voice this morning to defend us. Nobody. Not one soul. As far as they're concerned, he could have come into this house and killed us one by one. You got to look out for yourself."

By the time Grandmother finished her lecture, my brothers and I were already late for school. We checked to see if the coast was clear and then ran all the way.

5

By late morning, about the time we broke for lunch, the sting from the headmaster's flogging had cooled and I finally stopped crying. Every time I was flogged, I promised myself not to cry. But each time, even as the headmaster was lengthening the strap to measure me, I would start crying, silently at first, raising my hands to my face to wipe away the first traces of the tears that would eventually flood down my cheeks, and then loudly as the heavy leather made contact with my back. Usually, the weeping would have no effect, but sometimes, as if out of pity, the headmaster would give me two stiff lashes instead of the regular three, and I would run to my class, bawling and digging at my back from the pain. In terms of discomfort, seldom would one lash less make any difference, and most mornings I would sit wriggling on the hard wooden bench from the welts that ran down the length of my back to my bottom. For the rest of the morning, I would sit at my desk crying, my head buried in my hands, unable to see what was written on the blackboard in front of the class because of the water in my eyes.

When I had to write, the tears would splatter on the page of the double-lined exercise book, creating smudges on the pencil scribbles. No matter how I tried, I couldn't help crying. I just wasn't strong or hard enough, not like the bigger boys or Ollie and Grantley, who would come back from the headmaster's office with a wide grin on their faces, smugly denying that the flogging had had an effect on them. Their protestations always seemed to be so much truer with me standing at their sides, with the big teardrops splashing on my hands and the front of my shirt. There was no mistaking it: I was the crybaby of the class, if not the school and the village. It was a recognition that just as easily embarrassed Alvin and Chester.

"Somebody only got to raise their hand at you for you to start crying like some baby," Alvin would say to me in anger. And since I looked up to my eldest brother for guidance and approval, I would silently renew the promise to myself not to embarrass him anymore, that the next time I would walk up to the headmaster and take my flogging like a man. But it never worked, and every morning Chester and Alvin had to put up with the indignity of me and my tears. Finally, Chester and Alvin would seldom walk with me to school and would make sure that we weren't together in the line of late arrivals.

So I would crawl into my seat on the bench in the class, beside Ollie. Depending on his mood, he could be just as cruel as my brothers, calling me a crybaby and suggesting that my head had to be full of water for me to cry so much and for so long. Sometimes he would add to the pain by punching or kicking me under the desk. Once he even stepped on my blind toe, causing me to again howl in pain. From the look on his face, I felt he might have mashed me by accident. But I couldn't be too sure. So I continued to cry, while the other boys looked on and laughed.

"Why don't you all leave Howard alone?" Mr. Allen, the mild-mannered teacher, would say. I think he liked me, or at least pitied me, for he would often ask me to leave my place in the classroom and to sit by the open window, where I could look outside at the flat fields of green sugar canes in the distance, up to the Wards' house on the hill.

"You gotta learn to start getting to school early if you know you can't take the lashes," Mr. Allen said as I stood in front of him with tears running down my face. "Don't mind the other boys with hard backs. They're already accustomed to working in the cane fields. Beating them is like flogging a dead horse, a waste of time. But it is different with you. So you should get up a little earlier and leave home on time. You got a clock at home?''

I shook my head; the tears wouldn't let me speak, and Mr. Allen shrugged his shoulders as if to concede that he had done his best, that without a clock at home I was on my own and there was nothing more he could do.

At noon, I went home with Chester, walking as quickly as possible on the grass at the side of the hot tar road. Lunch was the remainder of breakfast and oat-flakes porridge. Sometimes cream of wheat or corn-meal porridge was substituted, but nobody in the house really cared for either one. Alma had it waiting for us, piping hot and still in the skillet in which it was boiled.

We hurriedly spooned it out of the plates so that we could leave the house in enough time to avoid another flogging. To get two floggings in one day was simply unacceptable. Often, I would leave without finishing the porridge, either because I ate too slowly or it was too filling. Most times, I would ask to exchange the porridge for a cup of sugar water, either plain or with some lime juice in it. We didn't have any ice, so we drank it like that. A special treat at harvest time was to get a cup of swank, made with the black sticky sugar-cane molasses instead of the regular sugar. It was a lighter drink and not quite as filling. Once in a while, Alma and Grandmother would give me the sugar water. Most times, they demanded that I drink the oat flakes and keep my mouth shut and stop complaining.

"You better eat what you got and thank the Lord for his daily blessing. I never met a little boy like you that could be so miserable," Grandmother said.

Somehow the swank was more acceptable in her eyes and, from a financial position, it was also easier for her to condemn the lunches that some students bought at the school. I would have done anything to be able to buy the ice-cold sweet drink from Mrs. Perkins's shop across from the school, and the two fish cakes and the salt bread that would have replaced the bakes. Chester never said anything, but from the look in his eyes, I knew he was thinking the same thing. It was different with Alvin; I had seen him sharing the forbidden meal with friends, so there was no reason for him to complain. I admired his approach and decided that I too would circumvent Grandmother's wishes and our poverty by making friends with the boys in our class with a bit of money in their pockets. I had to keep this plan secret, for Grandmother and Alma would have killed me for simply thinking of begging for food. We could never admit to anyone that we were hungry, not even if our mouths were white all over and we were about to drop.

When I returned from school in the evening, Grandmother was sitting waiting for me. I walked into the house after shouting "Good evening" loudly enough for her to hear. The last time I had entered the house without speaking, Grandmother gave me a smack to the head and reminded me that I wasn't a man yet and still lacked manners and respect for elders.

On this evening, she was sitting on the large rock in the back yard picking rice, the ritual of separating the bad and cracked grains from the good, before she cooked the daily meal. The cracked and black grains would be fed to the fowls the next morning, along with any of the cooked food that was left over; that way Grandmother could stretch the scratched grain. Picking rice was a time when she did most of her thinking.

"Come here, Howard, before you take your clothes off," she called to me. "Bring the black canvas bag underneath the table with you when yuh coming."

"Yes, Grandmother," I shouted.

"I want you to go down to Oistins and buy some flying fish for this evening," she said, placing the tray with the rice on the ground beside the large rock. Some of the fowls, thinking it was intended for them, rushed from under the cellar and had helped themselves to several quick pecks before she shooed them away.

"Me?" I asked. I was surprised that I would be asked to do such a chore. This was much more important than running to the village shop for a quarter pound of butter or a pint of rice. This was moving into the big leagues.

"Take this shilling here and place it in your pants pocket," she said, reaching into a little bag under an apron tied around her waist. "Take care that you don't lose it 'cause that's all the money I got for fish today," she continued. Although dollars and cents had been the local currency for some time, she still involuntarily referred to the silver twenty-five-cent coins as shillings, a conspicuous throwback to the days when England and the entire Caribbean used pounds, shillings, and pence as legal tender.

"When you get down to the fish market, I want you to wait around 'til the price of the fish starts dropping. Right now I hear they're selling ten for the shilling, but that's too high for us. That's for the white people that can afford to buy at them prices. I want you to listen carefully to the price when it starts to drop and when you feel it's low enough, move in and buy. But don't wait too late 'cause we still gotta eat this evening. You understand what I'm telling you?"

"Yes, Grandmother," I said, shaking my head, awed by the prospect of going to Oistins alone.

"Don't get into trouble with anybody, don't stop to play with any of your friends, and don't go in the sea when you get down there and soak up your good school pants. The salt in the sea water would make the pants rot and I ain't got no money to buy new ones just yet."

"Okay, Grandmother," I said and walked through the gate, first checking to make sure that I had the quarter in my pocket.

———

Simmonds's pub, a small lean-to attached to the front of another house by an almond tree, was across the road from the standpipe. This was the gathering point for the men and boys before they moved to the light when the sun went down and the electric street lamps were turned on. I had to pass the pub on my way to Oistins. When I was almost there, who should appear in front of me but Brutus, the vagabond. He had spotted me first and must have been hiding behind the pub; his appearance was so sudden that I couldn't run away and escape.

"Hey you, little boy, where you going?" he called out to me. In a second he was standing in front of me, blocking my way.

"Your grandmother's walking 'bout telling people that I pelt her house and that I stole her turkey. You know, I have five minds to give you a good slap 'round yuh fucking head to teach your grandmother a lesson."

He raised his hand and I recoiled. I was scared, breathing hard, and had no path of escape.

"You better leave me alone. Let me go 'bout my business," I said, trying to sound brave.

He swung his hand over my head and I ducked. I don't think he intended to hit me. Like a cat with a frightened mouse, he was playing with me, waving his hand close to my ears.

"Look at him ducking. I ain't ready to hit you yet. Not yet."

"Why don't you leave that boy alone, Everick?" Simmonds called from the pub, sitting as usual behind the counter. He stood up to his full height of about six feet and shouted to Brutus. "Let the little boy go on his way, I didn't see him trouble you this good afternoon. I don't know why people like you always looking for trouble, looking to get your ass hauled in front of some judge, so that you could start bawling that you ain't born with no luck."

"Where you going?" Brutus demanded, continuing to block my way. He was wearing long khaki pants and a white shirt with short sleeves that exposed his thick muscular arms. He was about twenty-three years old and his muscles were well developed. Needless to say, I stood no chance in a fight against him.

"I'm going to buy fish in Oistins," I answered meekly, trying to run around his legs. He grabbed the bag from me, looked into it, saw it was empty, and threw it into the air.

"Your grandmother can't even buy a proper bag for you to put fish in?" he asked as the bag came down like a parachute. He gave it a hard kick as soon as it touched the ground, his toe ripping a hole in the side. I rushed over and picked it up and placed it behind my back.

"So you going to get fish this evening," he continued, laughing and bending over to look me straight in the face. "Want to know what we having for dinner this evening? Well, let me tell yuh: a good soft juicy turkey. That's what. The same turkey that your grandmother was raising, that she said somebody stole from her. I don't know what your grandmother feeds them to make them so big.

"And another thing. I want you to deliver a message to your Aunt Pretty for me. Tell her that I still waiting for her, that when I get her down where I want her, she's going to open her legs wide and say, 'Everick, Everick, do it some more. You're too sweet.' "

While pretending he was cuddling Pretty, he closed his eyes and I took my only chance to slip past him. But I was not fast enough, for he turned around and gave me a hard slap to my head that caused me to stumble and my ears to ring. Water sprang to my eyes. Then he kicked me on my leg and tried to hit me again, but I broke into a run and made a quick dash down the road as if the devil himself were behind me. Brutus ran into the gutter beside the road as if searching for a stone or something to throw at me, and in my fear I increased my speed to get out of his firing range. I looked back over my shoulder to see Simmonds standing in front of him, preventing him from throwing a rusting milk can at me. When I was safely out of his way, I started to walk again and it was then I became aware of the burning in my foot. I had kicked the scab off my blind toe again and it was bleeding profusely. Painfully, I hobbled the rest of the way to the seaside.

As soon as I arrived in the fishing village, I forgot about the pain and waited patiently for the price to be announced. It was an exhilarating experience, playing between the various fishing boats on the sand and wading in the surf, washing the blood off my toe. The salt water burned, but I remembered Grandmother saying that sea water was alive, not like fresh water, and was the cure for all cuts, sores, aches, and pains. Every so often, I would gingerly put my hand in my pocket to check that the quarter was still there. Eventually, I found a piece of fishing nylon on the beach and tied a knot in my pocket to keep the money secure, and to give me peace of mind.

It was still early and the fish were still being sold at ten for a quarter. All this time the fisherman were landing literally hundreds of flying fish, several dolphins, sharks, and other big fish to add to those already on sale. The helping hands in the market would row small Moses boats out to the bigger launches. Starting before sun-up, the fishermen raided the fishing grounds, transferring the catch from the bigger boats to the smaller vessels. Then the fishermen would row for the shore, jumping out of the boat about fifteen yards from land and, with the help of the men on the beach, pull the small boat up on the sand. Having beached the boats and fish, the men would return to their spot at the western end of the market to argue politics and to play dominoes or draughts. The women, sitting on stools with the fish spread on crocus bags, would be cleaning and selling the fish at the side of the road.

Over the clutter of voices, I heard someone shouting, "Twelve for a quarter!" The price had dropped and I pricked my ears for further confirmation. Suddenly, the same words were coming from every fish seller's mouth. Some of the men who had either been waiting in their cars, or just drinking rum and beer in the shop across from the market, crossed the road, made their purchases, and disappeared. The brief flurry was soon over, to be followed by a heavy lull. Around us, darkness was quickly descending as the sun, like a big fire ball, dropped quickly into the darkening ocean over the horizon. Everyone was waiting for another price discount, which was inevitable, because the fishermen had caught a surplus this day. Without refrigeration, they had no choice but to lower the price before the eyes of the fish became too glassy. Nobody in Barbados would buy fish that were more than a few hours old. Time was the seller's biggest enemy, for the sun had now disappeared over the waters. The street lamp in front of the market came on and the men at the western end of the market carried the wooden tables under the light, resuming their games and chatter. At eighteen for the quarter, I was ready to buy. Suddenly, before I could advance the fifty yards to the nearest seller, the prices were in a free fall, with the women trying to outshout one another in a mass of confusion and noise. Twenty for the quarter, then twenty-one, twenty-two, twenty-three. I bought at twenty-five for the quarter and ran hard for home.

When I came through the gate, Grandmother, Pretty, and Alma were sitting around the fire talking and laughing. Alvin and Chester were sitting on the ground, poking pieces of twigs into the fire. In the half darkness, the white smoke was rising into the air, and the sparks were dancing above the flames.

"How did you do at the market?" Grandmother asked. "Somebody just passed through the village on a bicycle selling sixteen for a shilling."

"That ain't nothin'," I said proudly. "I got twenty-five for the money."

"What!" Alma asked incredulously. "Who's going to clean all of them fish tonight? What time we're going to eat, boah?"

"Count yuh blessing, chile," Grandmother said. "We three girls can lick these out in no time if we put some heart into it. Howard, empty the fish right there on the rocks and go into the house and bring out some knives."

I started to limp toward the kitchen and Grandmother noticed.

"What's wrong with you now? You hurt that toe again, boy?"

I thought of telling her about Brutus, but decided against it. No need for another cuss-out and I didn't want Brutus to come looking for me.

"Nothing," I said. "I soaked the foot in the sea water so it's burning me a bit now."

"That's good. The sea water is good for cuts. You hungry?"

"A little bit."

She uncovered the pot and took out two spoonfuls of the rice, added some salted cooking butter, and stirred it in a bowl.

"Here. Eat this 'til the rest of the food is done."

I took the bowl and spoon and ate the buttered rice. Until then, I hadn't realized how hungry I was.

6

It was seldom that all of us were at home together. I missed that—just sitting around the blazing fire, feeling the heat in the already warm night and enjoying the closeness. We would sit, secure in our being together, under thousands of bright stars, twinkling against a vast black background of eternity. Only when the fire was spent and the last coals from the wood had burned out would we retire for the night, Grandmother ritually throwing a pail of water on the fireplace to extinguish any smoldering coals. This night, however, was different. Although none of us would readily admit it, we were here together seeking protection from the evil that lurked in the dark world beyond the battered and poorly secured paling. Danger walked the streets and stalked us, it could descend upon us unexpectedly under the cover of darkness, when we were most exposed and vulnerable. Grandmother was still disappointed and frightened that despite her loud cries the previous night, nobody had opened a window or come over when the house was being stoned. When Brutus stoned the house again, in broad daylight, and nobody intervened, she knew for sure we were on our own.

As it turned out, Grandmother was skipping a night from church, and Alvin and Chester were grounded, mainly by a hunger that kept them from venturing too far from home, but also due to Grandmother's refusing to let them out of her sight until things were settled with the neighbors. Rarely would Pretty have an evening off work like this, and when she did, Alma would seldom leave her side, for they always had so much to talk about. Before the sun was up, Pretty was usually gone from the house to her place of work, to have breakfast ready and hot when her master and mistress and their two children got up from sleeping. Long after we had gone to bed at night, we would hear her heavy feet on the creaking floor near our heads. Even on Sundays, when Grandmother liked everyone to be home for lunch, Pretty was seldom with us. The domestic job demanded her attention seven days a week, and what hours were left had to be given to Henry, the boy-friend with the car, whom Grandmother had called a cultured, hard-working man. But when she was home, there was never a dull moment, not with that loud clear voice constantly ringing with laughter from deep in her chest, for she was fat, big boned, and lively, with boundless energy.

We looked on her reverently. She went every day into the white people's house, a place that in my mind was just short of being a palace, with real mattress beds, chairs, and more than enough food; the epitome of cleanliness, where every speck of dust was brushed away before it could settle and defile a piece of well-polished furniture or pollute the air. When I thought of living in England, I thought of the house Pretty described to us, the one that she kept so sparkling clean. The kind of house that made her smell so different when she returned home. That was the kind of house our parents lived in and we would live in when we joined them.

"But you ain't tell me yet why you home this evening," Grandmother eventually asked Pretty. We had all been wondering. "You and your boyfriend Henry got trouble or something, 'cause yuh know you young people can't 'gree too long."

"No. Nothing so," Pretty responded nonchalantly, obviously not worried about the state of her love affair. We were relieved, for our one tenuous claim to acceptance was the car with the bright lights that everyone admired so begrudgingly. If Pretty could succeed in snaring this town man, rich enough to own a car, then all of us would acquire some social status, for the entire village of Lodge Road could lay claim to only three cars. "He say that he got to work late and since me and the mistress didn't hit it off too good today, she told me I can go home, that she will cook her own supper."

"What happen'd then?" Grandmother asked, taking her empty bowl over to the trough with the other unwashed utensils.

"I can't understand them white people," Pretty started. "They think they can get water outta stone."

Any reference to the Maryshaws, Pretty's employers, was never to the individuals or even the family itself, but rather to all the white or half-white people that lived along the coast, on the best pieces of real estate. We talked about them as if they were aliens, hard-hearted intruders from another world. And in many ways that was how all the black people on the island viewed them, as a monolithic group that because of their wealth and color had no feelings for the rest of mankind. It was a small moneyed and influential group that enjoyed the best the island could offer; they lived and ate well and they kept to themselves. Their contact with poor people like us was limited to when they opened the doors of their immaculately painted and imposing limestone bungalows to receive one of us into their midst as a hired hand. They employed women in low-paying work as domestic servants and hired men as gardeners, butlers, watchmen, and handymen. They worked them into the ground and then discarded them like pieces of soiled cloth. The exceptions were the people like the Wards, the politicians, who still kept to themselves socially, but also descended upon us in search of votes.

Generally, however, we saw little of their world. Several methods were used to mark how far we could go. The most obvious was the high limestone walls encircling Top Rock, the whitewashed walls with the embedded broken glass on the top. It glistened in the bright midday sun and sent a clear message to anyone with strange ideas. Where there wasn't a wall and broken glass, there was rusting barbed wire with the sharp prongs; the black private watchmen with unrestricted license to mercilessly beat any unauthorized intruders; the sharp-toothed Alsatians that prowled the grounds; or, in the final resort, the guns of the householders.

This group of people touched every aspect of our lives, and yet they were so removed from us. Not only did they provide jobs, but they owned the places of business in the city and in the nearby town of Oistins, the stores and shops to which every family on the island was so indebted and whose books contained their names and how much they owed. They were also the barristers, solicitors, doctors, undertakers, and, as was the case with the Wards, the political leaders and the plantation owners. The Wards had a say in virtually every job held by people living in Lodge Road and the surrounding villages; they also ran the police force and the schools. Even the few blacks in the village that appeared to have a modicum of independence, such as the shopkeepers, were still beholden to them. It was the merchants in Bridgetown that had the importing licenses, and they were also the distributors and agents for foreign companies, with the right to advance goods to the shopkeepers on credit. Once he accepted, and acceptance was a prerequisite for future business, the shopkeeper was eternally in the merchant's control.

Our common ground with the wealthy was our faith and allegiance to the British Crown. Barbados derived importance from being a colony of Britain and each citizen's belief that our small country could become as great as England by copying everything they did, by getting to England to live and learn in their system, and by swearing our undying allegiance to their flag. This we did every morning in schools like Christ Church Boys' Elementary or in the private colleges along the coast.

"I went into work a little late this morning because of what happen'd here, and before I could change into my apron and start sweeping the kitchen floor, the mistress comes up to me just so and say that the master got something he wants to discuss with me. I said, 'Yes, ma'am' and took some coffee into the master bedroom right away. I can't understand why these white people can't sleep in the same blasted bedroom as man and wife; to tell the truth, it would give me less work to do if there was only one bed."

"White people like that," Grandmother said in her wisdom, spitting out the words as if to suggest that only a fool or the inexperienced would expect anything different. "You know they like to play that they so polite, that they so lovey-dovey when they get together in public. But when you see them sleeping in two different bedrooms, you know that something's wrong, that they ain't hitting it off too good. But you can never tell for sure. That's where black people can't hold a candle to them, can't beat them a-tall. If a husband and wife ain't seeing eye to eye, we would be cussing and telling off one another in public and the whole damn world would know. But white people are different; I guess that's why they got so much money."

"Anyway, I went into his room," Pretty continued, still sitting on the rock by the fire with her yellow sleeveless dress wrapped around her. "And he looks at me and tells me that he and the mistress are planning to have a couple o' friends over on Friday night. So he wants me to come in early tomorrow and work my normal hours cleaning up the place, then stay later through the party to help with the preparations, to cook the food, serve the drinks and only leave after I have cleaned up after them all. So I ask him when he wants me to come in and how much he's going to pay me for all that extra work. And you know what he says? He says that he can't afford to give me anything more. Can you imagine that? He wants me to work like a horse, and to come home tired as a dog, and not make an extra cent. I told him right so: that he can't be serious. I ain't no workhorse for nobody. Not for the money he does pay me when Friday comes."

"You see what I does be telling all of you 'bout these fart-frightened white people that got a little money," Grandmother said in disgust. She turned to look at every one of us individually, shaking her index finger at nobody in particular. "Boy, they still think we livin' in the days of slavery. That we don't know what money is. That's because we does rely on them for the few coppers every Friday night, that they can treat us like dogs, work yuh 'til yuh drop, and don't give yuh one damn cent extra. It ain't fair, not in the sight of God nor man."

"Then the mistress, not liking what I's say, comes in and says to me: 'Miss Howell, you can't talk to the master like that. I won't have it.' I just gave her the eye. The Lord knows that if looks could kill that this very woman would be dead right now. But I keep my mouth shut and then the master, as if he's some big shot, says to me: 'I expect you to be here tomorrow at five-thirty in the morning.' I shook my head and he said that I could leave now and do the rest o' my work. Then this afternoon, the mistress says I could go home a little bit early tonight, after I cook the children's meal, that she would put them to bed since I got to get up early the next day. So that is why I'm home now."

"Lord have mercy. Like the Devil's running loose looking for trouble and he can't find nobody to pick on but us," Grandmother said, bending over at the waist and holding her head in her hands. She stared into the flames and then glanced quickly at Pretty.

"So what you plan to do tomorrow morning, chile?" Grandmother asked, anticipation rife on her face. She didn't like the idea that the only steady income for the family, beside what Dad was sending from England, could be in jeopardy.

"Not a thing. Not one damn thing," Pretty said defiantly. This was expected since there was no way she wanted to appear trampled on. "I'm going to walk in that house at the same time that I'm accustomed to and see what she gotta say. She can only tell me to go back home, 'cause she gotta be a clown to think she can work me like that and get away with it."

"You don't got to do that, girl," Grandmother said gleefully. The approach was good, but unnecessarily confrontational, and white people always had the right to fire without giving notice. No need for Pretty to take such a risk. "Use the head that God give yuh, chile. Use it good. If you do it your way, she could fire you. When she asks you anything, tell her that you couldn't come in any earlier, 'cause when you was walking through Top Rock to get to her house, the police stopped you and wouldn't let you go. So you had to come back home and wait until the sun was up. They can't touch you if you say something like that."

"That's a good one," Pretty said, obviously relieved and impressed with Grandmother's wisdom. The answer was sure to go unchallenged. Of late, the white people of Top Rock had been complaining that the police were letting too many people use the area as a thoroughfare, that too many houses in the area were being broken into, and that people were vandalizing the well-manicured lawns and stealing the mangoes off the trees in the back yards. So the police chief, who himself lived in Top Rock, and whose wife was a good friend of Pretty's mistress, had put more policemen with bicycles on patrol in the area with orders to stop everyone. Several people taking a shortcut home through these exclusive areas, too tired to walk the three miles around Top Rock, had ended up spending a night at the police station or having to pay $1.25 in magistrate's court for loitering.

"It'll be a lie," Grandmother said. "But the Lord will understand. You know it makes me real mad, when I think 'bout them white people having their parties and dancing up on the lawns and at them hotels, and them is the same people that caused the governor to ban our own carnival some years ago. As long as I can remember, people could always take their children dressed in their nice pants and shirt to look at the flowers at the Governor's House on a Sunday evening. Then he started inviting only certain kinds of people to the New Year's ball at the Marine Hotel. We can't even go on the beach anymore, because he says it's private property. Then he bans the carnival 'cause one or two merchants in Bridgetown started to complain and wanted it stopped."

"Why would you mind if the carnival was stopped?" Alma asked. "You didn't used to dance anyway, not like the other people."

"Girl, shut yuh mouth, if you don't know what you're talking 'bout," Grandmother shot back, casting a quick disapproving glance her way. She still hadn't forgiven Alma for neglecting the lamp the previous night. "You talking 'bout since I gave my soul to Christ for the last time. Things changed since then. Since I cut out certain things from my life so as to make it wholesome for my Lord and saviour, so I can go to church with a clean conscience. But I was young, too, and I could dance like nobody's business, especially at carnival time. I only had to hear a little music and you should've seen me shaking my waist."

"I didn't know that," Alma said, looking momentarily ashamed that Grandmother would admit so easily and unabashedly to actually having danced in the streets. "I didn't know that at all."

"When I was young, I was real pretty. I had quite a few young gentlemen running me down. I could've picked and choosed whoever I wanted, but I had to go like a damn fool and choose your father and grandfather, that no-good, sweet-talking vagabond now living somewhere in 'Merica. He couldn't tell when he had something good. Too good for him, if you ask me.

"Howard," she said, turning to me and pointing into the darkness, in the direction of the opened back door, "go in there and climb up on that shelf and bring that tambourine for me."

I walked gingerly into the house, taking care not to hurt my blind toe, relying on my memory to negotiate from the bright wood fire to the darkness, then into the house with the pale kerosene light.

"Give me that instrument there," she said, taking the tambourine from me. "The Bible say: 'Use the tambourine and cymbals to make a joyful sound unto the Lord.' "

With that she started to shake the tambourine above her head, bringing it down with a resounding bang as she slapped the dried transparent skin with a hard hand. Then she started to sing, not a Christian song as we expected, but a calypso, one of our favorites by the Mighty Sparrow from Trinidad. Grandmother said she had seen him perform at the old Globe and the Empire theaters in town, long before Sparrow was mighty and all them big-shot people started talking about him, saying what a great poet he was.

'So they don't want Federation
They don't want to unite as one . . .'

She was up and dancing, using the words of the song and the demise of the West Indian political state to help us forget Aunt Pretty's problem and our loneliness in the village. We were laughing at her unconventional dancing, and singing at the top of our voices. Alma was also getting into the act, the two of them linking hands and circling and singing.

Soon, Pretty joined in the dancing, pulling her yellow dress up over her knees and twirling so that the bottom looked like a flare, like a tent around her legs.

"What's wrong with you, boy?" Grandmother asked, stopping to hold Chester by his shoulder and shaking him rhythmically. "You dancing too stiff, like you is some mannequin they got in the stores in town. Shake your waist, snap your fingers, get into the rhythm. And you too, Alma, is that how you going to attract the young men? Is that how you got Branford running after you when the night come? Yuh think I didn't know 'bout that?"

"What Branford you talking about?" Alma sucked her teeth in make-believe disgust.

"You think I don't know," Grandmother replied good-naturedly. "I told you before: I already pass all the roads that you'll travel in the years ahead. So you put that in your pipe and smoke it."

"Look at her face," Pretty teased Alma. "Look at how she's smiling when you talk about her sweet boy. But to tell the truth, Branford ain't too bad. He's a good-looking boy." Pretty sat down on the rock, the sweat pouring down the side of her face.

"You hear that?" Pretty asked, raising her hand in the air for silence and attention. "You hear that?"

"What?" Grandmother put down the tambourine.

"I thought I heard something just now, like a dog crying or something," Pretty said. The look of concern on her face quickly evaporated. Grandmother looked into the darkness beyond the paling.

"I ain't hear nothing," Grandmother said, still listening carefully. "You must be hearing spirits. Maybe that's why you hear the dogs howling. They howl when spirits are around, in the darkness. You know this is the time of the night that the dead that resting uneasy stir from the grave."

She flopped down on the big smooth rock, tucked her feet and the hem of her dress under her and stared straight into the fire. Each time the fire crackled or the flame leap up, it appeared to be reflected off her smooth, sweating black face, with her flat nose and big eyes.

"And the thing is that these spirits could be all around us. Even like now they could be attracted to this fire right here in this yard and we wouldn't know," she said, still trying to catch her breath from the exertion. "We would never know. Only the animals can tell when they're around and that's why when you hear a dog howling mournfully you have to watch out."

"These spirits, can they hurt living people?" I asked fearfully. These type of stories were usually very scary. Grandmother liked telling them, often saying that we, as young people, should learn the facts of life, both the good and bad.

"Sure they can," Grandmother said somberly. "Why else you think they'd come back to walk with the living? Because they are the spirits of wicked men, condemned to roam the earth forever, and they can only rest after they cut out the heart of some young person and offer it to the Devil as the price for peace. Sometimes if they know young children living in a particular house, they'd even stone the house so that the people inside would get frightened and run outside where the spirits can get them for the sacrifice."

She stared into the fire as if searching for answers to her own questions. Mine were more frightening, so much so that I could no longer find my tongue to talk. Even with the warm evening air, I could feel the chill running down my spine. I wished she would douse the fire with water, end the story, and let us all go inside the house and latch shut the doors and windows.

"That is why I keep telling you young children to stay close to the house at night. You never can tell when some man looking for a young person's heart might pass through this village and grab one of you off the streets. And the next thing we know, one of you will turn up dead in some cane field."

"Ma, how you know all these strange things that I don't hear anybody else talking about?" Pretty asked.

"The ways of the world," she answered. "These are things that my mother used to tell me as a child, around the fire like this at night, and she said her mother did the same when she was a little girl. These stories go 'way back to when the first Africans came to this island; they were the only ones that could explain why the dogs keep crying so much in the night. But as I was saying, these things happen to little children when they don't listen to their elders, who think they know life better than them."

A somberness descended over the evening as we each reflected on the story. It was getting late, and outside the crickets and frogs played their music in the grass. In the peaceful calm, we could hear one another breathing and yawning. Alma finished washing the dishes in the trough and took them inside the house.

The story had raised some questions in my mind. "How'd you know it wasn't the spirits?" I blurted out. My thoughts were running ahead of me.

"What?" Grandmother said.

"Last night," I continued. "When the house was stoned. How did you know right away it was Brutus?"

"Why you always have to be asking so many questions?" Grandmother snapped. "I think it's time to put out the fire and go inside the house."

She was angry that I doubted her. But I was scared and wanted answers to still my fears. "I think you boys should go and wash your face and hands and get ready for bed."

We walked over to the rocks and pebbles in the corner, beside the bath house for the women. The bath house was made of corrugated galvanized steel, rectangular in shape and with a floor of concrete. The draining was poor and the area was always soggy.

Before we could take a cup of water out of the barrel, the first stone landed on the roof and fell into the yard a foot or so from Pretty. Scrambling, we ran into the house and closed the door as more stones descended on us. Grandmother, Pretty, and Alma screamed at the top of their lungs. We three boys stood in the center of the house in mortal fear, unable to scream. It was hard to decide who to be scared of more: the angry Brutus Waite, or his dead counterparts who were looking for a boy just like me for their evil deeds. Outside, the fire burned itself out as we lay cowering under covers until daybreak.

7

The hot, steamy days dragged slowly by, as if each new day were competing with the previous one to see which could be hotter. The grass and shrubs beside the road gradually became scorched, and by midday the island was reduced to a simmering haze for as far as the eye could see, like pools of water in the distance on the black tar roads.

The lack of rain meant the reservoirs were at dangerously low levels, and the government took to circulating small yellow handbills urging conservation. The few old and battered windmills—throwbacks to earlier times when each village was responsible for its own water supply—continued to crank away noisily, the sails hardly moving in the placid air; the stainless steel parts gleamed in the sun, but brought almost no water to the surface. With their roots lifeless, the grass and vines could no longer hold together the powdery earth at the sides of the road.

A strong breeze would have no trouble stirring up a cloud of dust to blind passersby or to scatter it on the furniture in the houses. Sometimes the cloud whirled around in a spiral, like a small harmless tornado that would get bigger and more menacing, the bits of paper, cigarette boxes, and cardboard swirling uncontrollably in the wind to be deposited a few yards on. On such occasions, we would half-jokingly say the Devil was at work, busily trying to create a storm to cause destruction, trying his hand at a whirlwind. Some people took it more seriously. They felt that these were the symptoms of nature rising up against the people for even entertaining the idea that change was necessary. There was a price for everything.

It was the incessant heat, the blazing sun, round and red in the sky like a fireball, exacting a price of sweat and energy from the black sweltering bodies below, that set the tone and agenda of every passing day. By ten o'clock in the morning, most of the government casual workers who cleaned the trenches to eradicate the mosquitoes would be seeking shelter from its blazing rays, the backs of their shirts and bodices soaked with perspiration. In order to put in a full day's work, they had to leave home early, before the sun was completely up. So by mid-morning they would have completed most of what was to be done for the day; they spent the next few hours dodging the sun's fury. Most of the time would be spent around the standpipe, cupping their hands to the faucet for a drink, or under the shed by Simmonds's pub, talking and playing draughts. Or sharing a bottle of rum, getting drunk against the heat, hoping for rain to come and cool the road.

The lack of rain played havoc with the corn, and the young cane plants now drooped in the hard fields. They all suffered from a torturous withering from lack of water, as they struggled to find moisture deep below the surface, away underneath the big long cracks in the powdery black soil. Suffering the same fate was any notion of independence. It was when the sun was hottest that the political demonstration took place. The demonstration was a one-time affair that failed to catch the people's imagination. Herbert Ward and his opposition party had called a meeting for the next weekend, reasserting their strength and intention of winning the next election and of restoring the faith of the people in the British Empire. Until then, Mr. Ward said, the people unfortunately would have to suffer, paying the price for voting him out of office in favor of a bunch of uncouth idiots with strange ideas.

It was around this time that the shortage of food hit the island, giving Mr. Ward and his supporters even more to talk about. In fact, everybody talked about this hardship at the school's morning assembly, including Mr. Bradshaw, Pastor Allsop, and the superintendent. Nature's apparent reprimand became such a serious issue that the Ministry of Education took to sending out special flyers instructing us on water and food conservation and assuring us the government was doing everything possible under the circumstances.

In his morning lectures about the affairs of the world, Mr. Bradshaw talked about the need for the people of the island to share what little they had, and for all of us to remain strong in the face of adversity.

But Mr. Ward and the others would have none of this. They saw the hardships as simply a precursor of what would inevitably follow if the people were foolish enough to run headlong down the road to independence. Pastor Allsop said such affliction was truly a sign that the people of the island were hardening their hearts, were veering off the straight and narrow path in search of false gods. The one and true God was sending an unmistakable warning, he said.

All of this gave us more than enough to talk about in the schoolyard on afternoons when, instead of playing cricket, we hunted for shelter from the blazing sun. It was through these statements that we knew the heat of the political battle for the hearts and minds of all Bajans was turned up all the way. The old establishment, represented by people such as Mr. Ward, Mr. Burton and the superintendent, would do all that was necessary to stop what they called the giddy-headed young radicals, such as Mr. Bradshaw and the premier, from corrupting the people with their ideas.

I had just finished drinking my morning cup of cocoa when Grandmother called me back into the house. It was Saturday morning and for some strange reason she was not going to town to shop. She took down my pair of good pants from a wire hanger on the side of the house and told me to put them on. Then she handed me a faded short-sleeved navy blue shirt, which was getting a bit tight across the back.

"Go down to Top Rock where Pretty does work and she

will have something for us," she said, walking to the gate of the paling. She stood in the open doorway, inside the yard, and continued to address me. "You remember where Pretty works, where me and you went the last time when it rained?"

I nodded my head.

"When you get there, don't go to the front door," she instructed me, talking softly and slowly as if she were unsure of what she was saying. "Go 'round to the back and unlock the gate door, but look first and see that the big ugly dog they got ain't walking 'bout the yard. Don't take no chances with that dog. Anyway, Pretty's going to be looking for you, and will have a parcel for you to bring home. Take it and get back up here. Don't stop to talk to anybody on the way, yuh hear me."

I walked out of the yard with her instructions in my ear. I didn't like going into Top Rock. It was a strange, different world that I wasn't happy visiting. The walk was fine until I reached the big white limestone wall that marked the boundary separating the poor from the privileged class.

When I arrived at the gate, Pretty was looking through the kitchen window. She signaled for me to unlatch the door and to walk in and sit on a box in the garage. The garage was as big as many of the houses in Lodge Road and probably was better suited for living in than our home. Several months earlier, Grandmother and I had visited the house to see Pretty, and as soon as we were ready to leave, the clouds released a torrential downpour. We sheltered in the garage, even as the owner drove up in his car and looked suspiciously at us. Without saying a word, he closed and locked the car and went through the side door into the house.

Pretty opened the kitchen door and was about to step out when she heard footsteps. She relocked the door and placed the canvas bag on the floor beside the garbage pail. Then she tried to look busy. The white woman, in a one-piece green bathing suit, finished tying the straps behind her neck and opened the refrigerator door. She was a head taller than Pretty, slim with dark brown hair and long shapely legs. Black sunglasses were perched on her head, pulling back her hair neatly. Mrs. Maryshaw, I thought. Immediately, I remembered Pretty saying that the mistress and the master of the house didn't sleep together.

She said something to Pretty and, laughing, took a bottle of Coke out of the yellow refrigerator, pried off the top, and poured the beverage into a tall glass with ice. She then put on a pair of rubber sandals and slipped through the back door, heading for the lawn and the deck chair. As soon as she stepped out, she saw me sitting quietly in the garage. She was temporarily startled, but she quickly recovered, placing a hand over her mouth to stifle a scream.

"Can I do anything for you?" she asked. I stared at her, dumfounded, words failing me. She didn't appear too threatening, but I was wondering what trouble I might have caused Pretty. "Who are you? What are you doing sitting there?"

"He is my nephew," Pretty shouted from the kitchen door, coming up behind the mistress. She was smiling half-heartedly, not sure how the mistress would react. "He came to bring something for me. He's okay, don't worry about him."

"How far did you come in this hot sun?" she asked, turning and speaking directly to me. The tall glass came up to her lips, her long white fingers, the nails well shaped and painted red, curled around it.

"I come from home."

"All the way from Lodge Road; did you walk down here?"

"Yes ma'am. I . . ."

"And barefooted? You shouldn't have to walk on the hot road like that. Not barefoot. It's not good for someone as young as you. And look at the way you're sweating from the sun. It's too hot, eh? That garage is awfully hot at this time of the day. Don't sit there, go into the kitchen and have a seat."

Pretty quickly pulled up one of the chairs by the kitchen door, next to the refrigerator.

"Sit back in the chair and relax until your aunt is ready."

Hearing the conversation from the kitchen, the two children Pretty had talked so much about came to investigate. The boy was about my size and age and he looked at me and smiled. His face was clean, like he had had a bath, and his hair was greased. He was wearing a plaid shirt, black cotton long pants, and brown socks. Even Alvin and Chester who were older than me had not yet graduated to wearing long pants. In our world, only men wore long pants or the senior students going to the prestigious high schools. I stared at him and he smiled again. His younger sister, with a ponytail and short bangs on her forehead, took one look at me and returned to what she was doing inside the house. I was less of a curiosity for her.

"Say hi to the little boy, Trevor," his mother instructed, returning to the kitchen.

"Hi," he said. "How yuh doing?"

"Quite well." I remembered Grandmother telling me that I should always answer this way when anyone asked me how I was doing. The reply sprung automatically to my lips. The sweat was continuing to run down my face and I wiped it away with the back of my hand. The white boy looked at me and shifted his weight from one foot to the other.

"Trevor, go to your room and bring the old pair of black shoes that you don't wear anymore," Mrs. Maryshaw said. He turned from leaning on the side of the house by the entrance to the kitchen and disappeared. I followed him with my eyes as he passed the heavy mahogany chairs with plastic on them, the cabinet with the white plates, to the foot of the stairs that took him to the second level of the house. Pretty went to the oven and opened the heavy glass door. She tested the meat by jabbing it with a fork and turned it over in a big pan, the juices sizzling and a sweet smell escaping from the browning meat. With that finished, she closed the door with a bang and started to cut up the vegetables in the sink.

Pretty looked nervous and she kept glancing from the corner of her eye at Mrs. Maryshaw. Up close, I could see the woman's skin was an even brown all over. She walked through the kitchen barefoot, as Pretty and I watched her every move, wishing she would disappear, if only for a minute.

"Maybe we should give this young fellow something to drink. You hungry?" she asked, leaning against the fridge and looking straight at me. Before I could answer, she opened the fridge door and was peering inside.

"No thanks," I answered automatically, remembering we weren't supposed to accept food from strangers.

"All the same, a cold drink won't harm. What's his name?" she asked, turning to Pretty and keeping the door open.

"His name is Howard," she answered, smiling.

Mrs. Maryshaw stepped back from the refrigerator and I saw stacks of bottles and containers on the inside. It was the first time I had seen inside a refrigerator, although I had heard Pretty talk about the cold draft from the fridge that gave her bad colds.

Grandmother had warned her to be careful for that very reason. The white vapor seeping out of the fridge was the culprit as far as I could see and instinctively I swung my feet away so that they wouldn't catch anything and swell up. I had heard enough stories of people who had caught colds in their feet, which later became so swollen that they had to be cut off.

"You want a Coke or something?" she asked, surveying the contents of the fridge. "We used the last of the orange juice for breakfast. You think a Coke would do?" she again asked Pretty.

She handed me the forbidden drink in a tall glass like the one she had used earlier and I took it, taking care not to spill any. Slowly, I sipped it and savored the cold liquid on my lips. Ginger beer or mauby, no matter how much Grandmother swore by them, had nothing on this delicious drink. I wanted to gulp it down, but managed to control myself. I also remembered to leave a residue in the bottom of the glass as a sign of good manners.

Trevor reappeared with the news that he couldn't find the

shoes. He said they must have been thrown out with the rest of the clothes that he no longer wanted. In any case, it had been so long since he had worn them that he wouldn't know where to look.

"No, they're still at the back of the closet with all the other shoes. Go and look again," his mother said.

"I know where they is, Mistress," Pretty said. "I will get them."

Before she could answer, Pretty had disappeared into the house. Trevor looked at me and walked over to the refrigerator and took out a bottle of Coke for himself. He drank it straight from the bottle, the way the men in Lodge Road drank their beer at Simmonds's pub.

"Do you go to school?" he asked.

"Yes."

"You preparing for the Common Entrance Examination, too?"

"No, I ain't in Class Three yet."

"I am at my school and you must be my age," Trevor said.

"He doesn't go to the same school, Trevor," his mother said. "He goes to the government school and they teach differently. You begin preparing for the exam much sooner."

"Is that why none of their students pass? Our teacher says that," Trevor said.

"I don't know." His mother smiled uneasily. Pretty returned and put the shoes on the floor after dusting them off with the palm of her hands. Trevor looked at them and wrinkled up his nose.

"Try them on, Howard, and see if they fit," his mother said. "It's better for you to wear them if they fit than to have them about here. I don't think Trevor would ever wear them again."

"Go 'head and try them on and let me see," Pretty said. She was standing next to me, drying her hands on the white apron. The round white servant's hat looked too small for her head.

I chose to put on the left shoe first, taking care not to get everything mixed up. It would be embarrassing for Pretty and me if I chose the right foot for the left shoe. With a little discomfort, I slipped the left shoe on so I wouldn't hurt the blind toe. The length was fine but it was a bit tight across the instep. Pretty stooped and searched the front of the shoe for the tip of my toe and declared that it fit well.

"Try on the other one," the mistress said.

With special care, I did as I was told.

"Well, you have yourself a pair of shoes, young man. Do you like them?"

I looked down at the shoes and was pleased with what I saw. The black shoes looked a bit scruffy, but it was nothing that couldn't be fixed with an application of Nugget black polish and a sound brushing. The tips of the shoes were twisted, but the heels and soles were in very good condition.

"I think I like them," I muttered incoherently, overcome by the generosity of the givers, people who were supposed to know how to exact blood from a stone.

"What did he say?" she asked Pretty, a puzzled look on her face as if I were speaking a very strange language.

"He said thank you very much," Pretty replied.

"Oh. Don't mention it," the woman said, waving her hand in the air as if to dispel some irritant. With that she left the kitchen, pulled the sunglasses over her eyes and headed for her chair. Trevor went back into the house.

"Look like somebody get lucky today," Pretty said as soon as they were gone. I sat on the chair and carefully took off the shoes. "No. Keep them on," Pretty said. "Make them feel you really want them, that you're grateful. Anyway, you take up that bag down there and open it for me quick. Don't let anybody see what yuh doing, though."

Quickly, she opened the oven and took out the pan with the roast. She sunk a fork into a smaller piece and with one swift action placed it in a plastic ice-cream container on the kitchen sink and covered it.

"Here, put that in the bag quick, quick," she said. "Tell Ma that she can lick up a sauce to go with it. Tell her not to leave food for me because I'm going to eat here. Okay?"

Minutes later, I was on my way home with enough food to feed us for the day. When I was leaving, I shouted, "Goodbye and thank you" to the mistress, but she didn't hear, or if she did, she didn't acknowledge it. She was stretched out on her belly, as if she were sleeping. Trevor was looking through the front window as I left. He made a face at me, but I ignored him. As soon as I was out of sight, I took off the shoes and put them in the bag. They were pinching my toes. When I got home, Grandmother placed a bottle and some folded paper in each shoe to stretch them so they wouldn't pinch the next time I had to use them. Then we placed them under the bed. Chester reclaimed his old shoes that he had given up for me to go to church, and Alvin reclaimed the pair Chester had temporarily inherited. Grandmother no longer had to keep the promise to buy a new pair of shoes for Alvin.

"See what I tell yuh," she said, delighted at how everything had worked out so well. "Crab don't get fat if it don't walk out of its hole."

Still, Grandmother never explained to us why she didn't go to town anymore and why we had to get Pretty to steal some of her boss's food. She didn't have to tell us anything. We too had noticed that the postman was no longer calling with the brown envelopes with "On Her Majesty's Service" stamped on the front.

8

The November morning broke hot and steamy as usual. There was nothing in the air to suggest the day would end any other way, except for an occasional breeze that was trying in vain to bathe the scorched land. But the weather was all so deceptive, the torrid heat that quickly induced lethargy by relentlessly sapping our energies—as deceptive as Mr. Bradshaw would turn out for those of us who quickly marked him as just another headmaster passing through the school on his way to a secure government pension. The only difference between him and his predecessors obviously was his blackness, which caused us to be even more suspicious of him.

Instead of his color being a badge of honor, something that all of us could celebrate as a community achievement, it was a widespread cause of suspicion and fear. For although we knew that, at least on the surface, he was like any one of us in the district, we feared him perhaps more than any other headmaster just simply because he was one of us. Grandmother had said many times that any black man placed in authority was worse on his own people than any white man would be. This was an opinion commonly held across the island, part of the reason, she said, for black people never feeling comfortable enough to trust their own to be their political leaders.

"The higher the monkey climbs, the more clearly he does show you his ass," she had said, not specifically of Mr. Bradshaw, but of the few black people who had broken through to some form of respectability on the island. Invariably, these people thought it best to show they were no longer part of the unwashed by being harsh on those left behind.

"It is so damn easy to kick down the ladder after you've climbed up. That's why, no matter how hard it is working in the white people's houses, I would never advise a dog to work as a servant for one of those fart-frightened black people that come back from England with a little money. First thing they do is to buy one big monstrous house down in Top Rock and then forget where they really come from," Grandmother said.

From what Ollie told us he was hearing under the street lamp at night, Mr. Bradshaw was clearly in this category. Worse, he did not have to buy his big house; it came with the job. That in itself was even more reason for him to stay aloof and, by beating up their children, to take out his resentment on poor people for not being smart enough to keep up with him.

As it turned out, the house Mr. Bradshaw asked the government to buy for him was not in Top Rock or any of the more affluent areas. It was less than a mile from the school, beside the main road that ran through the heart of the district and in front of the school. We should have seen that this location was symbolic; it should have given us some idea of how Mr. Bradshaw thought, but at the outset nobody found it significant. We noted only that his choice for a home further complicated our lives. Wherever we went in the village, we had to pass in front of this house, which meant that every time any of us stepped out of our house—even on weekends when we didn't always have to be on good behavior—we ran the risk of getting into trouble simply by walking the road and being spotted by the headmaster. I lived in absolute dread that Chester and Alvin would do something to force Grandmother to follow through with her threat to place us in Mr. Bradshaw's hands. With Mr. Bradshaw living so close by, it would be easy for Grandmother to walk over to Mr. Bradshaw's house in a fit of anger and make these dreadful arrangements before she fully understood what she was doing. I wished Mr. Bradshaw would pack up and move to Top Rock where he now belonged and make life easier for us.

For most of this morning, Mr. Allen had taken the class under the large plum tree at the back of the school yard, where the branches and big trunk provided some shelter and also hid us from the view of Mr. Bradshaw. This way there was only a remote chance of the headmaster turning up unexpectedly in the class and possibly ending up flogging every one of us, although he hadn't, to this point, beaten us at all. The plum tree was just off to the west of the big wooden schoolhouse, the biggest of the three buildings in the school compound and which also served as the hall for all official occasions and from where Mr. Bradshaw would give his lengthy morning admonitions.

Recently he had taken to telling us how we must change and be prepared for all the changes of the future. Everybody quickly realized he was talking about independence because we all knew he was becoming a major player in the Democratic Front for Independence and was a good friend of the premier. That was how he got the job as headmaster in the first place, people said.

This morning, Mr. Bradshaw had spent almost an hour telling us about things happening overseas, specifically in Africa where he said the winds of change, winds of freedom, were blowing.

"More of you should be listening to the radio, to find out what is happening in the world beyond the shores of this island," he said, just when I thought he was ending the speech. "You should be listening to the BBC news, to the Voice of America on shortwave radio, even broadcasts from the Soviet Union and other places around the world. We live in a changing world. What happens in other countries will affect us. So you boys should be listening to radio, if only to the commentaries on the cricket matches in England, where our boys are making us so proud by destroying the Englishmen."

Eventually, every speech reached this point. He could go on for another twenty minutes talking about "the great exploits of our cricketing heroes." That was when we started listening to his speech. We all loved cricket; we were proud that our heroes were defeating the English, but we were constantly surprised that a headmaster would encourage us to think about this game, which everybody knew was played mainly by the riffraff of the island. But we were willing to overlook that, for it was known throughout the island that in his youth Mr. Bradshaw had been one of the best cricketers on the island and that if he hadn't been so pompous and bigheaded as a young man he would have been one of the heroes that represented us at the international level of the sport.

There were other things we were to find out about Mr. Bradshaw, but in the first two months of his appointment as the new headmaster we schoolboys were too much in fear of him to worry about his past or politics. Others in the village, however, did not have this fear and they were quite willing to fill in the blanks about the man who had been presented to us as an army officer who had bravely and selflessly fought for his Queen and Empire but who now belonged to a group of radicals adding to the hurricane called independence that was threatening this very Empire.

As soon as the morning exercises were over, Mr. Allen had signaled for two of the biggest boys to grab the heavy wooden easel and take it into the back yard. Another two took opposite ends of the portable blackboard. The easel was made of four long pieces of heavy pine wood, too heavy for me to lift. Mr. Allen walked ahead of the class with the pegs for the easel, two sticks of chalk, and the ever-present ruler.

By lunchtime the first signs of a major storm were upon us. Outside, the sky was turning dark and in the distance we could hear loud thunder. Big black clouds were rolling low over the island, blocking out the sun as we hurried home for lunch. The wind was gusting so hard that it was blowing the dry leaves and pieces of paper along the street.

Before we left home to return to school, Alma suggested that we help her bring in the day's half-dry washing from the line in the back yard. Then she closed the windows and spread the clothes on the chairs, table, and bed to continue drying. It looked as if the drought was about to be washed away, so we hurried back to school with the rain just beginning to fall.

Almost as soon as we were inside, the clouds broke, creating a torrential downpour, so hard that we had to close the windows and turn on the electric lights, something that we did about twice a year. Outside we could hear the heavy drops beating against the concrete and on the roof of the building as if the rain were trying to drown out our voices. A calm settled over the school and Mr. Allen, unable to talk over the noise of the rain, instructed us to read quietly to ourselves. There was a sweetness from the smell of the overdue rains on the parched earth, a coziness inside the building that calmed us, an insulation from what was going on outside in the wider world.

Suddenly, we felt an air of expectancy in the building. The students had sensed something happening, for Phillips, the head boy, was making his way from class to class with a thin red book in his hand; the traditional method used by Mr. Bradshaw to send a message to the school without calling a full assembly. When it was his turn, Mr. Allen read the message quietly and signed his name with the black fountain pen he always carried in his shirt pocket. Then he looked up at the class and smiled.

"When the rain holds up, you can all go home," he said, trying to sound disappointed. "The Ministry of Education is closing the school because we expect some bad weather tonight and they have to use the school as a shelter."

At that moment, out of the corner of my eye I caught a swift movement at the front of the school. I looked up and saw Mr. Bradshaw rushing over to the radio receiver hanging over the platform. He seemed to be in a big hurry. He reached out, twisted the volume knob, and pressed his ear to the radio. He seemed flustered. Mr. Burton passed in front of the platform and Mr. Bradshaw spoke to him. As they talked, other teachers started congregating around the radio. Obviously, something important was happening. It must be a really big hurricane that was threatening us, I thought. All the same, I was happy for a half-holiday from school, even if it was being ruined by rain.

Outside the school, Alvin and Chester were waiting impatiently for me.

"What took you so long to come out?" Alvin asked.

"I couldn't come out 'til Mr. Allen let me out, yuh know," I shot back.

"Don't give me no back-talk," Alvin said angrily.

By the time we got to the corner of Water Street and Lodge Road, beyond Mr. Bradshaw's house, the downpour had started again. Tired from running and needing to catch our breath, we took shelter from the pelting rain in the shop at the corner of the street. Inside, a group of six stern-faced men were standing under a large radio. Instantly, we realized something was wrong because there was no talking or arguing. All looked sad, standing with their big black arms crossed at their chest, listening to the humming radio at full volume.

The announcer on the radio had a foreign accent and there was a crackling sound in the background, indicating the broadcast was coming live from overseas.

"What you listening to?" someone asked the men. They looked at us as if to suggest we shouldn't interrupt. The rain was falling heavily, and with the high wind, we had to close the door to keep out the water.

"They shot the president," one of the men answered.

"What president?"

"There is only one president that I know 'bout." Little Foot John, leaning against bags of flour heaped one on top of the other, answered sharply as if we, being students, should automatically know who they were talking about. "There is only one president in the world worth talking 'bout and that is JFK. Sometime I wonder what that idiot Bradshaw does teach in that school."

Little Foot, obviously, wasn't his real name, but ever since he had contracted polio as a little boy, making one leg shorter than the other, the name had stuck with him. He was very broad and muscular in the shoulders and he walked with a pronounced limp in shoes that had been specially made for him. In spite of the handicap, he lived a full life, visiting the United States two or three times a year as a migrant laborer to cut sugar cane and pick fruits. These visits gave him the right to be an expert on America.

"We talking 'bout Kennedy, man," Little Foot continued. "Somebody just shot him dead."

We looked at one another, oblivious to who this great president was. We had never heard of him, but then again, Mr. Bradshaw had told us about a lot of other presidents and prime ministers with strange African names we couldn't remember, about people and countries we never knew existed. Still, this one must have been important, we thought, for the radio to be carrying a live broadcast on his death. It was just like when Winston Churchill died and we all assembled in the school to hear the BBC broadcast and then went to church and prayed for his soul.

"That is why we getting all this rain today," Little Foot said, "for this gotta be another sign that all these changes throughout the world ain't no good for anybody. I hear Mr. Ward say so himself and I believe it. You know all this independence foolishness people going up and down this peaceful island talking about; people like a certain headmaster at a certain school, if you know what I mean." He shot a quick look at us as if we were party to some great conspiracy. We paid no attention to the looks; Little Foot was like that. Everybody knew that since Mr. Ward was against independence Little Foot would be too. "I know something had to be wrong when I woke up this morning and instead of seeing all that heat and sun, we getting black clouds. Something had to be wrong as hell as . . ."

At that moment the broadcast from the United States was

interrupted. "See what I mean," Little Foot said. He tried to raise the volume higher, but it was already up all the way.

"We have a bulletin from the Meteorological Office at Seawell International Airport," the announcer said in a solemn voice. "This is bulletin number seven and we will be repeating it every half hour, until circumstances change."

"I know," Little Foot said, once again trying to raise the volume. "Storm in we ass tonight self."

The announcer went on with a warning that a tropical storm was ninety miles to the east of the island moving at twenty miles an hour to the west northwest. People in low-lying areas should evacuate to the schools, the announcer said, in case of flooding.

"Now we return you to the Voice of America and commentary on the death of the American president, John Fitzgerald Kennedy," the announcer said. The humming buzz returned to the radio. Little Foot John picked up from where he left off.

"I was there in the United States when he got elected and I remember hearing a preacher say that he was a gift from God to the American people, that God had sent him to deal with them wicked Communist people."

"Who you think killed him?" one of the men asked.

"Think," Little Foot spat out the word angrily. "Think. I don't think nothing. I know who it is and it can only be them Russians. But be Christ, yuh better listen to me good. You better pay attention good 'cause this might be the last day we living. Take my word, if them Americans find out that it was really the Russians that killed their president, well, everybody's in trouble. You know the Americans got their finger on the bomb right this moment, and could blow up the whole damn world." Little Foot flexed his right index finger as if pressing a button to act out what he meant.

"So when you think of it, all this rain has its meaning," Little Foot said, going to the shop door, opening it and peeping out as if to confirm that things were getting worse. "And the thing is that we right here on this island are also responsible for what's happening. We're connected." He returned to his position under the radio. "We only gotta look at how certain politicians, and here I include a certain headmaster who should remain nameless, but who lives in a great big house a few steps away from this very shop, a house paid for by the poor taxpayers of this country, but that's another matter," he said, glancing again at us as if searching our faces for a road back to his original thought. "But certain dishonest people of a certain political persuasion are spending their time cussing the church when the honest men and women of God speak out against them. It ain't good nor proper for people on this island to be walking up and down in the hot broiling sun behind banners saying they want independence when most of them can't even spell the word. You think God likes them things? You don't know that is why God sending a storm to cut our ass, 'til we learn a lesson. These changes ain't no good, man. Take it from me. I heard Wardie say so myself."

"What 'bout Wardie's daughter?" the man asking the questions continued. "People 'bout here saying that she ain't seeing eye to eye with her father; that she's siding with the very same people wanting independence. That is why she came back from England to live here. So what you think 'bout she?"

"What about Miss Ward? Anybody got any more lies to tell 'bout this poor woman? Any more stupid political gossip, if I may say so? Anybody got anything else to say, so that I can go and ask Wardie my own self?"

"Why'd she come back from England?" someone ventured, perhaps not too worried about such a powerful man as Mr. Ward hearing of these transgressions.

"Why don't you ask why Herbert Bradshaw come back too?" Little Foot shot back. "At least he came back with a clear mission to indoctrinate poor people. Miss Ward come back because she wanted to, this is a free country, and she can go back to England when she's ready. She ain't like Bradshaw. True, he was in the army but what good that do him? None.

Except that it allowed him to use the people's money when he came out of the army to go to university so that he can get a degree—in political science and philosophy, I hear Mr. Ward say—but he got this degree using the people's money and now he comes back down here criticizing the same people that sent him to university. How ungrateful can you get? Anybody got any more questions?''

Nobody answered. The announcer with a strange accent continued talking.

"Anyway, it don't look like the rain's going to let up tonight. Looks to me like this is an all-night rain, so I'm going to try hobbling across the road to get to my little shack," Little Foot said. He stepped briskly into the rain, closed the door behind him, and hurried across the road to his house. The men followed, pausing only long enough to pull up their collars around their necks.

Having caught our breath and realizing the futility of waiting any longer for the rain to let up, we decided to move along and take our soaking too. We left the American announcer talking about the slain president. It would be a cold and wet night, and it seemed nature was once again vexed with the whole world. Instead of trying to parch or starve us to death, it was now trying to drown us. Or so Little Foot said. We headed into the rain, still trying to figure out what it all meant.

9

In the warmth of the afternoon, Grandmother walked slowly down the dusty road, carefully balancing the large neatly wrapped official-looking box on her head. The box was wrapped with hard brown paper and covered with several impressive-looking English stamps. Grandmother's name and address were written in big bold letters on the paper and could be read clearly from several feet away. She laughingly called out greetings to virtually everyone in the rocky gap, including Mavis Thorpe, who, it seemed, was once again a friend.

"How you doing this beautiful evening, Mrs. Thorpe," she called, stopping to balance the box on her head. "We must always be thankful to God for his small mercies, for things like a beautiful and warm evening like this one."

"Yes, Mrs. Howell, I know what you mean," Mrs. Thorpe said, smiling broadly, clearly reading between the lines of her neighbor's forced good intentions.

Grandmother had caught me unawares, and more embarrassingly, standing in Mavis Thorpe's kitchen with a bowl of soup in my hand. When she appeared, I could not move. The newly restored friendliness between the two houses was tenuous at best and my appearance in the enemy camp was met with a cold stare. However, Grandmother had more important matters to deal with, namely making sure that her package stirred the jealousy of her neighbors.

Grandmother stopped in front of the paling door to continue the conversation. All the time they were talking about the heat of the afternoon, Grandmother was taking great care to innocently raise her hand every so often to touch the big box, to shift the load on her head. She did everything possible to focus attention on the parcel from overseas, short of talking specifically about it. But nobody watching could fail to understand the body language.

The first tentative words exchanged between Grandmother and Mavis Thorpe were at Christmas, three months earlier. But the relationship, as far as I could see, never really firmed up. In the safety of our house, Grandmother would tell us why we shouldn't trust Mavis Thorpe and her family, and that all of us should be careful about what was said around them, even when we were just playing with Theo and his brother.

"Just remember that every skin teeth ain't a laugh," Grandmother warned. "And he that got ears to hear, let him hear. That's all I hope I gotta say on that question. Just remember what happened to my turkey."

Still, the first attempts at reconciliation had been hers, mainly to lessen the tension, she had argued, and because the Bible demanded that we love our neighbors, even those that did us wrong. "We have to learn to forgive even if we can't forget," she explained. So one morning, just before Christmas, while Mavis Thorpe was bathing Theo in the back yard, Grandmother cautiously wished her a good morning and politely enquired how she was preparing for the festive season. Mavis Thorpe, taken aback by the direct approach, answered coldly at first; but answer she did, not wanting to rebuff a grown and experienced woman in front of the children. By evening they were once again standing in their separate back yards talking and exchanging bits of news, even laughing at the calamities and foibles of some people in the village. It was as if they had never disagreed. Every day the length of the conversations increased. Nobody mentioned the stoning of our house, the theft of the turkey, or Pretty's perceived pride. In the true Christmas spirit, nobody was anxious to pass judgment on anyone's Christian life.

But now Grandmother was standing in front of the door,

forcing Mavis to continue looking at the box on her head. She was careful to keep the parcel out of any conversation with Mavis. At least for now.

"What's that wicked gran'son o' mine doing over there at your place this good evening, Mistress Thorpe?" Grandmother said happily, holding the box with one hand. "Lord knows, I gotta put down real quick this thing here on my head before the load breaks my neck," she continued with a straight face, apparently forgetting the reference to me.

When I thought she wasn't looking, I eased over to Mavis's kitchen sink, placed the empty soup bowl and spoon in it, and wiped my mouth with the back of my hand. Theo and his brothers and sisters continued eating by the opened door. Mavis, Ismay, and Brutus got up from the table and peeked out the door at Grandmother.

"It ain't easy walkin' all the way up here from Oistins with this big able load on my head. And everybody knows that I's one woman that don't cry out about weight for nothing. I can carry a ton on this head o' mine when I ready. I'm going to have to send Pretty and her young gentle Henry in the car for the next one."

"You should count your blessings, Miss Howell," Mavis answered as I pushed as quietly as possible past her in the door. "Everybody ain't got a son in England that can send them something every now and then."

"You ain't lying, girl," Grandmother responded, pouncing on the opening. "I was the most surprised person on God's earth when the postman came and knocked on my door the other day. And it's so big and heavy that the poor postman can't bring it all the way up here on his bicycle." This wasn't true: postmen never delivered parcels. Grandmother was banking on Mavis, never having received a parcel herself, not knowing this.

"Anyway, let me go and take this heavy thing off my head and talk to yuh later. Say good evening to Mrs. Thorpe, Howard, and come with me," she said, turning to me as I made my way through the door. From the icy tone in her voice, I knew she was angry.

Grandmother stepped inside the house and closed the door behind her. She put the parcel on the floor in front of the bench, while Alma, Chester, and Alvin came through the back door and stared at it. I reached out to touch a piece of the string that was tied in a fancy knot.

"What you touching that for?" Grandmother shouted at me. "Let me tell you one thing, boy, and let me tell yuh for your own good. If I ever come home again and see you eating food at anybody's house around here, like you starving or something, yuh ass will be mine. The beating I'll give you, you'll piss straight."

I bowed my head and walked away, just in case she changed her mind and decided that it was best to drive home the warning with a smack or two around my head. It wasn't unusual for this to happen when she was really mad.

"You know, I come home good enough this evening, looking for somebody to help me with this parcel, and what I see: one Howard over there with a big able spoon in his hand mauling the food, like he starving and we don't feed him. Eating from the same people that I does warn all of you about over and over again to be careful with. You can't trust these people. I keep telling you that. But it's like I talking to a stone wall. But let me catch yuh over there again, giving the people something to cuss me about when they're ready. That is all I got to say to you."

All eyes were on me and I felt like crying. But I blew my nose instead and leaned against the house by the door. Chester looked at me as if suggesting with his eyes that I must have been crazy to accept the meal, no matter how hungry I was. But I didn't beg for the food. I had been playing with Theo, and then his mother had called us into the house, enquiring why, all of a sudden, Pretty was looking so fat. While they were talking, Mavis Thorpe took the pot off the kerosene stove and doled out a bowl for me. What was I to do?

This was the first time I had eaten with them and it was just a couple spoonfuls of soup with dumplings, sweet potato, and yams. It was no different from Christmas when the three of us went over to Mavis Thorpe's and ate pudding, coconut bread and ham. The precedent had been established, so I didn't see any reason to refuse the food this time. Still fearing the worst, I kept this explanation to myself. Like everyone else, I would rather find out what was in the box from England.

"I don't know why people vexing my spirit so," Grandmother said, cutting the cord around the parcel with our broken knife. The box was positioned between her legs and held there by the soles of her feet. She was bending over and turning it to get at the sides. It didn't appear to be too heavy. "I gone to collect the li'l parcel and that big-guts Postmaster General looks at me and says I gotta pay duty. Well, I look him straight in his bent-up face and ask him exactly what duty he wants. He says I gotta pay money and must open up the box to let him see what's inside it. So, I took out that letter that your father sent me and said look for yourself: used clothes. Pants and shirts that people wear in England and ain't want no more. He shook his head and told me to go along. He had to be mad as hell to think I was going to pay him any duty."

The parcel was now open and we could smell the sweet odor of another country. The twine was in bits on the floor and Grandmother had pulled off the brown paper and rolled it in a ball. She would keep it to help start the fire for cooking. Grandmother usually kept a bundle of old papers, newspapers, cement bags, and brown shopping bags for this purpose. She reached into the box and rummaged among the papers. Finally, Grandmother produced a tin still wrapped in plastic. Pictures of the horses and royalty covered it.

"Sweeties," Grandmother announced. "Your father don't forget to send the sweets, chocolates and things." She placed the tin on the table and suggested sternly that nobody touch it.

Eventually, she emptied the box of the six separate parcels. One by one she handed us our parcels. Hers contained three dresses, a black hat, and a pair of black and white shoes. The shoes slipped onto her feet easily and she walked around the house without any difficulty, smiling all over.

"How he know I want these?" she exclaimed. "Now I can wear these to church and nobody won't be able to say a thing to me. They can't pick their teeth at me. What he send you, Alma?"

"A sweater and a pair of pel'pusher pants," she said, holding the multi-colored pants to her waist. "I think I'll try them on right now and see how they fit."

Alvin and Chester were also ripping into their parcels. A blue police car with a siren fell out of Alvin's, and he grabbed it and started pushing it across the floor. It let out a whirring sound and continued on by itself, eventually disappearing under the bed. Alvin ran after it while Chester picked up a toy revolver he had received and pretended to shoot at Alvin. When he pulled the trigger, the gun let off a loud bang, releasing a cork from the nozzle. Alvin and Chester soon exchanged toys.

In the excitement, I was fumbling unsuccessfully to open the parcel with my name on it. Grandmother snatched it from me and placed the parcel on her lap. I was eager to see what toy I had received. I knew it had to contain one, because Alvin and Chester had toys and I had been promised at Christmas that my father would send me a toy in the new year. Christmas had come and found the three of us without presents. Even Theo and his brothers and sisters next door received clothes and toys from America, sent by their father.

I had asked Grandmother why we didn't have any presents; at first she told me to shut up and eat my food and be grateful that Jesus Christ had come into the world to die for our sins.

"Christmas isn't a time for toys and presents. Not even for filling up your belly like some hog. I don't know why some people does spend the Lord's birthday like that. So don't come asking me about presents and things. Two days from now I bet you that all them toys will be mashed up and all that money wasted. Them toys that you so breaking your heart after is only tin and some paint. A waste o' money. Money that they could've used to put food on the table."

That didn't stop my questioning and eventually she relented, promising to write my father and ask him to send toys for us.

The opened parcel revealed a pair of short pants, a short-sleeved white shirt, and a black bow tie. Grandmother threw the empty paper on the floor and picked up the pants. "Hum! It looks too big for you, Howard. But you can always wear it next year." As she spoke, she turned the pants around to examine them from every direction. "I think I'll give this to Chester and buy you another one."

"But Grandmother, there is . . . is . . . no toy in the paper," I said, hoping that somehow a car or something would materialize. I looked again in the box, rummaging among the papers, as water started to well up in my eyes. It was empty, except for mothballs and pieces of newspaper. I was devastated.

Everyone was happy but me. I sat beside Grandmother and asked her about my toy and the Christmas promise. She suggested I share Alvin's and Chester's. They promptly refused to let me touch them.

"I'll write and remind your father to send a car or something for you," she said, putting on the black hat and pressing it down on her head. "I'll write him. How this hat look on me head?" she asked.

"Push it a little to the side," Alma said.

With nobody noticing, I slipped into the back yard where I sat on the rock by the fireplace and cried silently. Sitting alone out there with the early evening darkness descending around me, I could hear the happy voices in the house like faint whispers. As at no other time in my life, I felt cut off from everyone, lonely and betrayed. It was easy for me, sitting in the warm dusk, to escape into my dreams and to wonder what it would be like to live with my mother and father, where they could see me with their own eyes and not have to guess about my size or wait for Grandmother to send them a measurement. They would do the right thing if I were with them, if I could talk to them and say what I wanted. It was understandable that they would make a mistake, for it must have been extremely difficult to keep track of my sizes now that I was growing so fast. Still, it hurt and I felt forgotten. Life would be so much easier if they hurried up and sent for my brothers and me to join them in England.

Mavis Thorpe heard the loud voices in our house and looked through the side window of her kitchen. She saw me sitting on the rock, chin resting on my knees, and must have sensed that something was wrong.

"What you doing sitting down out there like some loupie dog that lost its mother?" she called from the window. I wanted to explain my hurt and disappointment, but I couldn't. At the back of my mind was the warning from Grandmother never to talk to anyone about what was happening in our house. Already that evening, I had caused Grandmother to get angry and I knew it wouldn't be wise to offend her again.

"Nothin'," I answered, trying to sound cheerful. I stretched out my legs from the curled-up position and sat erect. "Nothin'. I'm just sittin' here by myself gettin' a little bit o' fresh air."

"I know what you mean. The evening's getting a little close with all this heat. I think it's going to rain real soon. You like what your father sent for you?"

"Yes, thank you." I looked around the black sky and saw no sign of rain, only bright stars for as far as my eyes could see.

"That's good, 'cause you and your brothers need all the help you can get. Anyway, don't sit down out there in the dew like that 'cause you might catch a cold. Go inside and get a hat to cover your head. Theo's getting ready to go to sleep now."

She closed the window and disappeared into the kitchen and then into the shed roof. Minutes later, a light moved through the house, and I saw Mavis Thorpe with a lighted lamp and a book in her hand going into the children's bedroom. If only Theo knew how much I envied him for having a mother.

The disappointment over the parcel was one of many I had faced in the three months since Christmas. It seemed as if the whole world was turning against Grandmother and our family, but that it had chosen me as the one to take home the message. In the weeks leading up to Christmas, Grandmother, as she did every year, sent the three of us into the rock quarry every morning before school to bring home basins of crushed powdery stone called marl. At six-thirty in the morning, we would get up from sleeping and walk to the quarry. Once there we would bend under the barbed wire and head for where the men with their sticks of dynamite, caps, fuses, and long iron drills had blasted the limestone rock the day before. We took with us a small piece of iron which we used to scrape the flour-like marl from between the boulders into heaps. We would carefully remove the pebbles and small rocks before filling the basins. Because Alvin was the eldest and strongest, he would help Chester and me lift the basins onto our heads and then strain to get his on his own head. Most mornings, we would make two or three trips, piling the marl in a heap in a corner of the yard. By the time we finished, the sun would be high in the sky and people would be asking us what we intended to do with all that marl, or joking that we must have mistaken it for flour. Or they would say that the people who owned the quarry should have us locked up for stealing. Everyone we passed had something to say, but we were forced to ignore them and keep our heads straight. We felt thoroughly exposed and embarrassed, but Grandmother never understood our feelings no matter how much we complained.

Grumbling, hungry, and running late for school, we

would wash the marl from our faces, hands, and feet and quickly put on our school clothes. The skillet of cocoa would be waiting for us and Grandmother would pour it steaming hot from the fire into our tin cups, cold cocoa and milk cans that a blacksmith had put handles on for us. Most of them were rusting from the bottom or the handles were breaking off. We hated going for marl, mainly because it ensured that we got to school late and had to face the wrath of the angry teachers.

Two days before Christmas, Grandmother spread the marl outside around the house. We had swept the yard clean, gathered up the leaves, and hoed the bush and patches of grass, while she went to town for the Christmas shopping. Grandmother took great care to spread the marl under the tree where the chickens and turkeys slept. It covered their droppings. This was our winter wonderland of snow, Barbados style.

It was on that day that the owner of the quarry, a short brown-skinned man named Archer, stopped me in front of the house and said he would be laying a complaint with the police against the three of us if we didn't pay him for the stolen marl.

"The amount of marl you got there in your back yard could fill a whole lorry," he said. "I want payment for a lorry load—ten dollars, if you please. So tell your Grandmother that for me. She knows where I live and where she can bring the money. Otherwise, I'm putting the three of you straight in the hands of the police."

Grandmother said he could do whatever he liked, but she wasn't paying him. This left the three of us wondering all Christmas if we were headed for Dodd's.

On the Saturday before Christmas, Grandmother woke me earlier than usual and said that I was to take the bus to Kendal Hill to visit some baker I had never met. I had only heard of

Kendal Hill, and in my mind it was a foreign village where several of my school friends lived. Early in the morning, even while we slept, she had risen and made the dough for the coconut bread that everyone ate at Christmas. Until then, it looked as if we were going to be the only family in Lodge Road to go without this specialty. Grandmother had sworn to us that never again would she ask Mavis Thorpe for the use of her kerosene oven. Grandmother didn't want to owe any favors to Marvis, just in case there was another big-time quarrel, which she felt was almost inevitable.

"Ask the bus driver to show you where Clements the baker lives," she said, helping to place the basket with the dough on my head. "When you get there, tell Clements that Mrs. Howell up in Lodge Road, a sister in the church with his wife, asked him to bake these breads. He is a good man and he got one of them old-time brick ovens. You ever eat bread baked in a brick oven?"

"No."

"Well, let me tell yuh, you don't know what you missing," she said, smacking her lips as if she was already eating the bread. "That bread is sweeter than nothing you ever tasted."

Clements's home, a two-roof house with a flat-topped shed roof, was some distance from the main road. The conductor irritably pointed it out to me, adding loudly enough for everyone in the bus to hear that he wasn't no guide, he was hired just to issue tickets and make sure the correct fare was paid. Neither was he supposed to be lifting big heavy bags and baskets that would only hurt his back. He had, probably out of pity, or to let the bus proceed, helped lift my basket out of the bus. I stepped gingerly into the gutter beside the road and waited until the bus pulled away. At the house, a tall, brown-skinned woman, maybe Clements's wife, directed me to a door in the paling leading into the yard.

Inside, the baker, a shortish, coarse-skinned man of about fifty years old, was chopping a table top full of dough and putting the big elongated pieces on a flat thickly greased slab of tin. He hardly noticed me as I entered the yard. He didn't even pause from the mechanical chopping and slapping of the dough. With sweat covering his flabby but naked upper body and face, he took up a long bamboo rod with a hook at one end and opened a small iron door in a brick wall. Behind the door were red hot coals, the heat waves shimmering, steam escaping from the door itself. With the bamboo stick, the end black from the burning, he pushed the slab with the dough on it into the oven and closed the door.

When he turned around, he looked surprised.

"What you doing here?"

"Good morning," I stammered, holding the basket on my head with both hands. "I's Mistress Howell's grand-boy from Lodge Road and she tell me to ask you to bake these breads for her."

"Miss who?" he shouted, impatient that I should be taking up so much of his time. He returned to the dough and continued cutting. "You mean Miss Howell from Lodge Road? She send you to me now, a day like today! Well, she must be fucking mad or something. Just before Christmas," he said, not even looking up from the table. He sucked on his teeth loudly, shaking his head. I remained standing with the heavy basket on my head, not knowing what to do or say. Apparently, Grandmother had not made arrangements with him beforehand. This was as much a surprise for me as it was for him.

"Your Grandmother's crazy or something," he continued. "She ain't know I got my own business to look after on a day like today? Christmas is my busiest time, all sorts o' orders to fill. People runnin' down my ass for bread. I can't even fill the orders fast enough for them. She gotta be crazy to think I got the time to bake bread for her now. And to make things worse she ain't even going to give me one blind cent when I done." He said the last words as if he expected me to respond, to contradict him. I didn't. He was right.

"I's a busy man," Clements resumed. "What would happen if I go around baking bread for everybody for free? Who would buy from me? Tell me that. I can't understand some people; they just ain't got no conscience, and at Christmas, too."

Still angry, but obviously softening, he pulled back the white flour bags covering the dough.

"Jesus Christ, you mean she couldn't even parcel them out. You mean that I gotta cut up the dough, too."

At any moment, I expected him to demand that I leave his bakery, that he had too much work to be bothered by me.

"All I can say is that you're going to have to wait. I ain't putting myself out for nobody." He put the basket on another table covered with dried flour, beside a garbage can filled with egg shells and butter and lard tins. I continued standing over the basket. "You can go and sit there by the side o' the house in the shade, out o' me way so I can get some room to turn 'round. I don't want anybody under my foot on a day like this. I'm too busy."

It wasn't until late afternoon that he got around to the bread and by then I was hungry and tired. To save time, he cut the dough in big pieces and put them on one slab. Then he went into the house and started parceling out his other orders. I sat in the back yard with the basket at my foot, wondering why the bread was taking so long to bake.

"Jesus Christ," Clements said, racing from the house. "You, I forget you're still here." He dashed to the oven and opened the door. When he pulled out the slab, I could see the black burns at the side of the bread. He looked at me and then at the bread.

"Christ above! I forgot," he said apologetically. "I was too busy. Tell her, she chose a wrong day, man. Wait 'til they cool before putting them back in the basket." He started walking back to the house. Before closing the back door, he looked over his shoulder one last time and said: "Tell your Grand-mother that I forgot. Take them two pudding breads over there on the table with yuh and tell her that I send them." Then he closed the door and was gone.

That Christmas we had no sweet bread. Grandmother

tried cutting away the burns but they were too deep. The remaining bread was too dry, too hard. When she asked me what happened, I told her that Clements forgot them in the oven.

"Why didn't you remind him, then?"

"He was busy inside the house, and I didn't know the bread was done."

"You's a damn fool, that's what. These things does only happen when you ask somebody to do you a favor. Well, I tried my best," she said resignedly. "We're just going to have to eat our turkey and drink the sorrel that I got drying out there in the back yard. Let's thank God that we live to see another day. I can't do no more, if you're going to sit down there in the man's back yard and let him burn up the bread. And besides, your father ain't sent one cent extra for Christmas."

So on Christmas morning the six of us went to the early morning church service and pretended that we were looking forward to the day's celebrations. Grandmother pinned an artificial holly with small red bells and a green branch on her chest. Pretty and Alma put on their best white dresses. In the cool morning, with the stars bright in the sky, we walked to the church and filled up half of one bench. At daylight, when the boys and girls were catching the bus for Bridgetown to listen to the Royal Barbados Police Band playing carols, we headed home and hid our shame behind the closed doors. Christmas was like any other day for us. Pretty spent it at Henry's parents. Grandmother slept most of the day. In villages across the island, everyone was celebrating, showing charity towards one another, even to the point that the politicians had temporarily set aside their quarrel over the independence question. It was different for us. Alvin, Chester, and I could only look forward to spending the next one in London, England. We had no other choice.

10

Grandmother walked slowly up the aisle of the church with Alvin, Chester, and me trailing. At every row, she hesitated long enough to speak to someone while keeping her eye out for a good seat. As a rule, she did not like sitting too far in the back, lest it be misconstrued that she was backsliding and had a guilty conscience. The back was reserved for sinners and people who weren't too sure of the status of their soul with God. Neither did she want to be too close to the preacher, just in case she had to make an unscheduled exit from the hall, maybe to take one of us to pee on the rocks by the olive trees that fenced in the churchyard.

Eventually, she settled for one of the rows by an open window in the middle of the church. When the preaching and singing got going, the small hall was sure to get warm and she would be glad for the fresh air coming through the window. Having chosen the pew, she stepped aside and with a nod of her head signaled for the three of us to file down the row and take a seat.

This was revival time at the Pilgrim Holiness church, the first night of a week-long odyssey when Superintendent Cox, the evangelist from the city of Bridgetown, would try to bring the Lord to the village. Revival meetings were held about three times a year, providing a kind of renewal for the congregation and the opportunity to increase its numbers. The hall was full of the regular worshippers and many invitees, for this was the time of year Pastor Allsop and the elders of the church encouraged us to invite a friend to come and worship. Even in

Sunday school, we were told that this was the best thing we could do for a friend.

"What time you got, Sister Welch?" Grandmother asked, turning to the woman behind her.

Sister Welch nudged the man sitting beside her. He was looking a bit uneasy, wearing a tight, starched suit.

"Seven 'clock," said the man, whom everyone called Dolphus the carpenter. He shifted his feet as he studied the watch on his left hand as if to confirm the time. Maybe he was also showing off that his daughter in New York had sent him the watch. "I got seven 'clock." He was Sister Welch's reputed husband, and she had brought him along in hopes that he would be saved. Grandmother made it well known to us that only an infusion of the Holy Spirit would stop him from beating his partner and children, spending all his money in the rum shop every Friday night, and staying drunk all weekend.

"Thank you," Grandmother said. "I guess Paster Allsop will begin the service soon. Like we got a real good turnout tonight, eh, Sister Welch?"

"Yes, praise the Lord," she replied, placing the black Bible on her lap. "The Lord knows we need a little righteousness 'bout this place. There's a lot o' souls out there cryin' out for a little salvation."

Before Grandmother could agree, there was a hush throughout the church. Pastor Allsop was standing at the podium. His guest, the Superintendent, was sitting on a highback chair on the platform, frowning at the congregation. Pastor Allsop raised his hands in the air, palms facing up, signaling the worshippers to rise.

"Shall we stand," he said. "Let us begin this special week of revival by asking God's blessing. Brother Brown, would you lead us in prayer?"

With a loud rustle, the congregation rose to stand with heads bowed and eyes closed. Brother Brown, a half-brother of the pub owner in the front bench, began his prayer, his voice rising to a peak. "And, oh Lord, bless the bringer of your word this night, endow him with special powers and strength that he would be a faithful witness in your name, dear Lord. That he would lead some poor forgotten soul that is reaching out to you even now in its hour of darkness and desperation, bring it into your light and happiness. And we thank you, dear Lord. We thank you. Hallelujah. Praise your precious name. Hallelujah. We thank you. Mmmmmm. Mmmmm. Amen, Lord, amen." When he was finished everyone showed their approval by saying their own amen. Brother Lester Brown was the best prayer in the church.

Evangelist Cox came to the podium. He placed the Bible on the top of the dais and flipped it open, almost absent-mindedly. Slowly he surveyed the faces below him, his eyes stopping momentarily on some new person in the congregation, someone he hadn't seen in the church before. He knew almost everyone in the village from his days as an electrician wiring the houses, and from toiling in the service of the Wards, ensuring their political victories. Instinctively, like the old politician he was, he was looking to see who wasn't there, more so than who was.

His eyes continued to travel around the church—searching, observing, probing. There was not a picture in the dour-looking building; some of the yellowish paint was peeling off the wall. Cracks ran from the ceiling down the wall to the back of the church, ending just above the pieces of brown wood over the door, the main entrance to the building. One or two of the glass windowpanes were cracked or missing. There was a crush of faces on the outside pushing through the open windows to see what was going on inside. Many more people were standing in the doorways and outside in the darkness beyond the reach of the light.

Someone in the congregation cleared his throat, the sound reverberating throughout the hall, causing the people to stir uneasily, expectantly. The preacher looked in the direction of the noise, slowly taking the white handkerchief from his pocket and wiping his face. He touched the open Bible, slowly letting his long finger run along the back bone of the holy book, as if trying to break the book's spine to mark the page.

Suddenly, Evangelist Cox slammed the Bible shut. He picked the closed book off the podium by a corner and waved it like a sword in the air.

"Lord have mercy," he shouted, slowly at first, repeating himself several times. "Lord," he paused for emphasis, "have mercy. There is so much sin in this village, on this very island. So much sin around here, and it has to be exposed. Exposed so the light of righteousness can shine in dark places, in the hearts of sinful men and women, who even now are plotting strange things for the people of this island. Lord, let thy holy word be a guiding light unto my path, so man will come in out of his own darkness, even if man doth like darkness rather than light 'cause his deeds are evil."

He placed the Bible on the dais and walked away from it. He surveyed the room, walking, almost prancing in the Spirit, to one end of the podium and then back to the center. Looking around the hall, his eyes were still moving, as if he wasn't finding the right words to convey how he really felt. Except for the heavy breathing, there was absolute silence.

"Pastor Allsop, there is a Bible passage aching in my heart: Second Timothy, chapter three, verse thirteen—'But evil men and seducers shall wax worse and worse, deceiving, and being deceived,' " he recited without consulting the Bible he was still waving. "Thus says the holy word, of what will happen in the last day." He paused again to look around the building, as if seeking to identify those wicked deceivers that had even infiltrated the church, as if all of us were suspect.

"Amen, Brother Cox. Amen," Pastor Allsop said. "Preach the Word, even if it must be used like a sword."

"I ain't sorry for stepping on anybody's toes, Pastor Allsop. They shouldn't have any corns in the first place, if you know what I mean. And besides that, you can't get no corns unless you wear shoes that pinch your toes. The same thing applies to having sin. You have to encourage it: listen, flirt, and then lust after it, after strange things and strange ideas that look so beautiful so as to entice you into sinning. Tonight I bring a message, as harsh as it is, that must be preached whether the people like it or not. As a man of God, I have no choice. For there is sin in this little island, in this village, in this church. In all of us. Things ain't right and God likes the truth, so I must be truthful and say it as I see it. Things are changing too quick on this island and unless we accept Christ and ask him to lead and guide us, then we will have to bear the consequences. So will you please rise and join me in singing? I feel the urge in my heart to sing."

Grandmother shook Chester, and the three of us got up with the rest of the congregation. At first only the voice of the evangelist could be heard. Then the pastor joined in. Then everyone, sinner and saved, who remembered the words was singing. When the singing subsided, Evangelist Cox kept everyone standing. He was now ready to begin his sermon. It was thirty minutes before he suggested that everyone could sit again.

"There is a strange thing going around this island these days," the preacher said. "Independence." He scoffed at the word as if it was bad medicine someone was forcing down his throat. "Independence. That is what some people are walking around this island talking about. Some people from whom you would expect better—people that are even responsible for the educating of our children. That is the most unchristian thing I can think of, brothers and sisters, for doesn't the Bible itself tell us that we should lean on Christ our savior? How can we be leaning on someone else and still talking stupidness about being independent, too? To all those in high places that would lead us astray, I'd say: read Daniel chapter 6, verses 26 and 27—'God hath numbered thy kingdom and finished it. Thou art weighed in the balance, and art found wanting.' "

He looked around the church. Everyone was listening attentively; even those outside were silent.

"We must choose our leaders carefully, good upright

Christian people. We have to stick with the tried and true, those that never change, like the Bible says, that are the same yesterday, today, and tomorrow. People like, if you want me to call names, the late Jacob Ward and his son Herbert Ward, people that we know and trust. Not people that would lead us astray with so much talk of independence, that would lead us down the path of destruction. I say to all you people in the hearing of my voice: rise up and assert yourself. Forget about independence and make a clear choice for Christ. For as the psalmist said: 'I will say of the Lord, He is my refuge and fortress: my God; in him will I trust.' "

For the rest of the night, Evangelist Cox tried to exorcise this sin that he had identified, that was eroding morals and capable of corrupting the entire island. Grandmother had some difficulty keeping the three of us awake for the entire sermon. I must have dozed off for when she woke me, Evangelist Cox was making the altar call for sinners to be saved. Brother Brown and another older man had grabbed the table in front of the altar and were moving it out of the way and onto the podium to make room for the kneeling worshippers. Evangelist Cox was leading the congregation in another song.

Suddenly, there was movement. From almost every row of seats, members of the congregation were heading for the altar to kneel and pray, many of them crying and begging God for mercy. I looked back to see Sister Welch nudging her husband. He shook his head and I pretended not to look.

"Dolphus," Grandmother said, opening her eyes and turning to face Sister Welch's mate. "Don't resist. Don't resist the spirit and harden your heart. That is all I'm going to tell you."

Then she, too, slipped into the aisle and walked to the altar, her dress making a whooshing sound with every step. She knelt next to Sister Welch. Pastor Allsop was standing over them praying almost as loudly as Evangelist Cox. He was walking along the side of the altar laying his hand on the crown of each person's head.

Just before I nodded off to sleep again, I noticed Dolphus walking quickly to the altar, as if he was hoping nobody would see him. When Grandmother woke me again, there was already a pool of water on the cement under the bench. I had pissed myself in my sleep. This was getting embarrassing, and I took pains on the way out to hide the big stains on my pants.

The rest of the revival week was anti-climactic. By the third night, the same faces were answering the altar call, not so much asking for forgiveness, as it was assumed they were saved from eternal damnation the first night, but to renew their life in Christ. Try as he might, Evangelist Cox could not get any more additions to the flock and this he took as yet another sign that the strange political wind blowing across the island was bewitching the people.

Fire and brimstone had lost its effect on non-believers and the hard-hearted. Some of them had even chosen to attend political meetings in Oistins and nearby Silver Sands on the same nights that Evangelist Cox was preaching. They were listening to men and women like themselves talk late into the night of a new salvation, a new Jerusalem, through political independence. The people of the island were flirting with taking unto themselves a false god, a demon in the form of independence, against which Evangelist Cox and his former employer, Herbert Ward, railed from their pulpits and platforms. Their failure to frighten the people into a mass rejection of the notion of independence was the first sign for Mr. Ward and the evangelist that they could be facing a tough fight. By the third night, the number of faces peering through the windows and doors was reduced drastically, and ample seats were available inside the church.

"Don't tell me at your age you can't read any better than that?" a familiar voice was asking. I froze with fright and didn't dare look back. It was my luck that this was happening to me. Immediately, I conjured up images of the entire class blaming me for what was obviously in store for all of us. I was getting all too used to this bad luck and hoped for a change. Still, my throat was stricken with fear and I had trouble getting my answer out.

Minutes earlier, Mr. Allen had asked a group of us to distribute the Second Standard English Primers to the rest of the class. Ollie and I were sharing a book, and we were supposed to read the passage silently and to answer the comprehension questions that followed in our exercise books. Instead, we had held the sides of our faces in our open palms and pretended to read, while we continued to talk. Usually, Mr. Allen would ask us to write the answers in our English books, which he would correct at home at night and return the next day. But this time, he hadn't marked the answers from the previous day, so he corrected the work while we read silently. Mr. Allen must have overheard us talking, for he called on me to stand in front of the class and read aloud. This is when Mr. Bradshaw decided to show up on his daily rounds.

"I would expect better from someone like you, Howard Prescod. Aren't you preparing for the Common Entrance Examination? How old are you?"

"Nine, sir. Ten in November."

I stared at Mr. Allen, who showed not a trace of feeling.

I turned around to face a questioning Mr. Bradshaw.

"Go ahead and read the passage for me again."

I started more hesitantly than before because of the fright, stumbling over the words.

"You can do better than that," he continued, walking slowly toward the front of the class. We all dreaded what was in store. "No boy in Class Three should be reading like that, picking at words like the fowls in the back yard picking corn out of the scratch grain."

The tears welled in my eyes and my knees shook. He looked blurred through the water, walking threateningly with long strides, his hands behind his back like an overseer at one of the plantations. The boards creaked with each step of Mr. Bradshaw's polished shoes.

The last time we had been this close to him was three days earlier at the final game of the school's cricket tournament, which Mr. Bradshaw had personally organized. He had bought the trophy himself that was awarded to the winning class. Because of Mr. Bradshaw's interest in cricket, most of the boys remained after school to watch the games instead of running off home at dismissal. There was a reason for this. We knew Mr. Bradshaw was likely to turn up at the tournament unexpectedly, the same way he had started to drop in on the classes for the older boys like Chester and Alvin. When we had returned to school after the Christmas holidays, Mr. Bradshaw was like a changed man, like someone who felt that he had spent enough time learning the ropes and was now ready to run things his way. This new attitude led to some open rows with Mr. Burton, many of them in the full view of all the teachers, and sometimes the students, but much to our misgivings Mr. Bradshaw continued with what appeared to be a new agenda.

One of the fiercest rows was whether the cricket tournament would be of any benefit to the school. Everyone knew what had happened. Mr. Bradshaw had argued that even if the boys were not exceptional players, the tournament would give them a chance to play together and to keep the older boys off the streets on evenings so they wouldn't be tempted by trouble. "Surely, a cricket tournament will give us a chance to use some of that expensive gear that is so carefully kept under lock and key in the teachers' room," he was reputed to have told Mr. Burton. "In the five months I've been here, I can't remember seeing the boys use any of that equipment once, not once. The purpose for having that gear is not for rats and mice to live among."

Mr. Burton didn't agree with his proposal and bluntly refused to organize the tournament.

"You can damn well organize your tournament yourself," he had shot back. "This government doesn't pay me enough to teach these hard-headed boys for a full day and then run some stupid tournament on evenings when I should be at home resting." Until then, nobody had heard of a deputy headmaster refusing to carry out an order from his superior. Everyone knew why Mr. Burton had acted this way; he had the backing of Mr. Ward, who was still head of the education committee. In a row between Mr. Bradshaw and any teacher, it was obvious Mr. Ward would not side with the headmaster because of his prominence in the Democratic Front for Independence.

Because of the row, the entire school and the teachers were on hand for the first game of the tournament. Only Mr. Bradshaw and Mr. Burton were absent when the two opposing captains walked to the center of the pitch and tossed the coin.

We had all settled into enjoying the game when Phillips, the head boy, pulled a ball to the longleg boundary. To our surprise, Mr. Bradshaw was standing there alone with his hands behind his back. Nobody had noticed him arrive. The fielder chasing the ball was just as startled. He added a few more strides in his attempt to run over and retrieve the ball.

But Mr. Bradshaw snared the ball as it was bouncing past him and, with a flat, well-directed throw, effortlessly returned it on the mark to an absolutely astonished bowler. It was so unexpected that the entire team stood its ground and stared at him, refusing to believe their eyes. No headmaster had ever done that before: picking up a ball instead of letting the poor student run all the way to the boundary and then back to the original position. Not even a teacher would have done what Mr. Bradshaw had done. And more surprisingly, none of us expected such an accurate throw from him, even though we had heard that in his youth Mr. Bradshaw was one of the best cricketers that ever came from our district.

But there he was on the sidelines, standing at the edge of the field watching the game. From then on, at some point in every game, Mr. Bradshaw would turn up to watch, the sleeves of his heavily starched white shirt rolled to the elbows and his collar unbuttoned. Even at the end of the tournament, we were still unaccustomed to seeing anyone of his rank and authority at our games and because of this, even as the tourna-ment was drawing to a close, some of the boys said they didn't feel as free when they knew he was watching. Mr. Bradshaw must have realized how inhibited he made us feel, for he never stayed for an entire game, although he attended every one of them.

We were just as frightened when he dropped into our classes uninvited. Now, he had stopped right in front of me, his massive presence inches from my shaking body. He turned and bellowed:

"Is there anybody here who thinks he can do better than Prescod? Speak up."

Nobody answered. The class was suddenly very quiet. Even though there were better readers, nobody volunteered. No one dared, not with Mr. Bradshaw standing there, his presence short and foreboding, threatening. He marched to the front of the class and stopped, waiting for a response. Still none came.

"You mean to tell me that in a class with some forty boys, that not one of you can read any better than that? How many boys on your register, Mr. Allen?"

"Forty-three, sir. There were forty-eight at the beginning of the school year, but five never came back from vacation."

"How many present and accounted for today?"

"Thirty-seven, sir." Mr. Allen took up the big flat blue register and flipped it open to double-check. "Yes. Thirty-seven."

"Good. Thirty-seven boys. And I suppose all of them taking the Common Entrance Examination in one or two years. The Common Entrance is an examination of two papers: simple arithmetic and reading and comprehension. How can you pass either if you can't read? What will happen to all of you if you don't pass this test? I'll tell you what will happen. You'll have no future—none whatsoever. If you don't pass the examination, you will lose the chance to go on to Harrison College, Lodge School, Combermere, or Boys' Foundation. You will lose your chance to study science, history, geography, mathematics, languages. You will lose your chance to further yourself, to pull yourselves out of this endless cycle of ignorance, poverty, and crime. You must understand how important all this is. Do you really wish to spend your life not having any control over it, working the plantation fields that belong to other people, doing the jobs no one else wants? To be slaves when you don't have to be? Is that what you want?" Sweat was pouring off him, his face was strained.

The entire school was stunned. Teachers in the neighboring classes were suddenly pretending to be busy while keeping an ear on what was going on in our class. Mr. Bradshaw's voice was overpowering, moving. No teacher liked the headmaster to walk into their class—which was the headmaster's right—and simply take over. It showed up those particular teachers and demonstrated their lack of control for all to see. If it wasn't so close to our morning biscuits break, many of the teachers would probably have taken their classes outside, under the big plum tree, to lessen the chances of the headmaster's intervention. As Mr. Burton had said recently, Mr. Bradshaw was becoming unpredictable, as if this independence nonsense was turning him foolish or crazy.

"Howard, go back to your seat. You, Oliver Mayers, next to him, take the book from him and read for me. How old are you?"

"Ten, sir. Ten in June, sir."

"That means you must take the examination next year, doesn't it?"

"Yes, sir."

"How many boys on your register are preparing for next year's exams, Mr. Allen?"

"All of them, sir."

"Are you happy with their progress?"

"Not really, sir." Mr. Allen faced the class with a look on his face that suggested he was apologizing for telling the truth. We could have killed him. "They have a lot of catching up to do."

"Okay," Mr. Bradshaw said, turning his attention back to Ollie. "Read for me."

Ollie glared at him. He raised the book to eye level and stared at it. No words came from his lips.

"Go ahead, read."

"He can't read, sir," someone in the back said.

"Who said that?" the headmaster thundered. Ollie looked around in spiteful anger, as if to ask the question himself.

Nobody answered. Mr. Allen, feeling embarrassed for his class and thinking it might be a reflection on him, started to explain. "You will find, sir, that very few of the boys can actually read. In fact, Prescod is probably the best of the lot as he does read the Bible at home for his grandmother. The others can't tell B from bull foot."

"I see," Mr. Bradshaw said thoughtfully. "This is a bigger problem than I thought. If they can't read . . ."

"I think the problem here is that they don't get enough chances to read," Mr. Allen tried to explain, interrupting Mr. Bradshaw. The headmaster didn't respond, and Mr. Allen looked uncomfortable, rushing on to further explanations.

"Some of them don't come to school often enough, they are always out of school doing something for their parents. Jones there in the back hasn't been to school for a full week yet this term, and we are now in the eighth week with only five more to go in this term. It's that bad."

Jones dropped his head on the desk. We expected Mr. Bradshaw to immediately haul him to the front of the class and give him a good thrashing.

"But all of them are trying their best," Mr. Allen continued, lowering his voice, as if pleading like a lawyer who had just admitted his client's guilt. "They would learn if they had a chance to concentrate on what they were doing. As it is now, they mind their smaller brothers and sisters at home when their parents have babies and must return to work. Some of them are already working as part-time gardeners. Take Oliver Mayers, for example. He works as a gardener after school. And Jones, he spends the long vacation and first part of the school term picking pond grass and weeds in the cane fields when he should be here. They don't get the chance to come to school regularly."

The boys in Class Three B were laughing. They had heard Mr. Allen's explanation and found it funny. They were brighter, and everyone said they had a better chance at passing than any of us in Three C.

Mr. Bradshaw stepped away from the blackboard into the hallway between the two classes. "Jordan, Oswald Jordan in Three B. I heard you laughing. Get up and read something from the book in front of you."

Jordan sprang to his feet, fumbling with the book and pages.

"Hurry up. You were the one to laugh at your fellow students. Now, let me hear you read." Mr. Bradshaw continued pacing between the two classes. "Let me hear you do better."

Jordan started to read, mumbling something.

"Louder, let everyone hear you."

Jordan tried again, but it wasn't much better. Fear was constricting his throat. The few audible words were coming out in scattered, trembling outbursts.

"Come out here, Jordan, and stand before me. Let the boys have a good look at you and let that teach you that it isn't fair to laugh at the misfortune of other people. Each one of us is our brother's keeper, and we must remember that."

While Jordan was making his way to the hall, Mr. Bradshaw turned his back to our class to address Three A, the elite of the third standards.

"Class Three A. Will the monitor get up and read something for me?"

"We ain't got no reading books, sir," the monitor pleaded. "We was doing 'rithmetic this morning. Reading is this afternoon, after lunch."

In the distance, the bell was ringing for the morning break. The rest of the school was going for milk and biscuits. Because the headmaster was dealing with Class Three, we missed our turn. Nobody complained.

"What language is the arithmetic problem written in? Isn't it English, too? If he can't read that would somebody please give him a book to read?"

Mr. Allen handed the boys in the back row of Three A his staff copy and signaled for them to pass it along. The monitor started to read, racing through the passage, but slurring the words.

"All right, all right," Mr. Bradshaw said. "All of you are in the same boat. None of you is better than the others. That is nothing to be proud of, and the unfortunate thing is that it isn't the fault of any of you. Neither is it the fault of the teachers," he added quickly as Mr. Burton, sitting in front of Class Three A, angrily glared at him. "The truth is I don't think one of you in any of these three classes could pass the examination if it was set today. Not one. And that is a pity. The biggest problem is that none of you can read properly. I'm going to correct that. I will be taking charge of preparing Class

Three for the examination. I will prepare my own curriculum and with the help of the teachers we will work with you if you are willing to learn. I will hold classes myself. Some of them will have to be after school and maybe on Saturday mornings, as well. We have a lot of catching up to do and we will start right away. The first thing we have to do is to take the three classes down to the library in Oistins. How many of you are members of the library? Let me see your hands. Raise them in the air."

He looked around. No hands went up.

"How many have been inside the library then? Show me the hands. There are almost one hundred and seventy-five of you boys in these three classes. At least one of you must have been inside the library."

No hands went up.

"Ah, well all I can say is that we have our work cut out for us. Tomorrow, I will go down to the library in Oistins and get some membership forms so that you can fill them out in school and take them in. We will go one class at a time for the next three days. We can't frighten the poor librarian with almost two hundred young men that can't read nor write turning up in the library at the same time. Tomorrow, we will start with Three C, right after morning prayers. Any man-jack who is here today and doesn't turn up tomorrow will have to personally answer to me. So tell your parents that."

I wanted to get up and explain to Mr. Bradshaw that he was putting me in a difficult position. Grandmother had strictly forbidden us to bring any library books into her house. She felt that the Bible and the encyclopedias that Dad had sent for us were all we needed and that all other books were the Devil's way of corrupting people. When the reader least expected it, the Devil would slip in a message that would drive out the godliness and set the reader firmly on a path of sin and destruction.

I had a bad feeling of what Grandmother would think about going to the library, about her reception to me bringing home books. But I had no choice. Maybe Grandmother would understand and relent. Once again, I wondered why I was always in the middle of these things and thought hopefully of life in England with my parents, where things would be so much easier.

"So Class Three C should come prepared to walk down to Oistins tomorrow," Mr. Bradshaw continued. "My advice is that everyone wears a pair of shoes—pumps or sneakers. The tar road is going to be very hot and your feet will need the protection. The next day we will take Three A and then on Thursday Three B. You can now go for your milk and biscuits, starting with Three A by the door. When you come back into the school, do it in an orderly fashion and don't disrupt the rest of the school."

Mr. Bradshaw walked away from the classes, heading for his office. He left us dazed at the turn of events. Nobody expected this. Mr. Toppin before him never had shown this type of interest. If he did, it would usually end with a flogging, beginning with the first boy in the first row and working over to the last one in the last row. This could be repeated over and over, by which time the students' backs would be bruised and sore, the headmaster dripping in sweat, saliva foaming at the corners of his mouth.

We had expected this treatment when Mr. Bradshaw barged into the class and found us unable to read. Instead, he left us thunderstruck, feeling a bit proud because of what he had said.

But how could I tell Grandmother I had to wear shoes to school? She would ask why, and why Alvin and Chester didn't have to wear them as well. And then I would have to tell her about the library. It seemed there was no way I could get out of telling her.

That evening I walked home dejectedly, thinking of when the opportune time would be to break the news to Grandmother.

12

The chance to tell Grandmother never came. By the time I got home, she was waiting for me, and in a very happy mood. She was sitting on the floor of the house, her feet on the back steps with the flowered dress lapped between her legs and a broad smile on her face. As soon as I entered, she called me over to her side, folding a blue envelope and putting it in her pocket. This seemed as good a time as any to raise the matter.

"How was school today, big boy?" she asked, throwing her arm around my back and hugging me. "Your father wrote you and your two brothers. I was just reading the letter. He keep asking why you and your brothers don't write. He don't know that the three o' you big enough to write him anytime you want, but that you and your brothers are just too lazy. That's what. The Lord knows I try my levelest best to get all of you to write. But nothing doing. Why you don't like writing your parents, Howard?"

Before I could answer, she reached into her apron and pulled out twenty-five cents. "I want you to go down to Oistins and get some more fish for me. Don't wait 'til the price o' the fish drop all the way like the last time. Tomorrow morning I'm going down to the post office and change up the five-shilling note that your father send for the three o' you. A little tra-la to keep in your pocket. Your father also said that he's sending me a little more money when the month comes to support the three o' you. Like he only now realizes that it takes money to feed and clothe you, three growing young men."

I thought of breaking the news to her then, but before I

could begin, she thrust the old faded canvas bag into my hand. It was lying on the rocks, inside out, where it was deposited every time someone brought fish home. The inside of the bag was washed with soap to kill the smell and rawness, and there it remained until the next visit.

"Take care not to cross the road like some madman when you walking. And hurry up and come back: I don't want you to get licked down by some car."

Within two hours I was back home. Grandmother and Alma soon scaled the fish, gutting them on the rocks and throwing the belly to Mavis Thorpe's cat which had strayed over at the smell. The old black and white cat was a constant visitor and nuisance. Grandmother also saw it as a threat to her chickens and young turkeys. When Mavis wasn't looking, we would douse it with water and send it scampering.

While Grandmother was steaming the fish over the blazing fire, Mavis appeared at her window and called out to her. Because she didn't work, Mavis would always finish cooking early, soon after Theo and the others came home from school. Usually, while they were eating, Grandmother was just planning what to cook. When they were getting ready for bed, we were usually eating. The only thing I liked about this arrangement was that it allowed me to brag to Theo that I stayed up later than he, that I didn't go to sleep with the fowls and chickens, like him and his brothers. Then again, they probably didn't piss their beds every night.

"You going down by the corner shop tonight, Mrs. Howell?" Mavis asked. The tone in her voice suggested she was going and that she might be looking for companionship.

"What happening?"

"You ain't hear 'bout the big political meeting tonight? That Douglas Leopold Phillips and his boys holding a meeting down there. They've been driving up and down all over the place announcing the meeting over a loudspeaker on a car all day. You ain't hear it?"

"Yes, but I did forget. I don't pay too much attention to

no politician," Grandmother said in explanation of her ignorance. From her answer, it was obvious she was interested. "You think that he'll have anything good to say? Anything that would make it worthwhile to make the people stand out in the dew all night?" Grandmother didn't really expect an answer. She chipped a piece of pine wood from a bigger slab and placed it in the fire. In a moment, the splinter was blazing, further illuminating the darkening yard with a bright glow, great black soot reeking of sweet pine rising around the pot. "These political meetings like to go on and on forever. You know how politicians like to talk."

"I don't mind," Mavis said, obviously delighted at the thought of attending the meeting. "Me and a couple o' the girls are going to wrap a few sweaters round our necks to keep off the dew. And we're going to stand up out there 'til the last word. Maisie might even bring out a bench from her house and give it to us to sit on. You know, I do like to hear my man Phillips talking. I hope they bring him on last. He does make everything plain, plain. Any fool could understand what's going on 'pon this little island when he done talk. That man's got the right ideas about independence—it's time we was masters in our own house. That is why the white people don't like him."

Never one to be left out of anything, Grandmother decided to pack us up and head over to the political meeting, her previous convictions and the stern warnings from Pastor Allsop be damned.

A large crowd was already assembled by the time we arrived. Most of the people were milling around in the evening's darkness, just talking and waiting for the rally to start. The numbers were swelling by the minute; the mass of people were spreading out in all directions. People were sitting at the edge of the darkness by the sides of the road, on bicycles, or leaning against the wall in front of Little Foot's brand new house. Still people were arriving, on foot, by bus, on the back of lorries, and by bicycle. Most of the women carried small wooden benches on which they could sit when their feet got tired from standing. We found a spot under an almost leafless almond tree to the left of the truck that would be the stage for the night.

Everyone was in a very lively mood, full of expectations, laughing and talking loudly, like they were at a reunion or something. Even the saved Christians who weren't supposed to look like they were enjoying anything were laughing and joking. Cars with license plates from outside the parish were parked along the sides of Lodge Road and Water Street, converging at the intersection where the meeting was being held. Since Mr. Ashby was the only person in Lodge Road and the surrounding areas to own a car, this meant that Mr. Phillips had succeeded in drawing a crowd from around the island, and that more importantly, the rich and white people were concerned enough about what he was saying to come and hear him.

Many of the car drivers were sitting on the hoods of the automobiles, or just standing around talking and laughing among themselves. There wasn't a woman among them. As a group, they were sticking together, and the majority of black and poor people were happy to keep it that way, to be separated from them.

Occasionally, a black woman would talk to one of the white men. Usually it was her employer or a past master. The conversations were short, stilted, the man almost whispering, the woman laughing frequently and shyly. The uneasy meeting was punctuated by mechanical laughter, until, mercifully, the conversation would end abruptly. They had nothing in common to talk about: different politics, different dreams, different ways of seeing things. They were anxious to escape to their separate sides of the invisible fence.

Grandmother, Alma, and Mavis had walked gingerly down the center of the road, whispering among themselves

and eyeing the strangers suspiciously. The five of us boys—
Alvin, Chester, Theo, Theo's brother Donald, and me—followed behind. We were happy to be attending our first
political meeting and were excited at seeing so many people in
one place. Theo and I hung back behind the others, but not so
far that the grownups would be concerned, to talk and shout
to friends at the sides of the road.

In front of the shop was a flat Bedford truck. The hood
was painted red, with a black top, but the paint was peeling
and the truck looked old and battered. On the back of the
flat-bed was a porttable podium that some men were securing
to the truck. An electric wire was run from the shop to the
platform and fastened to a long thin piece of wood beside the
podium. A string of naked light bulbs hung over the back of
the truck, which served as a platform for the speakers. It was
as bright as day on the back of the lorry, the strong light
contrasting sharply with the deep darkness a few feet away. A
group of men were preparing the platform, rearranging chairs
for the speakers, installing the portable podium with the letters DFI—Democratic Front for Independence—on it. They
tested the microphones, running wires across the road into the
crowd for heavy silvery loudspeakers that were hanging from
the trees. A loudspeaker was placed on the roof of the shop
and another was taken some distance down Water Street into
the darkness where it blared away at nobody in particular. The
organizers of this rally were not going to let those who
couldn't make it to the meeting miss the words of Douglas
Leopold Phillips. They could not drift off into peaceful bliss
with a loudspeaker blaring miles away.

The chief technician, a short man in a white T-shirt with
a pair of pliers in his back pocket, was testing the speakers,
knocking the microphone with his hand and listening for the
sound. When nothing came out, he started banging harder
and swearing. The connection clicked in just in time to register
a loud "Fuck" that echoed through the neighboring villages.
At the sound of the cuss word, everyone laughed and a chorus

of voices went out, causing the speakers to squelch. The workman looked ashamed and covered the microphone with his hand. When the feedback died down, he continued to tug at the wires.

"At least you know she working," someone nearby shouted to the workman. The sensitive microphone picked that up, too.

"She working too blasted good," he responded. "Anyway, I glad for that, 'cause when Dipper Phillips get going, there ain't going to be a fellow for miles around that could truthfully say he ain't had the opportunity to hear the gospel, the living truth. I tell yuh, not when I done here."

None of the speakers had arrived so the people in the crowd continued to amuse themselves. A bus passed, slowly driving through the crowd, passing the parked cars now cutting the already narrow road in half. It turned up Lodge Road, accelerating beyond the row of cars. The people in the bus leaned through the windows to see what was going on. Some got off and joined the crowd. When the technician was finished, someone turned on a record player and the voice of Jim Reeves was blasted over the area. In spite of the loudness, nobody paid any attention, at least not until the needle of the record stuck in a groove and Jim Reeves sounded like a man with a bad stutter. "Why all o' you don't clean the records before playing them," a voice shouted.

After what seemed like an eternity, someone leapt onto the platform to lift the needle off the record. A loud scraping noise reverberated through the speakers. People shouted at him. He tried to restart the music, but the record stuck just as quickly. Again and again, the luckless man kept trying, even as the crowd hurled a mixture of advice and insults at him.

"Why don't you throw away that damn Jim Reeves record," said a tall man, coming out of the bar near the platform. "Play something West Indian, something black. Play the Mighty Charmer if yuh got any calypsos. Play Nat King Cole, the Drifters, Louis Armstrong. Something the people know, not some foolish Jim Reeves singing 'bout some stupid Rolly Polly and nonsense 'bout eating biscuits and getting fat. Play Sparrow or the Blue Busters, put a little ska music in we ass tonight to warm we up for the Dipper.''

He disappeared again into the shop and joined a group of men drinking white rum and beer chasers. His advice must have turned the trick because the worker got the music going. This time it was Mahalia Jackson, singing spirituals, her rich voice soaring over the crowd and capturing our attention. Some of the women started to hum, softly at first and then louder. Eventually, it was like an outdoor church meeting, with almost everyone singing.

This seemed to satisfy everyone, including the tall man in the bar, for he didn't reappear. I had always been curious about what really happened in the bar and made up an excuse that I was tired and needed to sit. To my surprise, Grandmother and Mavis suggested that we boys might want to rest on the stoop of the bar. We took that a step further and went right in.

Inside the shop, the tall stranger was in an earnest argument with Little Foot, who was standing underneath the radio in a corner of the bar. Like everyone else, he was holding a snap glass for his turn at the rum bottle. As he talked, he hobbled around on his shortened polio foot. The men were standing around them, letting the two debaters go at each other. Ma remained impassive and unconcerned in the doorway, apparently oblivious to the argument, but willingly accepting the glass of rum when it passed her way.

"I don't mind you," the tall slim man was saying, stabbing a long finger in the air above Little Foot's head. His face was contorted with emphasis. "I don't mind you a-tall, Li'l Foot. I don't mind you a-tall. It is people like you that sells out yuh own black people and keep all of us down-pressed like this for so long."

"You don't haveta get so personal," Little Foot shot back. The strength that had been lost in the polioed foot over the years had been added to his boisterous voice. "You can't face the truth. That is what's wrong with you. When you losing an argument you does gotta get personal, calling people names and things. But the old people always say empty buckets make the most noise, if you know what I mean." He turned to the other men for support. Nobody said anything. The most he got was some noncommittal head shakes. A scramble for the rum bottle and the glasses ensued. Little Foot, undeterred, returned to the issue at hand, whatever it was. "All I'm saying is that I ain't following no politician down the road to destruction. Not me, Bosie. I have a brain o' me own in my nut here," he pointed to his head, "and nobody ain't fooling me. All o' you here like idiots ready to believe every and anything bigguts Douglas Leopold Phillips says. As if he is some god. But not me. I know better. I's a man that does travel and see the outside world. So I know better."

"You know better because you is a yard fowl, that's what," the stranger said. "You know what a yard fowl is. Every morning you get up from sleeping and go into the yard and shake a couple of grains o' corn in an old cup and sure as hell the yard fowls come running. Rain or shine the yard fowls there. Even if you only put rocks in the cup and shake them, the yard fowl coming. You is a political yard fowl," he said emphatically, stabbing his finger in the air again, this time closer to Little Foot's face. "Worse, you is a fucking yard fowl for the white people, for the Wards who own all the land around here and exploits the poor people of this island. I'm talking 'bout the said same Herbert Ward that's the big shot on the local council, on the education board, the same bigwig for this parish of Christ Church in the Conservative Labour Movement, the same Labour Party that does represent the white people and only remembers the black people at election time. You's a yard fowl for Wardie. You, Little Foot, the man that does travel overseas, always there at their beck and call, like the fowl in the yard."

"You talking nonsense, Charlie," Little Foot said, sucking

his teeth loudly. "Nonsense. Everybody 'round here knows I's a Labourite, born and bred, and I ain't hiding it. I would rather be a Labourite than a fucking Communist. That is all I'll say to people like you, Charlie."

"Communist. Communist." Charlie spat out the words as if they were poison. "Who's a Communist, let me ask you that right now? Who is a Communist? You only making me hot now."

"If you don't know who are the Communists, too bad for you." He was speaking to the whole bar now. "All o' you down here at this political meeting, taking everything Douglas Leopold Phillips saying, all this nonsense 'bout independence and things like that, as if you all playing you don't know Phillips and his people are pure Communists. Just like Castro in Cuba. If we don't get rid o' them now, the next thing we know we're going to be owned by the Russians. And everybody knows what the Russians are: Communists, people that get their kicks out of burning Bibles and closing down churches. Ask Superintendent Cox at the church if you doubt me. Barbados would be in nothing but trouble if that happen'."

"If what happen?" Ma said, taking the smoldering cigar butt from her mouth. She spat into the darkness, narrowly missing a woman who was sitting nearby.

"Close down the churches and burn the Bibles," Little Foot repeated, probably thinking he had found a vocal ally.

"Be Christ, that won't be too bad a thing to do, if I say so." She puffed on the cigar. "I always said this little island would be a whole lot better off if we close down a lot o' places 'round here we call churches and if people throw away the Bible. But nobody don't listen to me." She relapsed into silence, staring into the crowd, waiting for the next drink.

"Don't mind him. That is nonsense he talkin'. Bare nonsense," Charlie said. "I don't know why you scandalizing Mr. Phillips so. Is it because he's black, like one o' us? Or is it because he ain't a member of the Conservative Labour Movement, the same Labour Party that promises you jobs and keeps you drunk?"

"I won't take you on," Little Foot said. "You can't face the music. All I know is that Phillips, the said one that all o' you come to hear like a bunch o' sheep with no brains, will sell us out to the Communists."

He paused for effect, hobbled over to the counter, and poured a big drink. Little Foot added some water and drained the glass with a loud gulp, his Adam's apple bobbing up and down like a small boat in rough seas. When he finished, he screwed up his face and wiped his mouth with the back of his hand. The bottle was now empty. The man standing next to him took up the empty bottle, held it up to the light, and shot a disapproving look at him.

"Little, man," he said contritely, "you coulda left back a little piece for me. But no. You had to gobble all of it, man."

Just then, a tall, stout white man with long silver hair came into the shop and went to the counter. The regular drinkers made room for him and the woman acting as bartender stopped attending the man she was dealing with and turned to him.

"What can I do for you, sir?" she asked reverently.

"Gi' me a couple o' beers and two bottles o' rum. A white rum and a dark one. And gi' me a couple o' Cokes, too, and some glasses, and see if you can put all o' that on a tray for me to carry outside."

The woman turned to the red wooden box and brought out a block of ice, placed it on the edge of the box, and started chipping at it with an ice pick. She put the splinters in an enamel bowl, placed six glasses on the tray along with the drinks, and slid it across the counter to the man.

"Getting a bit chilly out there," the white man said to nobody in particular. "Gotta get some good grog to warm up the insides. What you think?"

"That's okay, man. We're just talking some politics before you came in. I was telling these stupid-ass people here that if we ain't careful, Phillips going to turn us all into Communists," Little Foot said, obviously hoping the white man would support his argument.

"Communists," he laughed loudly, taking up the tray. "Communists. I've never heard that one before. All of us Communists, eh?" He walked out the door laughing, leaving everyone unsure what he really meant.

Then Mr. Bradshaw came bursting through the door. It happened so quickly that Theo, I, and our brothers couldn't even think of bolting from the bar. We looked up and to our horror saw him standing right over us. He wore an open-necked white shirt, the sleeves rolled up to the elbow and a big gold crucifix on his chest. He looked different, taller in the informal clothes. "Good-night, Mr. Bradshaw," we said, springing to attention and saluting. "Good-night, sir."

"Good-night, boys," Mr. Bradshaw said. "Come to the meeting, have you?"

"Yes, sir."

"Braddie, you're a headmaster, you got more brains than all o' us put together," Charlie said to Mr. Bradshaw, who was now leaning against the counter, smiling and ordering a beer. "Tell Little Foot there that he's talking foolishness. Ask him for me what we'll get from holding on to the British coattails all this time. He will understand you more than me."

"Give Little Foot a chance. He's going to come around some day and see that independence is good for all of us," Mr. Bradshaw said. "And we *will* get independence whether we want it or not, because the British just don't want us anymore: they have their own problems. They are begging us to become independent, like Jamaica and Trinidad. If he wants to support the Conservative Labour Movement, that's fine. Just do so after the election, Little Foot."

The sting of the argument was gone. The men in the bar shuffled about, finishing off drinks, talking among themselves and leaving Charlie to pay for the rum. On the outside, some men were sitting on the platform. The chairman was standing by the microphone getting ready to speak. There was no sign of Douglas Leopold Phillips, although his deputy had arrived and was talking to a knot of people in front of the platform. From all indications, the meeting was about to begin, and from all appearances, Mr. Bradshaw was not going to be leaving the bar too quickly. The five of us didn't want to be that close to him, not after the events that had occurred earlier that day. My luck was unreliable at best so when the opportunity came, we slipped out of the shop, all saying good-night loudly enough for Mr. Bradshaw and the woman behind the counter to hear. We hurried back to join Grandmother and Mavis. By the end of the rally, I was so tired that I forgot to say anything about going to the library. Before I got up in the morning, Grandmother had already left for the city on the early morning bus.

13

Mr. Burton walked in front of the class, carefully reviewing the troops and muttering under his breath. His black-framed glasses were perched low on his nose, emphasizing the deep scowl on his face. Trouble was brewing. It was obvious to everyone that he wasn't in favor of our going to the library.

As fate would have it, Mr. Bradshaw had an unexpected appointment in town and would not be going with us to the library. At first, this seemed to be a stroke of luck. Surely the responsibility of taking us on our outing would fall to Mr. Allen, or better yet, it might be postponed, giving me another chance to raise the matter with Grandmother. Mr. Allen probably wouldn't notice or even care that I was barefoot. Unfortunately, Mr. Burton, head of the Class Threes and still deputy headmaster, was given the chore, with Mr. Allen just coming along for the ride.

Everyone knew Mr. Burton was a beater. Everyone also knew that Mr. Bradshaw and he fought openly about independence. Many believed that Mr. Bradshaw's intervention in our class was because of Mr. Burton's insubordination and might not have been bred of a genuine concern for getting us up to speed for the screening test.

In any event, I was shoeless and hung back to disguise that fact as we stood for inspection in the yard behind the school. Of course, Mr. Burton, who had never liked me, zeroed in on me like a gun to a target. I was exposed and expected the worse.

"Prescod, come out here," he bellowed. I walked slowly to the front of the class. I was the only one without shoes.

126

"Where are your shoes, young man?"

"I ain't got none, sir."

"What's that?" he asked, stepping away from me and pretending not to hear. "Speak louder for everyone to hear."

"I said I ain't wearing none."

"We can see that. We got eyes to see that you ain't got no shoes on your feet," Mr. Burton said slowly, walking around me, inspecting my clothes as well. "You ain't wearing no shoes although the headmaster, Mr. Bradshaw, said loud and clear for everyone to hear that he wants every man-jack in Three C to wear shoes today. You heard him say that, Master Prescod? You was listening, weren't you? Answer me."

"Yes, sir."

"So where are your shoes?"

"I ain't got none, sir."

"What?" he said in mock dismay. "Your mother and father are still living in England? Am I right or wrong? Your father, Frankie, who I taught before you and who never gave me any trouble, is still in England, in the army?"

"Yes, sir."

"And you mean to tell me that your father, living in England, where he could buy as many pairs of shoes as he wishes, can't buy you a pair o' shoes to wear to school? Not even a pair o' canvas pumps that cost three dollars? You mean to tell me that? Look at all the other boys around you whose parents got nothing, still living in Barbados, not making half the money your mother and father making. But they're wearing shoes."

I didn't answer. The humiliation wouldn't let me. Eventually, I tried to speak, to explain that things weren't the way he was saying. But only a small quivering sound came from my throat. I could feel the sun baking down on me, the sweat pouring down my back as the eyes of almost the entire school bore right through me.

"I can't believe that your mother and father are in England and you're walking around here in bare feet," Mr. Burton continued. "And look at your clothes. The pants are dirty and faded. You've been in that same shirt for the past three days now. Lord, you're going to the people's library, the least you can do is wear a change of clothes. Wear something good, like your Sunday school pants and shoes."

A cloud passed under the sun, showering the field with shade. Mr. Burton continued to circle me like one of those long-necked birds in the cane fields sizing up a dead animal. I was alone in the world and unprotected.

He stopped walking and was now standing looking directly into my face as he spoke. The loose top plate of his false teeth fell forward each time he spoke. His tongue darted out to push it back in place. He reached in his pocket and pulled out the rolled-up strap that had made his pants leg bulge. The strap was short and thin with a big double knot at the end.

"I gotta try and set you right. Otherwise you're going to grow up at Dodd's door, as good as a cent, before you get a chance to go to England." With that he grabbed the front of my shirt, pulling it to tighten it across the back. By then the tears were rolling down my cheeks.

"You ain't crying yet," he taunted. "I ain't hit yuh yet. But you can be damn sure I'm going to give you something to cry about. This ain't going to be no fly bite, I tell yuh. You will remember to wear shoes the next time we tell you to. Twelve, yes, twelve of the best in the backside for yuh."

His right hand was raised with the brown shiny strap in it. I heard the sound before I felt the sting and the burn. With each strike, he pulled the strap across my back, extending the burn from the knot. Mr. Burton was taking his time, slowly administering the whipping, enjoying it. A pleasurable sneer came across his face and with each lash, I was wriggling and rubbing my back, bawling for mercy. With the shirt pulled so taut, there was virtually nothing but my back to absorb the punishment.

"Now that I finish, I got five minds not to let you go to the library with us this good morning. And to think we're doing all this so a few more of you hard-headed boys can have a chance at passing the screening test. But it will be a big waste o' time, you watch my words. A waste of time. No amount of going to the library, study or getting extra lessons will help someone like you. You're hopeless. Go into your class. You ain't going with us if you ain't got no shoes."

I ran into the school overcome by humiliation and the stinging pain. He didn't even let me explain. How could I explain that Grandmother didn't like libraries, that I *wanted* to wear the shoes—the ones that Pretty's mistress had given me? That Dad was going to send me some clothes as soon as Grandmother sent him the right size? But she had not yet found the time to measure me, not even to buy the measuring tape. I didn't care if I passed the stupid Common Entrance: I was going to England anyway, regardless of what anyone said. I was going to leave school as soon as I turned twelve. I could get a job as a gardener, maybe cutting lawns or watering the roses. Nobody would ever beat me again without a good reason. I would never pass the Common Entrance Exam. I didn't want to sit the damn exam, anyway. Alvin and Chester had already failed it. I just wanted my mother and father to send for me.

"Prescod," a calm voice was saying, disrupting my thoughts. "Come, Prescod. Come and join the line."

I raised my head from my hands, from the hard desk, and through the tears saw Mr. Allen in front of me, almost whispering.

"Come and join the line. We are leaving for the library now and you are coming, even without shoes."

"But I didn't do nothin'. I didn't do nothin' and he just beat me like that," I protested between sobs, my body shaking. My back was sore from the flogging, burning from the knots. It felt like Mr. Burton had hit the same spot all twelve times.

"I know. I know," Mr. Allen said, still speaking softly and calmly. "I know. But you are getting to be a big man. Wipe your eyes and come with me. Things will work out some day. You're growing up."

He held my hand and led me out the door. I joined the back of the line, one step ahead of Mr. Allen, and headed off to the library.

"What you doing there so quiet at the table?" Grandmother asked as she came through the side door to the house.

"Writing a letter," I mumbled dejectedly. I had been searching for the elusive words that would express on paper exactly how angry and abandoned I felt.

"We've been looking all over the place for you since the sun went down. I keep telling you that you should come straight home when the school lets out, but you won't listen," she said.

For half an hour I had been laboring over the task of putting my feelings into words, but the page was still empty, the yellow pencil stub forlornly resting on the paper, my thoughts jumbled in my brain.

Passing behind me, Grandmother walked through the house, kicked off the canvas pumps on her feet at the back door and entered the yard. I had come home to a dark and empty house and had lighted the lamp, taking great care not to let it slip. That was the first time I had ventured to touch the lamp when I was at home alone. In some ways, from the way I felt, I didn't really care if I had dropped the lamp. Perhaps it wasn't possible that anything more terrible could have happened to me; my luck could not get any worse.

Even as I had reached for the lamp and struck the match, my hands were still shaking from the anger inside my chest, a hurt that was many times stronger than the pain caused by Mr. Burton's strap, worse than anything Grandmother could possibly do to me if I were to break the lamp.

All day, pain and rejection had consumed me like fire. I had alternated between lonely depression and the feeling that somebody had to be responsible for my condition. None of the boys in my class appeared to have things as tough as I; nobody else in the entire school was worse off than my two brothers and I; no family in the district, if not on all the island, was worse off than ours. Anyone could casually pick on us and make trouble with no fear of retribution. This was not fair.

In my heart, I felt something had to change, and I thought about it so hard that between crying and thinking my head hurt desperately by the end of the school day. After school, I went for a long walk, going nowhere in particular, but allowing my feet to take me where they wanted, as long as it wasn't home. I just could not go home and face anyone there. All of us were in the same situation. I knew that much. We were helplessly exposed and so vulnerable that anyone could take advantage of us at any time, none of us capable of helping the other. We had no way of fighting back. And because everybody knew that, we were easy prey, even for people like Mr. Burton.

Earlier in the day, I had seen the same looks of despair and hurt on the faces of Alvin and Chester. They were standing in the schoolyard, a short distance from the very spot where Mr. Burton had administered the whipping a few hours earlier. Everyone was talking about the beating, re-enacting the moments, laughing at how I had cried out and begged for mercy. Feeling terribly ashamed for me, my brothers could only look on, standing at the edge of the group of boys, as if they feared that out of anger they might inadvertently say something in my defense and also end up being dragged before Mr. Burton. There was no glory for them in my shame. They did not even come over to talk to me, not because they didn't want to, but because we were all so scared and defenseless. I felt as sorry for them as I did for myself, for I knew they wanted to tell me that I did not deserve such treatment. What they could not communicate with their voices, they did with their eyes and faces, with their silence and the nervous shrugging of their shoulders. They shuffled their feet in the dust and tightly folded

their arms against their chests as if they wanted to hide themselves within their own bodies.

The more I thought about these things, the more I wanted
to walk, to be alone, to sit down and write a long letter to my
father and mother and to explain that they should hurry up
and send for us. That was the only solution to our problems:
going to England and joining our parents. It was as simple as
that. We would escape from Brutus, Mr. Burton, the Sunday
school, and the shame of knowing what people in the village
thought and said about Grandmother. I craved a strong father
to defend us, a man to fight and stand up to anyone bullying
us, a man to take away our fear.

The only way I could let my parents know how desperately we needed help was for me to write them a letter, to ask
them what had been keeping them so long. Dad had asked
Grandmother in the last letter why we wouldn't write him.
Maybe now he'd figure it out. But not through one of those
letters that Grandmother forced us to write while she dic-
tated—through one written in my own words.

"Writing your father, eh?" she asked again.

"Yes."

Even without looking up, I knew she was sitting on the
large rock in front of the fire. I could smell the sweet odor as
more of the wood caught the flame, as the thin smoke drifted
into the house.

"Know what you're going to tell him?" she asked. By then
I could hear the crackling sound of the flames. Grandmother's
tone was not as abrasive as I had expected.

"I want to ask him when he's going to send for us, so
that we can get away from here and grow up in a country
where . . ."

"What did you do for Leroy Burton to beat you this
morning?" she asked calmly. As usual, she addressed the
teachers by their full name, a reminder that she had known
them when they were at school together. The question surprised me. She must have noticed my reaction, for she explained why she was asking.

"Alvin and Chester told me when they came home this evening that Leroy Burton called you out in front of the whole school and gave you a good beating. What you'd do for him to do that?"

"I didn't do nothing," I said emphatically. At that moment I had to make a quick decision whether to tell her about the trip to the library. I didn't feel like explaining the whole thing. I hoped that Alvin and Chester in making their report of what had happened had not told her everything. "It's just that he's a big bully; he likes to beat up poor little children that don't have any father to defend them. That's why I'm writing my dad."

"What you expect he'll do about it?" Grandmother asked, almost in a whisper. "He's all the way in England." I looked up from the table to see her big shadow, elongated across the yard, reaching into the house through the back door, like a fallen giant with humps in his back and waist.

"He'll send for me, get me out of this trouble."

"But you know he's planning to do just that. Things take time. The good Lord lets everything happen in its own sweet time," she said softly.

"They keep saying that they sending for the three o' us every year but nothing ever happens, and all the boys at school keep laughing at us and . . ."

"Could it be that they aren't in a position to do that just yet?" Grandmother asked. "You got to remember that your mummy and daddy love you; every mother and father loves their children. I'm as sure of that as I'm sure of a God above. As soon as your mother and father can see their way, they'll send for you. Just remember taking time ain't laziness."

"Well, if they can't send for me now, I wish they were here. I's their son. I need them now," I said, the tears flowing down my cheeks again.

"Count your blessings, son. The Bible says: the race is not for the swift, but he that endureth to the end. Remember that. Don't look at the bad side alone. Be strong. Everything is for a time. You should never give up hope."

"But all we have is you and you can't go and beat up Mr. Burton," I said, exasperated by her answer.

"That's true," she said, offering no apology. "I's just a woman and I can't beat up nobody. But brute strength ain't all. You must realize it's better to have something in your head than to be a bully. You'll see that's true when you get to England."

I looked at her straight in the face and asked the question that had haunted me for so long. "Grandmother, are we really going to go there, to England, I mean?"

Before she could answer, Alvin and Chester came barreling through the paling gate. Grandmother looked at them. "He's home," and after a long pause she added, "writing a letter to his father."

"We looked all over for him," Alvin said. He looked at me. "Where you went?"

"Nowhere in particular," I said. "Over by the quarry, up by Ma's house."

"You wasn't afraid Ma would do something to you?" Chester asked.

Grandmother lifted the frying pan off the fire. She looked slightly stunned, a bit sad.

"You must be hungry, Howard," she said. "Alvin, go there on the table and bring me a few plates. The little morsel of food I cooked this evening is warmed up. Come, Howard, come and get some food in your stomach."

I got up from the table and walked into the yard. Grandmother spread the four plates on the back-door stoop and piled on the fried rice. There was no meat. The four of us sat on the rock before the fire and began eating.

"Life won't always be this tough," Grandmother said. "Let us bow our heads in prayer and ask God's blessing for these few mouthfuls of food and for his protection. Also give us the strength within ourselves to forgive others that offend us." She said a short but rambling prayer. We ate in silence under a dark cloudless tropical sky, partially brightened by millions of stars. Only the sound of our spoons hitting the enamel plates and the cracking of the firewood broke the quiet of the night.

Halfway through the plateful, Grandmother reached over and hugged me and softly rubbed the spot on my back where the strap had left its mark. Gently, she took my head and rested it on her lap. Soon I was fast asleep.

When I woke up in the morning, I found she had rubbed some warm oil on my back. Someone had carried me to my bed. The white sheet of paper for the letter was where I had left it the night before. Much of the hurt that had made me want to write the letter was still there. I still intended to write it, but the urgency was now gone.

14

It took me a long time to get over this painful humiliation. It was worse than anything I had ever experienced. I took refuge in myself and plotted ways to get even, not only with Mr. Burton, but with all those boys who continued to tease and mock my brothers and me. Maybe when I became a man, when I returned from England rich, educated, and mannerly, as Grandmother promised, I would be strong enough to fight back. Nobody would dare look on any of my family as easy pickings. But until then I had to defend myself and avoid any situations that could lead to more painful beatings.

One solution was for me to not draw attention to myself. Instead of talking and playing with others my age, I began to spend most of my time going to the library in Oistins and reading. In the classroom, I talked less and concentrated on what Mr. Allen was saying. Without a question, almost blindly, I followed his instructions.

I was determined to set myself apart so that nobody could hurt me, so that I would not continue to embarrass my broth-ers, so that I wouldn't have to worry about who would prey on us next. Whether it was Everick Waite, his sisters, or Mr. Burton.

Although Mr. Bradshaw and some of the other politicians were preaching that the people on this island were one, that there was strength in unity and that we should all face the future together, I saw no proof of this generosity in our lives. It seemed to me that in the village of Lodge Road, the stronger people were only unified in preying on the weaker ones among them, who happened to be mainly me and my family. I didn't detect any feeling of charity for the unfortunate, no sense of protection, only a frightening and dreaded exposure of our nakedness from being totally defenseless.

In some strange way, the strong seemed to know which of the weak to grind into the dust. None of them, for example, tackled Ma even though she was an older woman, lived alone, and got drunk almost every night. When intoxicated, she was even more defenseless than any of us as she wobbled down the road, dragging her cane behind her, going home to a house up by the quarry, at the farthest point of the village by the desolate cane fields. Her house was always open but nobody dared enter; nobody gave a thought to stoning it in the middle of the night. There was no man in her house yet people knew not to cross Ma, for everyone knew there was a gun, and Ma would not hesitate to use it in her defense. She kept her trigger finger sharp by firing the gun into the cane fields every night. Those loud bangs sent an unmistakable message around the village. In the rum shops, her tongue was as sharp and caustic as that of any man, easily cutting them down in conversation and castrating them by drinking more alcohol than any of them. Nobody messed with her and for good reason.

"That Ma is quite a woman," Grandmother often said when we heard her dragging the cane along the street. "I think the good Lord meant for she to be a man but something went wrong. In all my life I've never seen another woman like Ma when it comes to holding her own drinking and smoking with the men. She could go home drunk as a bat and first thing in the morning she's so sober you won't believe she went near a drop of that stuff. I tell yuh, she was meant to be a man." Despite her criticisms, it was obvious Grandmother had a begrudging respect for this older woman, a fondness that showed in her voice when she spoke to a sober Ma.

Even if things were to improve as Mr. Bradshaw predicted, that would only happen slowly, and in the meantime the members of my family would be responsible for their survival. So I followed through on my resolve to keep to myself, to find amusement through books just as Mr. Brad-shaw suggested. This way I could escape from Lodge Road and from Christ Church Boys' Elementary School and I wouldn't even have to wait until I was in England to be freed of the hurt and the constraints.

But I still could not bring home the library books. And though I devoured everything I could get my hands on, I tried to do it quietly, hoping nobody would notice how often I visited the library and how many books I borrowed. Reading would become my sole entertainment. My reading was im-proving slowly, and there were still many books beyond my ability. I knew that on my own, improving my reading would be a slow and torturous business unless I got help.

I also realized that there had to be a life beyond books, and I could not help seeing what was happening in Lodge Road and in the island as a whole. For all the people's faults, there seemed to be a stirring among them, as if for the first time they were ready to question everything. Perhaps this wasn't a change in the people, but simply that I was beginning to see the world through different eyes and that, more importantly, be-cause I didn't like what was around me, I was magnifying the significance of some developments. It was all so ambiguous and contrary: people steeped in the old system talking about revolution; those for whom there was nothing to gain from remaining as they were still clinging to what little they had for fear of losing it; the strong preying on the weak but keeping distant from the weakest member in the village; people choos-ing between aligning themselves with the old establishment and England and having the faith to trust in an untried and unknown future. The village, the entire island, was like a pot nearing the boil. Either the lid would blow off, or the heat could be turned down to a simmer, ensuring that nothing of value would be lost.

Grandmother got caught up in the changes, too. At least, she was involved in the talk of change, change that she wasn't too happy with but which nonetheless she accepted as better than what she had endured for a lifetime. Perhaps the greatest change for Grandmother was that Alma had finally found gainful employment. It wasn't a great job, but enough to keep her out of trouble and to provide a few dollars weekly. More than the money was the experience, the chance to be employed, and to begin to break the cycle of poverty that was inflicted disproportionately on the women on this island. Although she did not say it, I knew that Grandmother was proud that not only her son was making a living for himself, but now her two daughters were employed.

"Girl, it ain't the best o' jobs 'cause you ain't working in no government office like all them white or brown-skinned girls that went to Queen's College school," Grandmother said, "but it ain't the worst neither. I could think of a lot of other jobs young girls of your age find themselves doing, and to tell you the truth, I wouldn't want any of them for you. At least you're working in a hotel and you don't have to break off your head heading heavy canes morning, noon, and night as if all women are just beasts of burden, like the donkey. You can make something of yourself by concentrating on your work and taking your time to learn life. Don't rush into anything that will tie you down for the rest of your life. Taking yuh time ain't laziness."

Alma, for the first time in a long while, was obviously in Grandmother's good books, which meant that—within reason—she was free to stay out late at night and she didn't have to hasten home to light the big kerosene lamp on the shelf. That created a dilemma for Grandmother: should she allow any of the three of us to touch the precious lamp, knowing the excellent opportunity there was for this prized possession to slip from our hands, or should she rush home early every night from selling her fruit to do the job herself? Grandmother settled for the latter, which meant she was always at home when I arrived and therefore I didn't dare bring home any of the library books. But even more important still was keeping myself out of trouble and avoiding the pain and embarrassment of flogging from anyone, including Mr. Burton.

15

Grandmother walked into the house and flung the bamboo basket she was carrying on the floor. She was angry and the rage was plain on her sweating face. Recently, Grandmother appeared to have a lot on her mind, to be short tempered, so I said nothing, just in case I was the cause. It was very unusual for her to come home so early on a Saturday. Usually, she would leave early in the morning, on the seven o'clock bus, and return late in the evening. The basket, now overturned on its handle in the middle of the floor, would be loaded with the week's groceries. We would be anxious to see her and she was always happy when she returned from town.

"Howard," she shouted to me while she walked from the house into the yard. She took a cup of drinking water from the barrel, bending deeply to reach the water. The barrel was almost empty and that made her angrier. "Where is your brother Alvin? Where is he? He playing he's a man these days but I'll put my hand to his backside rough, rough and make him know his place. Look at this." She pointed angrily to the barrel. "Look at this. I walked all the way in the hot broiling sun from Oistins, and I can't even get a damn drink o' water. Your brother's suppose to fill up this barrel every day, but he ain't got no time for that. Not when he can run 'bout the road looking for strife and trouble. Where is he?"

Alvin was out playing. Usually, he would stop playing an hour or so before Grandmother was expected home and start filling the barrel. All of us detested bringing water home from the standpipe in the middle of the village, for it was a tough task walking with the big bucket of water on your head and being splashed with each step. A few months earlier, Grand-mother had stopped me from going to the standpipe after Brown Sugar, the latest woman to live with Anson Pinder, had doused me with a bucket of water. When I returned home drenched from head to foot, Grandmother was incensed but could do nothing, certainly not anything that would bring us in conflict with a known jailbird like Anson Pinder. We left the matter in God's hands, as usual. Because Alvin was bigger, he became responsible for bringing the water home, a chore he always put off until the last moment. This time he was out of luck.

"Anyway," she said, swiftly changing the conversation, "I want you to go over to Babsie Bourne's shop up the road and see if Mrs. Bourne will trust us with some more goods. I don't like doing this, but God knows that is all I can do these days. What else can I do? I went down to the post office like some idiot this morning to see if your father sent the little tra-la that he's suppose to send every month to feed the three of you. And for the third straight month running there was no blasted money. Not a cent. And then the Postmaster General got the nerve to turn to me and say that it looks like we've been cut off. That no more money might be coming and that I shouldn't keep coming down there bothering his workers."

"What happen?" I asked curiously. It wasn't often Grand-mother was in such a foul mood. It wasn't often either that she spoke to any of us in such detail about money.

"How's I to know what happen?" she shouted, the anger still strong in her voice. "You ain't see me here in Buhbadus? I look to you like I living in England? So how would I know what's happening? This is three months running that I gotta be begging people that I don't even speak to for credit. You think that's fair? Tell me straight, that fair?"

"No," I whimpered indecisively, "I don't think so."

"Anyway you look in the basket over there and hand me the list o' things I was to buy in town today. You go to Babsie Bourne's shop and see if Mrs. Bourne can help us out for another week. Tell her I'll see her in the middle o' the week to fix things up. Otherwise, I don't know what I'm going to do."

I handed her the piece of lined white paper. She took a pencil stub from her hair and, dabbing the point on the tip of her tongue, started to scratch out some of the listed items.

"We can do without milk and salt this week and we ain't got to use no butter in the food." She drew heavy lines through the items, tearing the paper in spots from the pressure she applied. "We could even do without flour. No, we gotta have flour, 'cause we might use the flour for more bakes."

As it turned out, no amount of elimination would help. Mrs. Bourne had cut off the credit and was demanding that Grandmother clear some of her debts. I came home and told her, worried at what her response would be and how she would treat the bearer of such bad news. Surprisingly, Grandmother was serene, almost as if she wasn't disappointed, as if she expected it.

"When Pretty comes home tonight, she might be able to spare some extra money," she said ruefully. "Thank God that she's still bringing in a few cents. Otherwise, I don't know what we would do. Only God knows how long she can keep it up in the state she's in now."

As fate would have it, Pretty didn't keep it up for much longer. She was always a bit fat, but recently she'd been starting to blow up like a balloon, and she was tiring faster. Every time she bent over to pick up something heavy, Grandmother would shout at her. For the most part, Grandmother and Pretty always talked in code so we couldn't understand, but sometimes in the heat of conversation Grandmother set aside all formalities. Pretty's bending was such an occasion. "You better be careful," Grandmother would say constantly, wagging her finger disapprovingly. "Otherwise, you'll end up with the navel string wrapped around the infant's neck. You remember Elsie, her little angel came into this world that way, dead as a doornail, for the very same reason. You shouldn't bend over like that, take your time and stoop down. You also shouldn't look at anything that's ugly, or dead or deformed, otherwise that child could be born half-foolish or something so. I can tell you right now, I ain't want nothing that look like a monkey or no half o' idiot in this house.''

Mavis Thorpe and her sister were constantly asking me why Pretty was getting so fat. I had a fairly good idea but didn't understand the particulars. I also didn't want to give the secret away. So when they first asked, I told them that she was eating a lot of food. Grandmother always told us that only people that were eating well and who had a good mind got fat. The two were not mutually exclusive. Thin people were either suffering from malnutrition or had such bad thoughts that no amount of food would do them good.

"If it's food that making her look so, how come it's only her belly getting fat?" Mavis asked. I had gone over into the back yard to play with Theo when Ismay and Mavis called me to where they were sitting and started questioning me. I thought quickly before answering.

"Well, if she's eating a lot of food, then her belly bound to get fat 'cause that's where the food's going." They laughed loudly at what I thought was a pretty good answer.

Grandmother and Mavis continued to be on precarious speaking terms. Grandmother later confided to us that with things the way they were, she had no choice but to continue speaking to her, that she could never tell when Pretty might want help, and Mavis might be the only one available.

"Did the mistress give you anything when you was leaving for the last time?" Grandmother asked Pretty, who was sitting by the fire, folding some bleached flour bags. For weeks, she had been collecting the bags from the shops around the village. Grandmother and Alma helped her to hem the sides of the square pieces of cloth. "She give you anything as a parting gift?"

"No. Nothing. Not one cent," claimed Pretty.

"Them brutes," Grandmother replied without looking up from the hemming. "You mean to tell me that after six faithful years of service she couldn't give you an extra week's pay? You mean to tell me that? These people ain't got no heart a-tall, if you ask me. You know who she got to replace you, after she won't take Alma?"

"Some foreigner girl that just come up here from one o' the islands. She don't even talk too good and she can't do one thing in the kitchen, but that is their business 'cause that is what you get for being so cheap. They paying the poor girl half what they pay me, you believe that?"

"She ought to be lucky they ain't want her to work for free, knowing them," Grandmother said mockingly. "Did they say if you can come back when you get your strength back?"

"She didn't say anything, but I don't think she wants me back, not when she got this other girl to work for so cheap."

"All we can say is thank God Alma's working for them tourists at the guesthouse in Worthings. The money'll come in handy and the good Lord know we could do with it. By the way, you manage to set aside anything for the midwife?"

We sat in the yard, one of the few times in a long while we were together. Usually, this was a time for stories, singing, and dancing. This time it was quiet whispers as if the women didn't want the neighbors to hear, that they didn't even want us to know what was really going on. Nobody was laughing or happy. A pall hung over the yard, encroaching on us, like the darkness overtaking the light from the fire and the rays from the lamp in the house.

"Yeah," Pretty said slowly. "I've been saving since I found out I was in the way. I should have enough."

"Good." Grandmother continued staring into darkness. "Good. The Lord don't put on any man or woman more than he or she can bear. I had to tell that to Pastor Allsop last Sunday. I was so surprised when he asked me to stay after the

meeting, that he had something important to talk to me
'bout." Grandmother ducked her head slightly and turned
away from us. Her body hunched and she continued. "Then
I find out that he can't allow me to remain a full member of
the church anymore because, as he says, there is sin in my
house. He was thinking of reading me out of the church. But
he didn't, deciding instead to give me a back seat. He said I
could still come to church but that I have to sit in the back and
I can't share in the body of Christ at the breaking of the bread
until I set things right in my own house. Well, I had to tell him
that even Christ has his cross to bear, and that I was willing to
bear mine too without his adding to them. Christ overcame
his troubles and me and my children will overcome ours too,
I tell him. So I walked out and left him sitting there in the front
of his church."

The next Saturday morning we were hastily awakened by
Grandmother. In the bedroom we could hear Pretty groaning
in agony. Alma, looking frightened, was standing over a big
pot of boiling water. She poured the water in a white enamel
basin and carried it into the bedroom behind the drawn
blinds. "Give her the cloth to bite when the pain's coming,"
Grandmother said, "something to chew on."

"Alvin, Chester, Howard," she called to us. "Get up from
sleeping. Chester, bundle up the bedding and put it in the back
yard. Alvin, run over to Mrs. Blackwood's and tell her to
come now, that Pretty needs her. Then the three of you go
outside and play in the yard, stay out behind the paling, away
from the house."

Mrs. Blackwood came as quickly as she could. She was
about Grandmother's age but shorter, with a strict, no-non-
sense approach. When she arrived, she immediately took control of the house, telling Alma and even Grandmother what
they should do and how quickly. She was particularly caustic
with Alma. Grandmother wasn't too sure if her youngest

daughter was ready to witness such a painful experience, but looking tired and a bit confused she didn't intervene and easily surrendered the running of her house to this stranger.

"You come with me and watch," Mrs. Blackwood said, taking Alma's hand and dragging her into the bedroom. Behind the curtains we could hear them talking. "I always say that a girl your age ain't too young to see what's going on, what they getting into when they playing with men friends. You would be surprised at the amount of girls your age I help out when the week comes. And half of them don't even know what they gettin' into when they going out with these pissy boys 'round this place. So you better watch and learn 'cause first does come the sweetness and then the pain, and only the woman does get the pain, not the man. I always hear that what sweetens a goat's mouth does burn its tail later. The same thing is true here."

She was easier on Pretty, almost a different person, talking soothingly and promising her the worst was all but over. She saw us through the blind and promptly ordered us out of the house, shouting at us through the curtains. All this time she was holding Pretty's hand and pressing a wet wash rag to her face.

"What I tell you," Grandmother said, somewhat mildly reinforcing the midwife's admonition. "Stay outside the house. In fact, the three of you better go next door and ask Mrs. Thorpe to give you a cup of tea this morning. Tell her Pretty's time come. Now get out of the house."

We moved quickly and as soon as we stepped into the back yard, they shut and latched the door behind us.

By the time we returned home tired and hungry in the evening, the family had increased by one and Mrs. Blackwood was gone. Grandmother allowed us into the bedroom to take a quick peek at the little boy sleeping on flour-bag sheets in a cardboard box on the table by the bed. Before entering the room, we had to scrub our feet and hands and had to promise to walk on our toes and keep quiet. We did as we were told, smiling sheepishly at the baby, making faces and such. Then Grandmother sat on her favorite spot on the rock in front of the fire in the yard as Alma left for some Saturday night dance. When we went to bed, Grandmother was still sitting quietly before the dying fire, seemingly oblivious to the wood burning out. There was a dazed look on her face as if she were being hypnotized by the glowing embers.

Eventually, I dropped off to sleep waiting for her to come into the house. By then, Alvin and Chester were sound asleep. Pretty continued to snore lightly and occasionally a weak sound would escape from the box on the table. As far as I knew, Grandmother spent several more hours in the dark yard under the stars, no doubt praying to and thanking God for the safe delivery of her grandson, wondering how she would feed yet another mouth, and especially worrying about what Alma could be doing under the cover of darkness.

16

For a Saturday morning, the road ahead of me was practically deserted. With an exercise book in my hand, the flimsy back long torn away from the fragile binding, I gladly left home, looking forward to getting to the classroom early for the lessons Mr. Bradshaw was giving outside regular school hours. Getting there early gave me the chance to spend more time with the library books.

A white and brown dog, every one of its ribs showing through the stretched skin, started crossing the road with a line of puppies trailing behind. It was Mrs. Jones's dog and it was returning home from a morning walk. As I passed in front of Mrs. Jones's house, one of the puppies, brown all over with a white patch around its dewy-looking black eyes, broke away from the line and started running behind me, eventually catching up and smelling my naked feet. It was a beautiful pup, playful and plump.

As I reached down to pick it up, it started licking my hands feverishly as if I were an old friend. The two of us hit it off immediately. For a long time now, I had been disappointed that Grandmother didn't like dogs or cats and wouldn't let us have pets—because they ate too much, she said, too much of what we didn't have to spare.

I had been borrowing books from the library, stories about animals and birds, the adventures of pirates and explorers. But my favorite had been about dogs, large adventure dogs that had a mind of their own, even though they couldn't talk; I had my eyes out for a dog of my own, even though I knew Grandmother would object. I dreamt of bringing the animal home; of sneaking it through the back yard when Grand-mother, Pretty, or Alma wasn't looking, and leashing it under the house, out of the way of the women. Then I would take him out when no one was around and we would run across the pasture and in the cane fields and have fun. When nobody was looking, I'd sneak him back in.

I picked up the puppy by the back of the neck and cradled it in my arms. It whined happily, hardly resisting.

"Don't hold him too close to you," a voice from the darkness called to me. "It's got a lot of fleas and they will get in yuh clothes and bite you up."

Mrs. Jones pushed her face through the window for me to see.

I put the exercise book and my homework on the ground and started to pet the mongrel. It curled up in my arms in a ball, slapping the tip of its tail rhythmically on my chest. Underneath my fingers, I could feel the warm bundle of flesh and hair, its little heart beating gently. Every so often it opened its small black-edged mouth, exposing tiny pointed teeth in a yawn, flicking out a small pink tongue, long enough to lick my hands. Then it curled up tighter against my chest. I didn't care about the fleas.

"You like that puppy? You want one to keep?" Mrs. Jones continued. One of her biggest concerns was to get rid of nine puppies. She had no intentions of keeping them but she didn't want to destroy them. She was offering them to anyone who wanted a watchdog and had posted a hand-painted sign to this effect on the side of her house.

"Yeah. Can I keep him?"

"Okay. I'll give you one when they're weaned," she con-tinued. "Right now they got to live on their mother's milk. They can't eat anything solid yet. When they're big enough, I'll give you one."

When I arrived at the school, the night watchman was still opening the doors. He looked surprised at seeing me and asked why I was so early. "You lookin' for something to thief now?" he asked, keeping a close eye on me as I walked past him into the classroom. "You better be careful, 'cause if anybody say they miss anything, I'll come looking for you. I tell you that."

I sucked my teeth at him, walked into Class Three C, and pulled my book out of the desk. I flipped it open and started to read. In the months since we had joined the library in Oistins, I had gone through the entire small collection of West Indian authors. I was now reading some of the books on Africa and I was liking them. I was so engrossed in the book, I didn't realize time was going by so quickly. I had lost track of everything except the story.

"What are you doing, Prescod?" said a voice above my head. It sounded familiar but unusually gentle. I looked up to see Mr. Bradshaw standing by my desk. Beside him was a tall white woman in shorts, her skin brown from the sun.

"N-nothing, sir," I stammered, scrambling to my feet. I nodded at the woman and she smiled back at me. The book I was reading fell to the floor and I bent over to pick it up.

"You can sit down," Mr. Bradshaw said, his voice soft and gentle. "What you doing with that library book there? You brought it from home?"

"No, sir. I can't take home any library books. My grandmother won't let me, so I read them at school. I stay at school on evenings and read them, or on Saturdays I stay here until the watchman locks up the school after the lessons you give us."

"That's admirable," he continued, sitting at the edge of the desk. To my surprise, he wasn't angry that I was leaving the books unprotected at school. "I was talking to the librarian, Mrs. Small, and she tells me that you're in the library constantly, that you hardly keep a book for more than a week and that you borrow some interesting titles."

"I'm sorry, sir. From now on I'll try to keep them for the full two weeks, but I read them so fast that I usually finish one book a week. So I carry it back as soon as I finish."

"You don't have to apologize, Prescod," he said, a wide grin breaking out on his face, showing his white teeth. "What I'm saying is that you are doing the right thing. You should continue to use the library as much as possible. It certainly won't do you any harm and you must realize by now that there is so much to learn and that you can never learn everything in school."

"I know, sir, I like to read." I waited for him to say something, but his attention and eyes were now on the woman.

"This is one of the boys I've been talking to you about." Mr. Bradshaw turned to face her directly. "You know, the children whose parents are living in England or America."

"Aren't these boys eventually going to England to live with their parents? If I was their mother, I'd certainly want them with me. In fact, I wouldn't leave them in the first place," she said. She continued to smile at me.

"Well, yes and no," Mr. Bradshaw said, waving his hand indecisively. "Some of them will get to England, but many will not. It will be hard for them to accept, and we in the schools and the party will have our work cut out for us to get these near-orphaned children to think like Bajans. There is little that really can be done. How do you get a child to realize his or her parents can't send for them, that they could grow up and become old men and women, never seeing their parents again. *You* know—it isn't easy for most of the parents living in England or America, no matter what some people think."

"How's he doing at school?" she asked. Before Mr. Bradshaw could answer, she turned and put the question directly to me. "How are you doing? You think you're going to pass the examination?"

"I hope so." This was the first time I had admitted such feelings to anyone.

"That's another thing," Mr. Bradshaw continued. "Before I started giving the private lessons, you hardly heard any of them talking about passing the exam. Now they have hope and some pride. Ain't that so, Prescod?"

"Yes, sir."

"You must keep it up," Mr. Bradshaw said, taking a step away from the desk as if getting ready to leave. "The improvement is showing in your work. If you continue as diligently as you are, I'm sure you can pass the exam. But you must continue working hard." He paused for a moment, looking puzzled. "Tell me," he asked, "why can't you take home the library books?"

"My Grandmother don't like it." I didn't feel like explaining further and hoped he wouldn't press the issue.

"I'll tell you what," he said, after a moment's thought. "If you ever want to read or borrow a book, feel free to come and have a look at my little library. I have a few books you might like. Just come over when you're ready, as long as you promise to take good care of the books. Remember they belong to me, not the government.

"Oh, by the way, Prescod," Mr. Bradshaw added as he was about to leave. "This is Sandra Ward."

This was interesting. "*The* Sandra Ward?" I asked.

"The one and only," she laughed. "Nice to meet you, Howard Prescod."

The two of them walked away, leaving me behind to finish the book I was reading. My jaw almost dropped off my face. It took me several moments to take all this in. I decided it wasn't a time to be shy.

"Can I take a look this afternoon, sir?" I called after him.

"At what?" he asked, again looking and sounding puzzled. He flashed a quick glance at Sandra, who was now holding his hand. They obviously weren't expecting an instant response.

"Your library, sir. This afternoon."

"Absolutely. When you're ready, come over." They walked toward his office and I watched them until they were out of sight. They looked strange together. It was the first time I had ever seen a black man and a white woman holding hands and joking with each other like close friends.

That afternoon after the watchman had returned to close the school, I went to Mr. Bradshaw's home. When I came through the door, Miss Ward and Mr. Bradshaw were talking in the back yard in the shadow of a large almond tree. They looked a bit surprised to see me, and I wondered if I was intruding. On a table in front of the chairs under the tree was a large pitcher half-filled with what looked like lemonade. At the creaking of the door, Miss Ward looked over her shoulder and Mr. Bradshaw stood up.

"Oh, it's you, Prescod," Mr. Bradshaw said. "What can I do for you?"

"The library, sir. I was hoping you'd let me . . ."

"But you couldn't have gone home since this morning," Sandra said. "You have on the same clothes and you have the books in your hand."

"No," I said, somewhat embarrassed by her observation. I had hoped that I would encounter Mr. Bradshaw alone and that he would have simply shown me into the house, to the library, where I could then be abandoned. "I was at school reading and then it was time to close up."

"You haven't had lunch yet?" Sandra asked. It was more a statement than a question. I self-consciously shifted my eyes to my feet.

"No. We don't eat until late in the evening on Saturdays," I explained. "So I don't think my Grandmother done cook yet."

"Well, have something to drink. Brains need nourishment too; not only books." She poured some of the drink from the pitcher into a glass and handed it to me. I hesitated for a moment.

"It's only a drink," Mr. Bradshaw said. "To help cool you down. Sandra, maybe we could give him a sandwich or something to eat."

She disappeared into the house and returned shortly. By then I had drunk half the contents of the glass. "I hope you like peanut butter," she said. I nodded, took the sandwich, and quickly polished it off and the remainder of the drink.

Inside the big house, everything smelled musty and strange, much like the smell at the Maryshaws' house in Top Rock. Mr. Bradshaw led the way and I followed, blinking my eyes in the darkness after the bright sunlight outside. We walked past the kitchen, beyond the dining room, which was almost as big as our entire house, and then into a little room on the side of the house closest to Water Street.

Mr. Bradshaw pushed open the glass door and peeked in. "This is my library," he said. "I do most of my reading and writing in here." On a desk at the side of the room was a pile of papers. I recognized them as the exercises Mr. Bradshaw had given us earlier that morning and which he had brought home to correct. But there was more: rows of books, magazines, letters, and photographs were stacked on numerous shelves. He pulled down a few of the books and asked, "What do you like? Here's something you might want to read. You ever heard of Hiawatha, the brave Indian?"

"No, sir."

"Over there are some more books you might like." He pointed, as if he had not heard my answer. He closed the book about the brave Indian and handed it to me. "Some of them are books the government sent out for us to review, to find out if we would like to have them in the schools. Just be careful with the books. And return them to the shelves, too."

"Yes, sir."

"And if you're taking a book home let me know," he said. "I'll leave you alone, now. When you're ready to go, give us a shout out in the back."

When I left later that evening, Sandra was still there and they were eating at a big table in the kitchen. Mr. Bradshaw was sitting at the table and she was standing, serving the food from an aluminum pot. It was macaroni. I stared for a moment without their knowing. They laughed and did a lot of touching. I couldn't hear what they were talking about and they obviously weren't aware of me watching. It was fascinating: a white woman serving a black man! I had to tell Grandmother and Pretty about this when I got home. Black people were supposed to be domestics in the white people's houses, to do the cooking and waiting on tables. I couldn't wait to tell Alma, Chester, and Alvin. They wouldn't believe it.

"Good evening," I said eventually.

"You mean 'good-night,' Prescod," Mr. Bradshaw said. "If you were coming in, you would say 'good evening.' But you're leaving for the night so it's 'good-night.' "

I was baffled.

"Don't confuse the boy," Sandra said. "Good-night, Prescod. I hope you enjoyed the books."

"I did and I want to take this one home to finish," I said, holding it up in the air.

"Good. But will your Grandmother allow that?" Sandra asked, now sitting at the table.

"I don't know," I answered. And I really didn't, but felt that maybe Grandmother would give in considering the books were coming from Mr. Bradshaw himself. I said good-bye. Mr. Bradshaw nodded his head and continued eating.

I stepped out into the twilight and started to walk home. When I got there, Grandmother was in the back yard bending over the pot on the blazing fire.

"And where you've been all this evening, young man?" she asked, hardly looking in my direction.

"Nowhere," I said, giving the familiar fall-back answer for all questions I didn't want to answer.

"The sun's gone down long-time since and it's only now that you decide to drag yourself through this gate here," she said. She was stirring the pot with a big wooden spoon, holding the end of her apron with one hand so that it would not fall into the fire.

"What's that you got there in your hand? I keep preaching my lungs out to the three of you not to bring home anybody's books." She tasted from the pot and knocked the spoon against the rim several times.

"You should make use of what we have in this house, 'cause you and your brothers just don't know how to care for books; you read the books with greasy fingers and you always find a way to tear off the backs. I don't have any money to buy backs for anyone books that you destroyed."

"It's from Mr. Bradshaw," I said.

She fell silent. The response seemed to surprise her. I continued into the house.

"Well, he's the headmaster and if he's foolish enough to let you bring home his good books, that's his business," she finally said. I had expected a more negative response, maybe even for her to order me to return the book first thing in the morning. Instead, she seemed ambivalent about me having the book, but more concerned that I be careful in handling it.

"But how come you got one o' Humphry Bradshaw books?" she asked after I thought the matter had been put to rest. "Where you see the headmaster to get a book from him and how comes he had to choose you to lend his books to? He lends his books to other boys, too?"

I had to tell her the truth, and risk stoking her anger. Between kneading the corn-meal dumplings and peeling the sweet potatoes and plantains, Grandmother listened, interjecting only once to ask if I was telling her that I had spent the evening at Mr. Bradshaw's house.

"I don't know why you have to go and draw up in the people's house for, lessons or no lessons," she said.

"But Mr. Bradshaw keep telling us that we should spend more time reading," I reasoned. "He keeps saying that the boys that have radios at home should stay home and listen to them. That way we'd know what's going on in the outside world. Since we don't have no radio to listen to, maybe we can read a bit."

"I don't know," Grandmother relented. "All the same, that Humphry Bradshaw's full of a lot of strange ideas, so he don't need me to tell him what to do. Strange ideas, if you ask me. And besides, it's his own books. If he wants you to mash them up, it's up to him. I just hope he knows what he's doing. And since he ain't no fool, he don't have to hear from me to know that I won't be giving him one blind cent when you destroy his books. You hungry now, or you full your guts with his food, too?"

"No," I said. "I'm a little bit hungry."

She didn't respond but ladled out two bowls of soup for us. When the others finally came home, they had to help themselves to the food kept warm in the pot over the dying coals. Grandmother had turned in to bed early, and I was sitting at the table finishing the book I had borrowed from Mr. Bradshaw.

Three weeks later as I was returning home from school, Mrs. Jones asked me if I was ready to take the puppy. Until then, I hadn't really expected her to keep her word. She and Grandmother weren't hitting it off recently, since Grandmother had been so late with the rent and eviction was surely pending.

"Yeah!"

"Here he is, then." She pushed him into my hands. "Remember to tie him up outside when you get home. Keep him tied until he gets the smell around the house and learns the yard. Otherwise he'll keep running 'way from home and coming back to his mother."

When I got home, Grandmother was sitting in the back yard holding the baby. She took one look at the puppy and frowned. I braced myself.

"What you got there?"

"A puppy. From Mrs. Jones."

"Who'll feed him? You think we can support another mouth 'round here? Where will we get the food from, huh?"

"I'll give him some of my own food," I called from the kitchen where I was tearing strings of cloth to make a leash. I tied a noose and slipped it around the compliant puppy's neck. Surprisingly, Grandmother did not pursue the matter;

instead she was tickling the baby and bouncing it on her breast.

"What you doing?" Alvin shouted. "You'll choke the puppy. You can't tie a knot like that, otherwise each time he pulls, he'll draw the knot tighter and tighter until he kills himself. Let me show you how to tie a dog."

He took the cloth and made a double knot. We tied the puppy to an iron stake in the earth at the back of the paling. Next to it we put a can of water. The puppy was at home and the three of us boys were equally happy to have him there. Grandmother said if we planned to keep him we may as well bathe him to get rid of the fleas, before they infested the house. When we tried to do that, he started to bark at the top of his little voice, rolling in the dirt and muddying himself. We loved him, and I called him Tupper, the name of the hero in a series of adventure books I had borrowed from the library.

17

When Pretty came through the gate, Grandmother was still sitting on the rock, her face in her hands, her body bent forward at the waist. The fire had all but burned out, except for the glowing coals.

"What you doing there, Ma?" Pretty asked softly, walking awkwardly into the yard, breathing heavily. Since the baby, she had shed some of the extra weight, but she was still a bit ungainly and tired easily. From the sound of Pretty's voice, we knew that bad news was coming. I paused in my reading to hear what she was saying.

"Me? I'm just sitting here . . . thinking," Grandmother said. "You know sometimes that is all you can do. Sit and think. Think 'bout life and thank God that you still got breath in your body, no matter what people say. The same God that made the stars up above, the crickets out there in the field, the very same God made you, too, and the one good thing about him is that he don't take sides. He ain't unfair."

"How's Anderson? He sleeping?"

"Yeah. But I think he'll get up soon. The little sugar water you left for him can't keep him going too long. He needs something more solid."

"Did Alma buy the milk for me?" She sat on the rock beside Grandmother and kicked off her slippers.

"Alma ain't got no money," Grandmother said. "You're going to have to run down the road and buy the milk yourself."

"I can't," Pretty said. "I ain't got no money, neither. I keep waiting and waiting for Henry to come home and he hasn't turned up, so I had to come home when it got too dark outside. I even had to walk all the way up here from Oistins because I spent the last five cents for the bus. I was hoping he would give me a drive home."

"Where is he tonight?"

"I don't know. He told me that he had to go for an interview this evening but that he was eventually going to come home and meet me."

"What, he's changing his job? What does he want an interview for, anyway?"

"To go away."

"Where's he going? You never tell me that he's going anywhere. Where's he going?"

"He wants to go to New York later this year, if possible."

"What about you and the baby? He just can't leave you two like that. Can he?"

"I don't know, Ma. I don't know," Pretty said. From the sound of her voice, I could tell she was close to tears. "Things so hard 'round here, so hard. No work. It might be best for him to go 'long overseas and send back some money. He says that he won't leave me out, though. But I don't know."

Mother and daughter sat in the darkness together, alone in their misery. Grandmother didn't want to frighten her daughter but she had told us all more than once about how so many men leave young women behind, with a child or two, promising to send for them but only to write back later to tell their mother or sister to tell the woman they had married some American or English woman.

Grandmother said that even the men who did get married couldn't be held down so it didn't make any sense trying to put pressure on Henry to walk Pretty down the aisle before he left. Grandmother's husband was young and strapping when he left: a proud and godly man, with a quick smile and a promise to move the world for his son and two daughters. He had vowed to send them to university in New York; in short, to ensure them a better life than the inevitable cycle of un-wanted pregnancies and long hours of working in the cane fields or in the white people's houses that was part and parcel of life in Barbados.

But the letters stopped coming, and it was ages without a word from New York. Then, a few years back, Grandmother received a registered letter from some lawyer with a New York address saying her "estranged" husband wanted a divorce, and could she please sign the enclosed forms. The lawyer went on to say that the divorce should be straightforward since the couple had been living apart for so long and her husband was willing to admit he had committed adultery. As if she cared about that, as if his screwing around with another woman was news to her. After all, what was she to expect, seeing they had been apart so long? She wasn't an idiot, neither was she foolish to things of the world. She didn't bother finishing the letter but instead threw it into the fire, under the brown enamel kettle that was boiling water for a cup of cocoa. The letter and envelope disappeared in grayish blue flames, and in the ashes she could still see the marks of the typewritten name, taunting her, like the marks on her heart and her memory.

"You know, I don't blame Henry for wanting to leave, to make something for himself," Pretty continued. "There ain't no jobs here, anyway. I spent most of the afternoon walking around Top Rock, going to people's houses asking for work. But nobody's hiring. Not a soul. I even went back to my old mistress and ask if she got anything, and she just took one look at me and said no, real sharp, as if she does eat razor blades or something. She didn't even ask me how the baby was."

"You will find a job somewhere. You're young and strong and things will work out. Just remember the good Lord don't put a sparrow on this earth without a branch or a worm for him."

"But where?" Pretty asked with frustration in her voice. "I even went into the supermarkets in Bridgetown and asked them if they needed any cashiers. But they ain't want nobody."

"I know what you mean." Grandmother's voice was low.

"You got to go soon and buy the milk before the child gets up."

"You got anything to lend me? I will give it back tomorrow."

"Girl, I had to give my last dollar fifty to Dudley from down the road this evening. And you know that nigger man up and cussed me real bad just because I didn't have all the money to pay him when he brought the few donkey cart loads of grass to stuff the bed with."

"I'll have to credit the milk then," Pretty said, an air of hopelessness in her voice. I knew she wasn't looking forward to the walk, nor begging the shopkeeper. "I got to go by Babsie Bourne's shop and asked Mrs. Bourne to help me out. I can't keep giving the little boy sugar water with bush in it. That is why he's pissing so fast. The tea ain't got no body in it and he keeps passing water as soon as he drinks it."

"Wait, Pretty. Don't go so fast," Grandmother said, rising from the rock and coming to the door of the house. "Come here, Howard. Put down the book you're reading and come here."

She turned back to Pretty. "I was thinking that it might be best if we sent little Howard for the milk, up to Simmonds's shop, not Babsie Bourne's. You see, he's a little boy and I can't see them so hard-hearted that they'll turn him down in the middle of the night. But if he doesn't get it from Simmonds, then he can try Babsie Bourne's, not before."

"Run up there quick and see if he's reasonable," Pretty instructed me. "Make sure you mention that it's for the baby. If they don't want to give you a tin of baby milk, ask for condensed or evaporated milk."

"And let me tell you, Howard, that from next Saturday on I want you to go down to the supermarket in Top Rock and sell some eggs for me. We got to make some money somehow," Grandmother said.

"But I got lessons on Saturday," I protested. Besides, I hated having to carry the big heavy basket with the eggs. "The exam's in six weeks' time and Mr. Bradshaw said he wants everybody that's taking the exam to come every day for the lessons.''

"Tell Mr. Bradshaw for me that you got to eat too, Common Entrance or no Common Entrance Examination. In any case, you might be only wasting your time, 'cause I can't see you passing no exam. You run 'long to Simmonds's shop, and make sure you don't bust that blind toe again, 'cause it looks like it's getting better.''

In spite of Grandmother's hopes, I returned home empty-handed, explaining that the shopkeepers said we should be paying off the debts rather than asking for more credit.

"At least we got sugar in the house," Grandmother said, trying to put a good face on the situation. "He's a strong baby and he's come through a lot already. He'll live.''

Grandmother began mixing the sugar water. Pretty was in tears as she went into the bedroom to be with Anderson. Grandmother stayed out in the back yard alone and was still out there in the darkness when we fell asleep.

18

Heavy rain pelted down on the roof, drenching the area surrounding the large gray stone house. Off to the side, pools of
water were forming, small pools, like isolated lakes where the
cracks in the earth were deep. Others merged into larger
pools, or the water formed small streams that rushed down
the sides of Water Street.

By the time I got inside the house, I was completely
soaked. From the heavy dark clouds hanging low over the land
it looked like a long rainy night ahead. It was the type of storm
that would cause floods, the waves bashing so heavily against
the rocks along the coast several miles away that we would
hear it in Lodge Road. On nights like this, Grandmother liked
to remind us of the flood that lasted forty days and forty
nights, and how the people drowned because they wouldn't
listen to Noah. And because there was no Noah in Lodge
Road, Grandmother had to employ all her ingenuity to keep
us dry. It was not easy to keep track of all the leaks in the
ceiling, or to prevent the torrent of water outside from washing away the four large limestone corner blocks on which our
house was propped. Getting a fire started with wood that had
been drenched thoroughly was no easy chore either. She had
to light the fire in a corner of the house so as not to smoke us
out into the rain like bees. At the same time, she had to take
care not to burn down our home by being too generous with
the kerosene oil. In place of coal, which was too expensive and
would only blacken her hands, Grandmother used bits of
wood, splitting them into smaller pieces to fill the bowels of
the iron coal-pot burner that she also pressed into service on

nights like this. A burner would be placed on top of the flat piece of galvanized metal to catch the ashes falling from the burning wood. Once there was a flame and the first smoke had escaped from the house, she would put the remaining pieces of wood by the side of the coal burner so they would dry, or at least partially dry.

However, none of this would be a problem where I was going. In a way, I felt as if I were cheating, removing myself from the cocoon of the family by heading over to Mr. Bradshaw's. Grandmother liked to joke that when my brothers and I grew up and were working, when we got to England and the big jobs that awaited us there, we would forget her, forget all the experiences we had shared as a family, forget even to drop her a line every now and then. I made a promise to myself not to let this happen, but at the same time I felt as if I were already proving her right by heading for the shelter and comfort of Mr. Bradshaw's home instead of staying with her and the others. Without even leaving the island, I was setting myself apart.

I made my way up to his house and quickly entered by the front door. "With all this rain, I didn't expect you this evening," Mr. Bradshaw said as I came through the door. "But I should know by now you are a determined boy." He locked the door behind me and began walking back to the living room. From the kitchen, I could see a man's feet in brown sandals.

"You had anything to eat yet?" Mr. Bradshaw asked when he was almost out of the kitchen.

"No. I just got back from the supermarket selling the eggs," I said, taking care to speak correctly. Mr. Bradshaw had demanded that I speak proper English on all occasions. I tried to speak slowly, thinking before letting anything escape from my mouth. However, no matter how I tried, the words sounded foreign, as if coming from someone close behind me. But I continued to persevere.

"When I saw how the rain was falling and how black the

sky was, I decided to come down here right now," I said.

"You're very dedicated." He pushed past me and headed for the living room.

"I cooked some coucou and steamed fish, so fix yourself something to eat. You can go into the library and do some homework afterwards. You didn't miss anything too much this morning; it's mainly math revision and reading. I don't think I'm going to try to teach anything new, just reinforce all we have covered so far and hope for the best. Your problem is different from the rest of the class: most of the boys are good in arithmetic but poor readers. It's the other way around with you. You still have a good chance if you concentrate a bit more on arithmetic, so go into the library and practice the problems I left."

Mr. Bradshaw was the only person Grandmother would allow me to take food from, and I was glad for this because he and Sandra were good cooks. Just as I was about finished eating the steamed shark and coucou they had cooked, the telephone in the kitchen rang. I got up from the table in the middle of the room and answered. It was Sandra and, rather than shouting for Mr. Bradshaw from the kitchen, I went into the room to get him. He and the man in the brown sandals were deep in conversation, gesturing emphatically even as I entered the room.

"Telephone for you, Mr. Bradshaw."

"Did you speak to Mr. Mohammed? Don't tell me you've lost your manners," the headmaster said. He got up and started to leave.

"Good afternoon, sir."

"Good afternoon, youngster. How are you?" he asked.

"Quite well."

I looked at the stranger, who was dressed in a long white robe like a woman's dress; on his head, which was shaven, he wore a small white cap. He stared at me as if he found me strange. I felt uneasy in his presence but didn't know how to take leave of him.

"That was my lady," Mr. Bradshaw said, returning to the room and rescuing me from the uncomfortable situation. "I want you to meet her before you go back. Anyway, as I was saying, we have a lot of work to do. The majority of people on this island don't recognize the significance of what's happening later this year, why we are so excited. We're creating a political revolution of such proportions that life on this island will change for everyone. But most Bajans are sitting around without a clue. Watch this, for example," he said, turning his attention toward me. Again, I felt uneasy and started to back out of the room.

"Don't run, Howard. I have something to ask you. What is the significance of November thirtieth?"

The answer was simple and I wondered why he was playing games with me. I was also glad he remembered. Maybe I would get a gift.

"It's a very special day for all of us," he continued. "What is it?"

"My birthday, sir. I'll be eleven years old on November thirtieth. Why you asking?"

"You can't be serious," he said, laughing loudly at what he must have thought was a funny reply. "You see this boy standing here," he said turning to his friend and putting an arm around me. "This boy is magic. He's going to turn out to be something, an example of what we can do on this island. And the good thing about it is that he is willing to learn and he does so quickly. A bit of a late starter, but I haven't met anyone his age with such a voracious appetite for books. He reads everything he comes across."

"You know, Brother Humphry, we're still looking for a place to set up a mosque, where we can worship in peace. Away from the harassment of the racist police in New York and Chicago," the stranger continued. Mr. Bradshaw sat on the chair by the window and looked quizzically at him. I didn't know if they were through with me and if I was free to get back to the homework.

"Since Brother Malcolm died, we've found out that the police have infiltrated our places of worship and are trying to divide us, set us one against the other."

"Uh hum," Mr. Bradshaw said. "I am hearing you, Abdul, but why are you telling me this?"

"We would like to set up that mosque here, on this island," he said. "And I am hoping that you, as a Brother, would help me to meet the right people. We like what we see on this island, and we feel that among black people, our own people, we can plant our seed and let it grow and nourish. We can set up a community that is different, that is set apart. We can do things to make this little island stand out like a pearl in the rest of the world—as a paradise for black people. We can show the world what black people can do and achieve."

"What made you choose Barbados in the first place?" Mr. Bradshaw asked.

"It's funny," the stranger continued. "I had forgotten about you since I last saw you in London. And let us be frank, this island is about to become independent. We feel that the poor black people on this island have been exploited enough, just like our black brothers and sisters in the United States. Now, if we can help mold an independent Barbados into a self-sufficient state, we would be sending a clear message of hope to blacks all over the world. A message that says we can cut ourselves off from the white man and be strong."

"But the Barbadian population isn't all black people," Mr. Bradshaw said. "What would we do with those that are not black—cast them into the sea?"

"I don't see the powerful white people that control the country worrying too much about black people here," Abdul said. "With independence you'll have a chance to change that. The shoe would be on the other foot. And with our mosque here, we could draw on our experiences in the United States and guide this island on the right path."

Mr. Bradshaw shook his head. "That's not what independence means at all. We are not interested in segregation, we are not interested in fighting the civil rights battles of the United States, we are simply looking to make a new society where every member, black, white, yellow or half-caste, can reach their full potential. That is what independence means for us."

"Brother Humphry, you're being too idealistic," Abdul said. "In the few days I've been on this island I've found out that this society isn't as united as you are making out. Many people out there do not support independence. Many people do not support your party; and you have an election to fight later this year. There can be no doubt that our help would be valuable and be worth the effort."

"We've never fooled ourselves that this would be an easy task. We knew we would have to spend a great deal of time educating the people, both black and white," Mr. Bradshaw said. "An independent nation as small as this one cannot have these divisions."

"That's why we are willing to help," Abdul said. "If you will set up a meeting for me with the premier, so that I can discuss buying a plantation and setting up a mosque and a school, my organization is prepared to make a financial donation to your party and to provide support during the election."

The stranger got up from the sofa and gathered up some papers. He placed them in a black briefcase and turned to Mr. Bradshaw.

"No, Abdul, I'm not the idealistic one," Mr. Bradshaw said softly. "Do you realize what would happen if the people on this island found our party discussing such matters with you? No. I think that if you want to set up a mosque, you'll have to do it on your own. This is still a Christian community and the people have a very low tolerance for other religions. But we will also allow freedom of religion after we have become a nation and you will be free to preach your gospel then and to win as many converts as you can. But you'd have to do it without the government's help, or at least my help."

The stranger let out a sigh and turned away, preparing to leave the house.

"Let me give you a ride to wherever you're going," Mr. Bradshaw said, taking his hat from the rack. He put on a black raincoat and the stranger buttoned on his as well.

"Coming with us, Howard?" Mr. Bradshaw shouted to me.

"No, I'm going to stay here and read. I still have homework to do and I feel a bit tired."

"If you want, you can go into the extra bedroom and sleep for a while. I'll take you home when I get back. Your Grandmother knows you were coming here, nuh?"

"Yes, sir."

When the car pulled out of the driveway, I locked the door behind me. It was getting darker and it was still raining hard, a steady beat playing on the roof. It must have been the long walk in the sun earlier in the day or the long period without anything to eat, but as soon as I got into the bedroom, I immediately and unintentionally fell fast asleep.

I woke up to bright sunshine and the sight of Mr. Bradshaw and Sandra standing by my bed.

"Ah, you're awake," Sandra said. "We have some breakfast for you."

"Grandmother," I panicked. "She's going to be angry with me for staying out the night and not telling her."

"Don't worry, we stopped by your home last night and told her you might stay over," Mr. Bradshaw said.

"We saw the little dog that you always talk so much about," Sandra said. "It was standing in front of the house as if it were looking for you. When we called it, it ran away; otherwise, we would have brought him for you."

But I had bigger worries. I cautiously slid my hand between my belly and the bedspread and to my horror and disappointment it was soaked. I felt like dying.

"Don't feel too badly," Mr. Bradshaw said. "Most boys your age have the same problem. It doesn't last forever."

"We were planning to go to the beach and have a picnic," Sandra said, also pretending that the soaked bed was routine. "Want to come with us? And don't worry, you can have a bath and wear a pair of Humphry's pants and a shirt. So get up and take a bath and get some breakfast." She playfully slapped me on my bottom and walked out.

Still embarrassed, I waited for Mr. Bradshaw to leave before jumping from the bed and running straight to the bathroom. When I returned, a pair of pants and a shirt, still in the plastic wrapping, were on the bed. The sheets were hanging over the door of the bedroom.

My embarrassment soon turned to excitement as we got into Mr. Bradshaw's car and headed out to the beach for the day.

19

"So you now decide to come home, eh?" Grandmother said as I walked gingerly into the back yard. She was sitting in the early evening darkness in front of the fireplace, as if she were waiting for me. "We left your food out on the table since lunchtime. I've kept looking out for you to come home today, and no sign of you. Not a word. And, besides, you know that you were supposed to be at Sunday school."

I stood in front of her, not knowing what to expect. As she spoke, Tupper irreverently bolted from underneath the house and began jumping all over me, licking my hands, feet and face, obviously not the least concerned with the gravity of the situation. I tried but could not control him.

Was Grandmother angry? I couldn't tell. The words were those of anger, but the tone was different, as if she did not have the energy to do more than scold, as if she were going through the motions, doing what she half-heartedly thought was necessary. She wasn't talking to me alone, but to Mr. Bradshaw as well, and even to herself, thinking aloud.

Ever since her chat with Pastor Allsop, I had noticed a change in Grandmother, as if she had lost some of the fire of her conviction, as if she had given up trying to influence the outcome of what was happening around her. She even refused to spend the quarter for the weekly bingo game, giving up her sole source of recreation, and abandoning the dream of winning the $1,000 first prize. She was preaching less to us, talking less about the hardships of the world and about our mother and father in England.

When I got out of the car, Mr. Bradshaw said he would

accompany me and have another word with Grandmother, but I ran ahead in the hope of heading off any confrontation. But because of the short distance from the car to the house, Mr. Bradshaw was not too far behind me and I knew that from where she was sitting, Grandmother had seen him coming and had heard the leather bottoms of his shoes crunch on the pebbles strewn around the house. I think it was for that reason she wasn't shouting at me and that she didn't try to hit me.

"Where you've been all this time?" she asked.

It had been an enjoyable day. So enjoyable that I had forgotten about Sunday school entirely. Well, not that I had really forgotten, but I had decided not to remind Mr. Bradshaw and Sandra that while I was sitting under the casaurina trees at the edge of the beach, watching the waves break on the blue Caribbean Sea and eating corned beef sandwiches, I should have been in Sunday school learning the weekly Golden Text from the Bible.

Even though Grandmother had been banned by the pastor, she still insisted that we go to church every Sunday afternoon. No matter how we protested, none of us could get out of this. She was so steadfast on this score that it was clear she saw the three of us as the last hope for reconciliation with the church, particularly since Pretty made it clear that she no longer had time nor use for Pastor Allsop and his elders. Alma simply stopped attending, no explanations offered. But as Grandmother said to us virtually every afternoon as we headed up Lodge Road, a Sunday wasn't blessed unless someone brought home the gospel in his soul. And Sunday, no matter what, was always the day she considered the most holy, the one that set the tone for the week.

Despite the tough times for the family, Sunday remained that special day, the only real family day when all of us were together for lunch. It was the day Grandmother ensured that there was a bit of meat or fish, a few slices of beets, a couple of lettuce leaves and boiled sliced string beans, even if it meant using provisions that would be needed during the rest of the week. Grandmother had always maintained that even the poorest of the poor should have a good meal on Sunday, a tradition our foreparents in slavery several hundreds years earlier kept and passed on to us. She had no intention of letting this generation be the end of the line for such a proud practice in our family. So every Sunday at noon, we filed out into the yard and bathed and then dressed in our school clothes in preparation for the meal Grandmother would dish up.

"I think I'll have to start dealing with you, Howard, different, very different," she continued. "You're getting big; you opening up your eyes to the things of this world and I don't know if I can handle you anymore. It's good you're getting an education but remember where you're from."

"How're you this evening, Mrs. Howell," Mr. Bradshaw said, coming through the paling gate. Tupper began barking loudly and yapping at his heels, as if he wanted to attack him. I intercepted and pulled the dog away and Mr. Bradshaw moved closer to Grandmother. Sandra was sitting in the car. "Enjoying the fresh evening breeze?"

"Not really," Grandmother said gruffly. "There ain't nothing to enjoy these days. Not with the way things turning out in this world."

"You sound angry to me," Mr. Bradshaw said.

"Well, wouldn't you be vexed too, if you had a little boy that stays out all night and day and nobody don't know where he is or what he's doing? Won't you get angry, too?"

"Well, you knew he was with me," Mr. Bradshaw said. "I dropped by last night and told your younger daughter where Howard was. Didn't she give you the message?"

"I got the message, all right, but that ain't what's bothering me," she said, putting a few dried sticks on the coals. "You know what the people around here would say when they see this little boy at your house almost every day. They'll say Miss Howell ain't capable of raising these three children on her own. You know what the people are like around here; how they like to talk; how they'll look at me. Or maybe you don't care."

"But that's not true," Mr. Bradshaw chuckled. He sat on the rock beside Grandmother and she moved around, out of her favorite spot, to make room for him, as if purposely putting some distance between them. I wished he would just turn around and head out of the yard.

"Sandra waiting by herself?" I asked, hoping he would get the hint.

"I don't think there's been a parent around here that has called on me to discipline a child. I don't think that happens anymore. At least, not since I took over from Mr. Toppin."

"That's what I'm worried about," Grandmother snapped, jumping off the stone to fan the coals with a large piece of cardboard. "I don't want to be the first. Howard ain't giving me no trouble; he ain't heading for Dodd's or anything so, so I don't want people to think that I can't control him; that I had to up and ask you for help. We's a poor but proud family, Mr. Bradshaw, very humble, and we'd just like it if people stopped noticing us."

"I wouldn't worry about that," Mr. Bradshaw said. He wasn't laughing anymore. It seemed that he was beginning to take her seriously, as seriously as she wanted to be taken. "If I were you, I wouldn't worry about what people are saying, anyway."

As they talk, I noticed Mr. Bradshaw constantly looking through the back door into the house. As far as I knew, he had never been inside this yard, so he must have been seeing for the first time the conditions under which we lived. From where he was sitting, I knew he could see Pretty's feet hanging over the edge of the bed, where she was having a nap with Anderson.

"I know that," Grandmother said, almost blurting out the words, as if she had been waiting for the right moment. " 'Cause you've probably heard by now what the people around here say about you. They see you walking about the place holding hands with this white woman, a big headmaster like you, showing no respect, setting no example for the young people."

"Do I sense you aren't so angry about my behavior, but about the woman I'm with?" Mr. Bradshaw asked, dropping his voice to the deep schoolmaster's tone. He still didn't sound angry.

"What you mean?" she snapped back.

"That she is white." His voice was softer, as if Mr. Bradshaw had been reminded that although he was the first black headmaster in the island, he was still talking to a woman who could be his mother, whose children he had played with, a woman who knew him under different circumstances.

"Well," Grandmother said, once again fanning the fire. Puffs of white smoke escaped from the coals, but the wood wasn't catching. "Well, yes. How come a black man like you, a man of the soil, a grass-roots man that grew up among the people, how come you couldn't find a black girl, to put in that big house the government provided for you? Why you had to go and find a white woman, a woman that could buy almost any house on this little island, that don't need you to help her? Answer me that?"

"Well . . ."

"No 'well,'" Grandmother said, growing angrier, as if she had finally thrown off what she had held back earlier in the conversation. She was becoming her old self. "You're just like all other black men we got around here, if you ask me. They get a good-paying job and they run off to New York and the first thing they do is look for a white woman, a woman that otherwise wouldn't even look at them, wouldn't even cut her eye at them, if you weren't who you were, if you weren't important."

"That's not true, Mrs. Howell. That's not . . ." Mr. Bradshaw seemed to be at a loss for words. I went over and sat on the doorstep to the house. It was getting dark; I could hardly make out the faces of Grandmother and Mr. Bradshaw from where I was sitting. I sensed that even though they were close, they, too, couldn't tell the expressions on each other's face, and this, perhaps, gave Grandmother her momentary boldness, her chance to thumb her nose at authority.

"And another thing that got people talking: you's a member of the DFI, the party that's walking up and down the length and breadth of this poor island talking about one thing and one thing only: independence. It's as if it's the song the sick cow died on. Only confusing the poor people's heads, with your lot saying one thing and Wardie and his people saying another. And all this time, you running around the place with a Ward, the daughter of the very man that's against the same independence that you and your party are fighting for. What's going on here: who's fooling who? Tell me that?"

Mr. Bradshaw took the cardboard from Grandmother and starting fanning the coals, giving her the chance to take over her place on the rock. When the fanning didn't help, the headmaster took a stick and, squatting before the smaller stones forming the fireplace, adeptly stirred the coals, moving some of the ashes to the side and then repositioning the wood. Another quick fan with a sudden burst of energy, as if throwing off his pent-up frustrations, and the sticks broke into flames, throwing brighter light on our faces and illuminating the entire yard. The cracking of the firewood caused Tupper to stir, but I patted him and he resumed a prostrate position with his paws stretched out in front of him, his head buried between them.

"Like you still remember a thing or two," Grandmother said by way of congratulation. "I mean, you's a man that accustomed to fancy gas stoves and things like that, not like poor people that got to use firewood. But you ain't lost your touch."

"Mrs. Howell, I have not changed," he said, retaking his seat. I thought he would be angry at Grandmother's remark, for knowing her, I was sure she had chosen her words carefully and wanted to reinforce the notion that Mr. Bradshaw, although being black, was no longer one of us. But he didn't respond that way, and I felt that Grandmother was surprised. Immediately, she began reacting to him differently, making room for him beside her and cracking a slight smile. "I'm still the same man that grew up around here. Because you see me going around with Ward's daughter or living in a big house doesn't mean one damn thing. She's a woman and I'm a man, the same man that went to school at Water Street, that used to play cricket with your son Frankie. I . . ."

"Look, I only telling you what the people saying," Grandmother protested. "You don't have to behave as if it is me that making these things up. You's the one that say only a couple minutes ago that what the people talking about don't matter. No need to get angry with me."

"I ain't angry," Mr. Bradshaw said, breathing loudly. "It is possible for people, like Sandra, to disagree with their family, to move away from them."

"That's what I was talking about earlier," Grandmother said, again dropping her voice. "Howard, bring a couple of cups of water so I can make some tea for the headmaster."

"It's fine. I don't need any tea," Mr. Bradshaw said.

"Too proud to have a cup of tea with poor people now?" Grandmother teased as I filled the pot with four containers full of water and placed it on the fire. I went back to the doorway.

"Anyway, that's what I was talking about. You take Howard and look after him. How do you think his two brothers feel? They have to stay at home with me and take what I can afford to give them; no more, no less. They can't run over to you. How you think they feel? I think the three o' them should be treated the same way. They're brothers."

"Don't forget I'm trying to help Howard to pass the Common Entrance Examination," Mr. Bradshaw said, looking across at me. "Isn't that so, Howard?"

"Yes, sir."

Grandmother cupped her head in her hands and stared

into the fire. For a moment it looked as if she were no longer listening to the headmaster. The water was beginning to boil under the blazing flames, the pressure of the steam causing the lid to flap. But she made no move.

"I'm just trying to make sure that he and as many children as possible get a fair chance at passing the examination, of making something of their life. So that under independence, they'll . . ."

"I don't know about no examination," Grandmother said. "The truth is I was thinking, only thinking mind you, that maybe Howard and his two brothers are getting to the point where they should be looking for a job. Most children their age are leaving school, anyway. And we need the money. When their parents send for them, then they can go back to school in England."

"But he's just a little boy," a voice said out of the darkness. It was Sandra's. She had grown tired of waiting in the car. She walked from the darkness into the light of the fire, casting a long shadow up against the house. Tupper started to growl again and to paw the ground, and I struggled to keep him under control.

"How you doing there, Miss Ward?" Grandmother said. She jumped to her feet and forced a smile, the kind that always sprang to her face when she was talking to anyone that she felt to be superior. "How you doing, and how is your father, old boy Wardie? Sit here." She offered her seat beside Mr. Bradshaw. "Howard, go inside the house there and bring a bench for the lady to sit on so this hard rock here won't sore up her bottom."

"It's okay. I can stand," Sandra said. "It's just that it's getting late and I wanted to get home to change out of these wet clothes. Your grandson is very good, a well-mannered boy, Mrs. Howell. You should be proud of him."

"I was telling the headmaster here that I try my levelest best to keep them on the straight and narrow path," Grandmother said. "All I hope is that he will take in a bit of the learning, the learning that people like your father and his father before him have helped to provide for every child on this island." Then she appeared to remember the point on which Sandra entered the conversation and felt the need to explain, almost apologetically. "I don't mind admitting it to the two of you, but things are rough, rough, and I need every cent I can get. That's why I was thinking, and I was only thinking, mind you, not that I had decided anything, but I was thinking that if he could find a job, maybe a little gardening job after school, that the few dollars would help us out. He won't have to leave school altogether just yet. And as I said, I was just thinking."

"I wouldn't do that," Sandra said. "I'd give him a chance to sit the examination. Then let's see what happens."

"I don't know," Grandmother said. "You want a cup of tea? The water's boiling," she said, raising the lid and peering into the steam.

Chester and Alvin came through the door at that moment and almost dropped dead when they saw Mr. Bradshaw and Sandra in the yard.

"Good-night," they shouted and slipped into the house to take off their shoes.

"What they're doing here?" Alvin asked me when he thought nobody was listening. "You're in big trouble!"

"No," I said.

"Boy, you're going to get it for not coming to Sunday school," Chester said. "Grandmother said she was just waiting for you to come home."

"I know."

Sandra and Mr. Bradshaw turned down another invitation for tea. Grandmother didn't press them. She later admitted to us that, in any case, she didn't have any tea in the house. As they were leaving, she asked Sandra to give her regards to Mr. Ward and to ask her father what was to become of all the people walking up and down the island looking for work but unable to find any.

"Don't worry too much," Mr. Bradshaw said. "Things are tough now, but they will get better. That is the message that we want to leave with the people: that things can only get better. Independence will give us the chance to make sure that things get better, for all the people on this island."

Then, almost as if Mr. Bradshaw wanted to prove a point, as if he didn't care what the people were saying about him, he threw his arm across Sandra's shoulders and walked into the darkness. Minutes later, we heard the car doors slam, the engine start and the car roar off down the rocky road.

"I don't mind what he's saying," Grandmother said. "But he sees things a lot different from the way we poor people see them. I don't mind his fancy talk about things getting better."

I turned and went inside, deciding it was better to get to sleep before Grandmother turned her anger on me again. This time I didn't wait for Chester to spread the bedding; I lay down and promptly fell asleep.

20

But life did not get any easier, although Mr. Bradshaw had promised it would. In the weeks following his visit, Grandmother said she found herself on a roller coaster, bouncing from one loop to another. Most disturbing was the news that Alma had lost her job.

"What you mean, you ain't got no job!" Grandmother yelled. "Every morning you leave here bright and early saying you going down to the Wards' guesthouse in Worthings to work. How you mean you ain't got no job?"

"The job ended three weeks ago. The people down here from Canada went back three Thursdays now. Since then the housekeeper tells me they ain't got no work for me, that they ain't got no more reservations for the rest of the year. Anyway, she says that sometimes people turn up when you don't expect and if I want to come and check every day and see if anybody come in, it'd be up to me and on my own time."

"But you only had the job for two months. You mean you can't keep a job for longer than that? What's wrong with you, girl?"

"See what I mean," Alma said, throwing her hands in the air in disgust, stomping her feet. "I knew you'd start getting on me like this, that's why I didn't tell you anything in the first place. I can't give myself a job. If the people gone back to Canada, what you want me to do? You don't think I know that things are tough for us since the boys' father stopped sending any money? How do you think it makes me feel? At least the mistress left a couple of dresses for me before leaving for Canada."

"You sicken me," Grandmother said, rocking the baby. Pretty had gone into town to visit Henry in the hopes of getting some money to buy milk for Anderson, the baby, leaving him in Grandmother's care. "To tell the truth, you's my daughter, but you sicken me. You can't even keep a job for more than a month. Everybody else your age has a job and they're supporting themselves, making something of themselves, but not you. I don't know what's wrong with you. We must all be cursed."

That was a week ago, and the reality that we were penniless with no income to speak of in the near future frightened Grandmother.

"Sometimes, I wish trouble would set up like a rainstorm, so I could see it coming and run and hide," she said, taking me into her confidence as a greater gulf developed between her and her two daughters. Chester and Alvin were seldom at home, so often I was the only one around when she wanted to talk. Since her chat with the headmaster, I noticed she was treating me differently, talking to me more.

As I stepped into the back yard to start collecting the eggs to sell to the hotel in Worthings, Grandmother called softly to me. "I got to talk to you and your brothers later, Howard. I got back the letter I wrote to your mother and father."

I thought she was going to scold me again for not writing the letter that I was still mulling over in my head. I had not rushed to send it off because Grandmother had said on several occasions that she did not think she had a correct address for my parents in England. That became the excuse for my putting off writing the letter. But I had not given up on writing to them. In fact, I was debating in my head if I shouldn't tell them about the independence issue at home and also ask them about some of the things I had heard Mr. Bradshaw and Sandra discussing about England. From what they were saying it appeared to me that England was more bad than good, but I knew they were wrong and that life could not be as harsh for immigrants as they claimed. Still, there were doubts in my mind because I knew Mr. Bradshaw and Sandra had lived in England and would know what they were talking about.

The only people who would tell me the truth, tell me what to expect when I joined them, were my parents, and I could only find out by writing them, which I planned to do as soon as I sorted some of my muddled thoughts.

Instead of scolding me, Grandmother had more troubling news to unburden on me.

"The letter came back yesterday," she said. "I don't know what to do. I can't get water out of stone."

In a desperate bid to make contact with my father, to implore him to start supporting us again, she had sent a letter to the last address she had for him. It had come back with the words "No longer at this address" scrawled almost illegibly on the front of the envelope.

"There's nothing more I can do," she said. "Things too tough and I don't even know now if your mother and father living or dead. So I got to make the decisions on my own."

During these times, and against her better judgment, she allowed me to spend more time at Mr. Bradshaw's. I knew she felt that, with the political climate heating up in anticipation of the vote on independence, it would have been better to keep me away from him, but she also knew she had to be practical; that even if she agreed with Mr. Burton and Mr. Toppin and distrusted Mr. Bradshaw's politics, because of his generosity she had one less mouth to feed. So most of my conversations with Grandmother were now restricted to early morning or on nights when she would ask me to read the Bible.

As I stepped through the back door with my hands full of eggs, Grandmother was already sitting on the rock. I could tell that she was reflecting on all that had happened and that, if she had slept at all last night, she must have been up very early worrying. She looked tired, old, and listless and it was only Tuesday.

Alvin and Chester came into the back yard, followed by

Pretty with Anderson in her arms. Grandmother took a sip of her hot cocoa.

"You going into town today, Ma?" Pretty asked.

"Why you ask?"

"I see you up so early. I thought you're planning to catch the first bus to town this morning."

She did not respond. But we could tell she was thinking, even as she held the tin cup in front of her lips and blew silently on the escaping steam.

There was a time, just a few months ago, when going into town was not such an unlikely venture, but was, in fact, something she looked forward to when heavy problems descended like lead on her shoulders. As soon as she would get into the crowded bus, someone would recognize her and they would talk so much that by the time they got into town whatever it was that was bothering her wouldn't appear that important.

The few trips to the city were now strictly on Wednesday mornings, walking the back roads so the women passing on the bus wouldn't see her as she sneaked in and out of the grounds of the big bakeries, buying, of all things, stale bread. She had first heard of getting cheap bread from a friend who kept pigs. When Grandmother had heard of this, she had laughed with the rest of the girls behind their friend's back. They didn't believe the bread was for the pigs. Grandmother knew how vicious the women could be, and she now felt ashamed for having been so heartless.

But with no money in the house, with Alma unable to find a job, and with Henry getting ready to leave for New York, leaving Pretty and Anderson behind, she told me she had decided to go to the bakery—not to buy the bread, but to go to have a look, to examine the barns and bins that contained the rejected bread, to find out if what people were saying was really true.

When she came home she slowly went through the loaves, breaking the breads and the cakes and smelling them for age, carefully inspecting them for discoloration, gingerly tasting for mustiness. To her surprise, she found most of the bread looked and tasted fresh. She ate some and it didn't kill her, even if with each swallow another bit of her pride slipped down her throat.

Sending us to work was drastic action, but that was the only choice left.

"I don't want to do it," she said, "but things are real hard and we could use any money we could get. I was hoping that your father would have come through; that was my last hope. But the letter came back."

We knew that as soon as she could make the arrangements, my brothers and I would drop out of school and enter the working world.

"But the Common Entrance Exam's coming up soon and you told Mr. Bradshaw and Sandra that . . ."

"I know," she interjected. "But what can I do? I don't feel too good doing what I know I gotta do, but what else can I do?"

I knew she had no choice, but it hurt nonetheless knowing that my school days were over. That surprised me, for a year or so earlier I would have leapt at the opportunity to leave school, to join former classmates who were working as gardeners and the like. Once I would have salivated at the thought of having my own money, as they did. But obviously I had changed and I did not want to be a gardener or a member of the government's road repair crew, although I didn't really know what I wanted to be.

Most of all, I wondered what Mr. Bradshaw would say when I told him that there would be no need for me to continue attending the special tutoring for the Common Entrance Examination.

Once again, our little world had been dealt a crippling blow. For the first time it dawned on me that running away to England to join my parents might not be an escape, might not be an option, after all—especially if my parents didn't surface and resume writing Grandmother.

I finished washing and grading the eggs before putting them in the basket and setting off for the hotels in hope of a quick sale, quick enough to allow me to return home with the basket and still get to school on time for what looked like the last of my school days.

21

"Miss Howell! Miss Howell!" The man's voice was calling urgently from the outside in front of the house. "What you're doing in there, girl?"

Grandmother put down the rice she was picking over for the evening meal and went to the opened side door. Waiting for her was Little Foot. With surprising speed and agility, he skipped over the bread-and-cheese tree fence separating us from the neighbors.

"What you're doing out there, Little Foot? You're bringing something for me now?" Grandmother asked jokingly. She pushed open the other half of the door and stepped to a side.

"I'm coming 'round with Mr. Ward to find out who's comin' to the political meeting Saturday night. You know we're having a big, big meeting by the corner shop. People from all over the island are coming. We'll show Douglas Leopold Phillips and his tribe how to hold a real big-time meeting 'cause, with what they had the other night, they're only making sport when they say they know how to hold really big meetings. If you think Phillips had people at that meeting, you ain't seen nothing yet. Come Saturday night and see for yourself."

"Where's Mr. Ward?" Grandmother asked. She looked past Little Foot, searching for the politician. "Looks like he gone back home, yuh," she teased.

"Nah, man. He won't do that," Little Foot said, climbing into the house and sitting on the bench beside me. I moved over to give him more room. "Let me sit here and rest my foot while I wait for him to catch up," he said, breathing loudly. Little Foot looked at me and I stared back at him. "I'm suppose' to go 'head o' Mr. Ward and tell the people he's coming, but although he's got two good, strong feet and I only got one," he pointed to the disabled leg, "he still can't keep up with me. He gotta stop and talk to the people, and you know how the people 'round here like a piece of talking."

He shifted his position and looked at me again, this time smiling broadly. The sweat was running down his face, as if it were coming from a single source in his thick knotted head of hair. The sweat settled on his upper lip and on his nose and formed little rivers that ran into his eyes or down the corners of his mouth. I smiled back at him and he slapped my back as if I were a man like him.

"This boy's getting real big, eh," he said approvingly. "I could remember when he was a little dot, no bigger than this." He held the palm of his hand flat to the floor, indicating the height he remembered. "Now you're almost a man. Boy, time does really fly."

"You ain't lie," Grandmother said, noncommittally. She continued to look for Mr. Ward, but he hadn't appeared yet. "And he can eat a lot, too."

"You're comin' to the meeting or not?" Little Foot persisted, changing the subject again. "Tell me now, Miss Howell: Let me know if you're a Labourite supporting Mr. Ward or if you're a Dems for Big Guts Phillips."

"I ain't one thing," Grandmother said teasingly, but also playing it safe. "I don't trust no politician. They're all the same, coming around and promise yuh anything at election time and then you don't ever see or hear from them again. Christ is my politician. He is the only person I can rely on and he's never let me down yet, not once."

She went to stand by the back door, her head almost touching the ledge with the small bottles of medicine.

"But Mr. Ward ain't like that," Little Foot said defensively. "You know that for yourself, Miss Howell. You know that any cat or dog can walk up to Mr. Ward and ask him a question. I mean, we all know that Phillips gotta call the election soon; the Queen in England done tell him: no independence without elections; to let the people decide if they want independence or not, so he got to call the election soon. You know he likes to force things on people. But Mr. Ward ain't like that."

The side door creaked as Mr. Ward entered, holding the two halves for support. He was wearing the white cork hat as usual, but this time he was dressed in khaki pants with white pump shoes and a flowered shirt that looked too small for him. The front of the shirt was unbuttoned, showing his protruding belly and the red hair of his chest. His armpits were soaked with sweat.

As soon as he entered, Grandmother shot me a quick glance, a signal to vacate the bench. Herbert Ward, sighing loudly, sat down heavily on the bench beside Little Foot. I parked myself out of the way of the adults, but still in a position where I could observe everything.

"I ain't like what?" he asked, still catching his breath. He looked tired and worn and his eyes scornfully flitted around the house. "What was that the two of you were just talking 'bout?" he asked, lapsing smoothly into vernacular.

"I was just tellin' Miss Howell that you ain't like the other politicians that come 'round here only at 'lection time beggin' for votes. You ain't like that," Little Foot testified emphatically, looking at the politician for support. "I keep tellin' these people around here that you're different. That without you I wouldn't have that big wall house down there at the corner of Lodge Road and Water Street, right where you'll keep this big meeting Saturday night. And I don't mind saying it to your face, Mr. Ward," Little Foot said, looking straight at him, while the politician nodded his head in agreement, "it ain't me alone that you helped. You'd help anybody that wants helpin'."

"You can bet your last dollar on that," Mr. Ward concurred. "You don't remember seeing me driving through this village every week? I'm in my office in Oistins at the Southern District Council, or at my office in the Parliament Buildings when the House's meeting and anybody—anybody—can walk in any time of the day or night and talk with me. You know that good enough, Mrs. Howell."

"I ain't say not." Grandmother backtracked from her earlier professed indecisive position, obviously hoping not to offend this powerful politician who could very well be the next leader of the island, our first prime minister, after independence. "You know me, I like to talk plain and all I'll say is that you have to pick and choose the politicians you support real careful. I have to look after myself, my children, and my grandchildren and we all got to be picking and choosing."

Anderson started to cry. He'd been sleeping and the voices must have stirred him.

"How's the young fellow?" Mr. Ward asked. He bent over the box by the grass bed and started to pat the back of the baby gently, talking almost in a whisper. "You go back to sleep, you hear, big boy. You go back to sleep. That's a good boy." Anderson curled up and began sucking his thumb. Mr. Ward's crooning worked magically; Anderson was soon fast asleep and Mr. Ward started to look more at ease in the surroundings.

"How's his mother keeping?" he asked, sitting on the bench again, checking his watch. He glanced quickly outside, as if telling himself that he must be moving on.

"Can't get a job. Can't find nothing to do," Grandmother said, throwing up her hands as if she were giving up on the world. "The same for my other daughter, Alma. She can't find nothing to do since she lost the pick at your guesthouse earlier this year. You ain't know of anything?"

"Why you didn't send them to talk to me?" Mr. Ward asked, getting up and taking the cork hat off his head. He fanned his face with it. Wiping the perspiration from his forehead with his hand, he said, "I don't like to say it, but that is what you get for voting in a bunch o' Communists, who ain't got the people's interests at heart, who're only looking to live like lords off the poor people, while the people can't even get a job to put food on the table for their children. That never happened when my father was in power. And the news about the foolishness happening on this island is spreading around the world. Every year my guesthouse used to be full with tourists from Canada, England, and the States twelve months a year, but look what's happening these days. You see for you ownself the tourists ain't coming no more." He waved his head in disgust and lifted his hands to the heavens as if seeking divine inspiration. "But we will change all that when we get back into power, right after the next election."

He started for the door, putting the hat on his head. Little Foot got up and left ahead of him. Soon we could hear him calling at the next house: "Miss Thorpe. Miss Thorpe, what you doing there, girl? I got somebody that you should talk to." The voice surged back into our house. Mr. Ward's ears picked up and he checked his watch again.

"Got to go," he said apologetically. "Tell the two girls to come and see me tomorrow. I'm looking for people to join the gang cleaning the streets. It ain't too hard work, although it's in the hot sun. Tell them to come and see me. The money ain't bad and they get Friday and Saturday off, with half-days off on Thursdays."

"Okay," Grandmother said. "You got anything for a' old woman like me to do?"

"You can come, too," Mr. Ward said, winking and stepping through the door. "The more the better. But I want all of you people to remember that these are vestry jobs. Not from Phillips. I hope everybody remembers that when the time comes to vote. Remember your friends, that's all I'll say for now."

He gingerly placed a foot on the limestone steps. Grandmother rushed over to the door and watched his departing back. A broad smile came to her face. I came to the door and stood beside her.

"You see that, Howard," she said, laughing, clapping her hands in glee when he was out of earshot. "God promised to always protect his people. Only God knows how much my heart was hurting when I was thinking how in the next few weeks the three of you boys would have to leave school and look for work if things didn't get any better. That it wouldn't even be no use you sitting the Common Entrance Examination in five weeks' time. But, thank the Lord, I put the matter in God's hand and asked him to deal with it, to take charge. Look what happened today. He ends up sending work right into my house. Praise the Lord."

That was the best news I had heard in some time. None of the three of us wanted to leave school. I had talked to Mr. Allen and he had said that maybe when I got older, when I joined my parents in England, I could return to school, the same way he was planning to go to the University of the West Indies in Jamaica to study economics as soon as the present government got back into power and kept its promise to make university education free of charge for everyone that qualified. "Of course, it will be easier for you when you're in England," Mr. Allen had said, without much conviction. Still I didn't want to leave school, as I suspected that even Mr. Allen believed that once I left, it would be the end of my academic training. More than that, I was enjoying the lessons with Mr. Bradshaw and I was always looking forward to my surreptitious visits to the library and to reading the books from the headmaster. Now, it appeared, I didn't have to leave school, and we all had Mr. Ward to thank for this. Grandmother would later make it quite clear when explaining our good fortune to Pretty, Alma, Alvin, and Chester that she would accept any day the certainty of jobs from Mr. Ward over something mysterious and far-fetched from Phillips called independence.

I was turning away from the door when I heard the scream from Grandmother. She had stepped into the back yard and was frantically pointing in the direction of the house cellar.

"Look at the worthless dog!" she screamed. "Look at him!"

"Who?"

"That dog of yours. Look at him there in the fowl nest eating all the eggs. I know it was he that was stealing all my eggs every day!"

She threw some loose stones at the dog. Tupper ran out and disappeared into the Thorpes' back yard, crossing the back-door step just as Little Foot and Mr. Ward were quietly leaving with scowls on their faces.

"He's got to go," Grandmother said. "We got to get rid of that damned dog real soon. I swear to God, we can't have no dog 'bout here, especially a dog that steals eggs."

For me, one crisis had replaced the other. One look at Grandmother's face made it clear that she would never forgive Tupper.

Until he was exposed, Tupper was showing all the signs of a good watchdog, responding to my training, to the tips I had read in the library books. So it came as a big disappointment when Grandmother remained so unyielding in her demand that I get rid of him. Throughout the night we would hear Tupper underneath the cellar barking loudly at the footsteps passing in front of the house. This made us feel secure, knowing nobody could creep up on us in the middle of the night without Tupper sounding the alarm. Maybe this was the reason our house had not been stoned in some time.

On her trips home late at night, Ma had become one of his favorite targets. He would run after her and yap at her heels, staying out of reach of the ever-present cane in her hand. No amount of cussing and swearing would have any effect on Tupper, a point that wasn't lost on Ma, who promptly switched to threatening to poison the animal. When that threat failed too, she promised to take Grandmother to court if the dog bit her.

In the days since Grandmother first talked about getting rid of Tupper, Chester, Alvin, and I had tried our best to cure the animal of its faults. We had tried several things, some that we had learned from the boys at school, and others we had improvised. But nothing worked and the unreformed Tupper grew even fonder of the eggs.

I had returned from the shop with the weekly groceries, intending to leave again as soon as I had hung the basket on a long spike nail on the side of the house.

"Didn't I tell you to get rid of that dog?" Grandmother asked. "I want you to throw that damn dog in the well."

"What well?"

"The one by Ma's house. Put the dog in this crocus bag and throw them in the well. You might as well get it over with now."

"But that would kill him," I protested.

"Better him dead than eating all my eggs. This morning I even saw him chasing the fowls as if he wanted to eat them too," she said.

I looked at her and to my horror saw that she was serious. She handed me the crocus bag and turned to go back inside the house. In her mind, it was an easy and straightforward matter. I had brought the dog home as a puppy; it was now up to me to get rid of it.

With no choice, I whistled softly and Tupper came running, wagging his tail. He continued running behind me, jumping and leaping on my back, licking me all over with his long pink tongue. This way, it was easier than trying to get him into the bag.

Eventually, we arrived at the well. It was one of several holes dug across the island by the government to facilitate drainage and prevent flooding when it rained heavily. The holes were dug as deep as the water table in the limestone rock that formed the foundation of the island.

Tupper saw a mongoose and, like a true adventurer, chased it into the field, yapping loudly. This reminded me of the adventure books I had read, the ones from the library about the boys in England about my age who took their hounds hunting. Watching him run around so spritely, I instantly forgot the purpose for our stroll. We didn't have foxes or rabbits, but the island was awash with mongooses, the brown furry animals that were just as much a threat to the island's poultry as Tupper was. We searched for wild animals in the grass and between the cane fields, but with no luck. A couple of times we spotted field mice, but they disappeared in the brown grass before we could get near to them.

When we were tired, I sat by the well and Tupper rolled over in the grass beside me, chewing on a stick and panting loudly. Occasionally, he raised his long ears, rose on his hind legs, and tensed his back as if getting ready to attack. But usually it was only the wind blowing through the top of the canes and the branches of the trees around the well.

Without my noticing, time was slipping away and darkness was descending. I finally became aware of the stillness of the late evening turning into early night, of the cane fields and the pastures, that surrounded us. In the distance I could see the yellow light from the lamps in the houses. I had to go. I didn't know what to do with Tupper.

Obviously, I couldn't take him back home. At the same time, I couldn't bring myself to put him in the bag and throw him into the well. Even if I wanted to, Tupper wouldn't let me. He thought it was a game and chewed on the mouth of the bag.

Killing the dog immediately would be more humane than letting it suffer for days in a dark well before it died.

Under one of the trees by the cane field was a heap of stones. They had been plucked from the fields during the past plowing. I went to the heap, took up a sizable stone and aimed it at the dog. The first landed at its feet and bounced over its back. Tupper chased after the stone, thinking I had started another game. I threw another stone; another chase. This time I waited until Tupper was closer and took better aim. The stone struck him and he howled in pain. But instead of running away, the dog continued to run toward me as if seeking my protection from the stones raining around him; he stupidly didn't realize the pain wasn't the result of a poor aim during our game but that I was deliberately hurting him. Through my tears, I could see him coming toward me, jumping out of the way of more stones, taking some of them on his back, but determinedly moving forward.

Finally, Tupper was right in front of me, whimpering from the pain. Then he careened over. He was dead.

I dropped the stone and ran away, not stopping until I was home. Grandmother never asked what happened.

22

"Look like the day of reckoning coming soon, er, Mrs. Howell." Mavis Thorpe leaned out of the back window of her shed roof.

"You ain't lie, girl." Grandmother rose from the rock where she had been sitting most of the evening staring at the pot on the fire. Her elongated shadow fell across the yard and against the back of the house. Mavis's voice, coming so unexpectedly out of the darkness, seemed to have startled her.

"The Bible's predicted these are definitely the last days we're living in. You only have to look around at all the strife and confusion to know that the Lord's soon coming for his world. Every man, woman and child will then have to stand up and give a reckoning for his soul."

"I was talking about the elections," Mavis explained. At that moment, Grandmother must have heard my footsteps approaching from the darkness, for she snapped her head around in the direction of the paling door as I came tottering through it with the heavy bucket of water on my head.

"It was just on the six o'clock news that Phillips called the election to decide this independence issue once and for all."

"For truth?" Grandmother quickly adjusted to the fact that the conversation was about more worldly things. As I passed by her, some of the water splashed from the unsteady bucket onto the ground and into the fire. Grandmother frowned at me, but continued her conversation. "That's going to be something else, to see how the people'll vote. I don't like elections."

As she talked, her mind still seemed to be elsewhere. She

put another bunch of twigs in the fire. The blaze leapt up over the top of the pot and then fell back just as quickly. Slowly, she walked back to the stone and resumed sitting, this time facing Mavis. That was my fifth bucket of water for the evening and I was now thoroughly soaked and tired from all the walking. Under my breath, I cursed Alvin. It was his chore to bring the water from the standpipe in the middle of the village, but even though school had finished three hours earlier, Alvin was not yet home. With Chester out searching for grass to feed the sheep, it fell to me to fill the water barrel in the corner of the yard.

Lately Grandmother had been demanding that I do more of these tasks, partly, I suspected, because Chester and Alvin were seldom at home and not because, as she said, I was getting big and had to start contributing to the family. At times, she would mumble that Alvin was getting out of hand and wasn't obeying her anymore. Flogging Alvin was a waste of time, she said; he might be headed for trouble and Dodd's if my mother and father didn't send for him in England, where he would at least have a man to discipline him. More of his tasks were falling to me as he asserted more of his teenage independence.

"You should've heard Big Guts Ward on the people's radio just now bragging about what he would and won't do if he wins the election," Mavis continued, leaning further out of the window in an apparent attempt to bridge the gap between the two houses. "I just hope the people of this island ain't so foolish as to put back Ward and the white people in power again. This island's progressed far enough in the four years that my man Phillips's been in government and I want it to stay that way."

"You never know how these things will turn out, girl," Grandmother replied. I dumped the water, throwing more of it on the ground than in the barrel, making the ground at the foot of the water container even muddier, and prepared to make another trek to the pipe. Not only was I tired and wet, but I was hungry and the smell of food on the fire only made things worse. With the sun fading fast, my clothes were getting cold from the wet; the muscles in my neck were sore from straining to steady the bucket on my head and tensing my body to prevent the water splashing with every step.

"People are funny; you can never tell how they'll vote," Grandmother said, stoking the fire. "You can never tell what devils an election could bring out in people. I hear a lot of them saying they don't know anything about this independence thing, but I know they'll still go out and vote when the day come."

"You plan to vote?" Mavis asked.

"Me? I ain't plan to vote for one soul but Christ, the Truth, the Light and the Way. I'm tired telling people I have enough problems of my own without having to worry about politicians that ain't got nothing better to do than to walk up and down this little island begging for votes and only confusing poor people's head. Politics ain't going to put no food on my table."

"I can tell you right now how I voting," Mavis said, realizing that Grandmother would never commit herself. "Only Phillips and the DFI can get my X on election day. I'm a die-hard independence supporter."

"I'll wait to hear what they say from the platform," Grandmother said, softening her stance in the name of prudence. "If I feel independence is what poor people like me need, then I'd vote for it. If not, then I won't. In fact, I might not even vote."

Grandmother broke off the conversation with Mrs. Thorpe to say, "Make that the last one you're bringing." I was surprised, as the barrel was only a quarter full.

She added, "Run along and bring that last bucket o' water. But make sure you wash your feet at the pipe. Walk on the grass at the side of the road on your way back. It doesn't make no sense bringing home the water and then wasting it to wash up for the evening. If you see that brother of yours standing under the street lamp, tell him I say to come home right now. But remember to wash up yourself; it'll help you sleep better."

Mavis took her elbows from the ledge. "I think I'll go now and bathe Theo before it gets much darker. Then I'll help him with his homework. You know the Common Entrance Examination just around the corner and we got to do what we can to help these children to open their brains. Tonight we practicing spelling."

I walked through the door into the darkness. In the distance, the street lamps on the main road had been turned on, but I was afraid to walk in the dark to get to the main road. Most of all, I feared that someone would attack me. I knew I had no choice but to venture into the darkness and to walk as quickly as possible. Grandmother would not have it any other way. My only hope was that on my way home I would meet Alvin and Chester—Alvin might even carry the bucket, leaving me free to run if anyone attacked us.

"This is going to be one hell of an election," Mavis's voice trailed after me. "Everybody's saying that this is going to be the nastiest campaign we ever see on this island."

"Nastiest ain't the word," Grandmother said. "You mean dangerous and spiteful. A lot of people'll get hurt before this voting's over. A lot o' poor people will have to swallow their conscience and laugh and grin in the politicians' face to get by. Them politicians have a long memory when they have power."

As I walked down the street, I realized that, long before the radio's announcement, I could have told them the official campaign had already come to Lodge Road. Even though I had seen men in a truck driving through the village and pasting large posters on street lamps, shop doors, houses and the walls of the standpipe, it did not occur to me that anything unusual was happening. The women were talking about the coming election and how the Conservative Labour Movement candidates had taken the lead in getting their message and posters out. The posters, with the CLM's symbol of a big black bell with X beside it, were everywhere. The people discussed how the Democratic Front for Independence was far behind in the race, as if unprepared for the fight that it had started.

This election would have nothing to do with me. I just wanted to fill my bucket and get home to change my clothes and eat.

Perhaps sensing how the political winds were blowing, Grandmother soon decreed that I should spend less time at Mr. Bradshaw's house.

"We got enough to do in this little shack to keep you busy," she announced several days after the discussion with Mavis. "I don't want you to keep running over to Bradshaw's house every chance you get. You can never tell who might be watching you."

"Who might be watching him?" Pretty asked, putting a spoonful of rice into her mouth. She was sitting on the rock beside Grandmother, who was holding Anderson while Pretty ate from the plate in her hand. "He's just a little boy. Why would anybody waste their time watching what he's doing?"

"Politics is a funny thing," Grandmother cautioned, dropping her voice almost to a whisper. "I don't want to have to spell out everything to everybody. You can never tell who's walking the road, listening, in the dark of the night. All I'll say is that he that hath ears to hear, let him hear. Take my foolish words and inwardly digest them to pick sense out of what might sound like nonsense. The same goes for you two." She nodded in the direction of Alvin and Chester, who were sitting on the steps at the back door. Alma was sitting in the doorway. I was sitting with my back against the house and feeling pleased that Pretty had caught Alvin trying to sneak away and had forced him to get the water that evening. Alvin didn't seem to mind.

"I don't want anybody to accuse me of being political one way or the other. I have to keep food in this house. I would advise you all to listen to me and be very careful with what you say around people for the next little while. Be very, very careful. I beg yuh, for everybody sake."

Without her having to explain, we understood what Grandmother was getting at. She was protecting the three jobs Mr. Ward was providing and she did not want to be seen as politically ungrateful by appearing to be in cahoots with the other side. At the same time, she knew that if the independence movement won, our indifference would be remembered and we would be at the mercy of the rulers of the young nation.

"But what about the lessons?" I asked.

"What lessons?" she answered. Grandmother appeared to have forgotten the prohibition she had just imposed on me.

"The lessons that Mr. Bradshaw gives on Saturday mornings," I said. "For the Common Entrance Examination. Do I still go to the lessons? At the school."

"All I am saying is that I don't want you in the man's house," she said. She seemed reluctant to commit herself entirely.

"Ma, you can't stop the little boy from going to the lessons," Pretty said. "There'll be a whole classful of boys there so nobody can't single him out. They would have to single out everybody. You know he needs the help for the exams."

"And it would keep him out of the house too, from getting in people's way all the time," Alma added.

"I don't understand these young people." Grandmother turned her attention to Anderson and tickled him under the chin. "But they will learn the hard way, won't they, Andy? They will learn the hard way and then it'll be too late. But they wouldn't be able to say I didn't warn them."

I took this to mean that Alma and Pretty had won their case on my behalf. I could continue attending the lessons as long as I stayed away from the house, where I might be seen going through the door just ahead of some DFI members. I knew that I would have to disobey Grandmother. I had to go to Mr. Bradshaw's house. *He* had the books I needed; his extra tutoring was my only bet, whether Grandmother knew it or not.

23

As we soon found out, political campaigns can pick up and carry along impartial and reluctant observers, just as a flooding river gathers up everything in its path. Grandmother watched helplessly, even resisting passively, as the competing campaigns unfurled, as people on the island got sucked into the swirling political debate whether they wished to or not. There was no escaping the demand to choose and participate. People were relentlessly bombarded in shops, on the streets, in the buses and wherever a small group gathered.

At first, Grandmother professed to have absolutely no interest in what was happening around us. But as Pretty, Alma and Alvin brought home news and Mavis Thorpe provided daily commentaries, it became more difficult for her to remain aloof, although she fought strenuously to keep the encroaching politics, and what she anticipated as the ensuing heartaches, as far away from her doors as possible. But as virtually everyone on the island became immersed in the election, Grandmother simply had to capitulate under the relentless efforts to win her vote; in the end, it was impossible to consider that she might be the only person in the entire island not to have a say on the independence question.

In no time, Phillips quashed the early campaign dominance of Mr. Ward and the CLM by pulling off the biggest political coup in the island's history. When nobody expected it, Phillips astounded everyone at a mammoth political meeting in the city by announcing that Sandra Ward would be running for his party. More than that—she would try to defeat her father in his Top Rock constituency!

"When he said that, the people at the meeting got so quiet, Ma, that you could've heard a pin drop," Pretty said. "All you could hear was Phillips saying that when we get independence we will show the world that all Bajans can live together, that this ain't going to be like places in Africa or the southern United States where black people got to be marching every day for the right to vote. At first the people didn't know if Phillips was a mad man or if he had sold out to the white people. So they said nothing."

Pretty, Alma and Mavis had gone to the meeting in one of the buses provided by the DFI. The meeting had been advertised for almost a week. Men in cars with loudspeakers on the roofs came through the villages several times a day reminding everyone to come to this important meeting. The streets were littered with the seemingly millions of handbills that were printed with Phillips's face on them and distributed for this main event.

The buses had arrived in the village as soon as darkness fell and were promptly packed as the men and the women piled in, many of them standing in the aisles, others leaning out of the doors and windows. Nobody seemed to mind the tight squeeze. As the bus carrying Mavis and my aunts pulled off, the people started singing hymns and party songs, blowing whistles and drumming on the sides of the vehicle.

"Listen to all that ruckus," Grandmother said as the bus speeded out of the village. "I can tell this is going to be more than just a meeting."

Alvin, Chester and I didn't go to the meeting, so we stayed at home with Grandmother. I knew she was anxious to hear about the meeting and couldn't wait until the three women got back to tell us what had happened. She said she had better things to do than to spend the night in the dew listening to politicians, but I didn't see her making a good use of her time. We sat on the rock in the back yard waiting. I think the truth was that she just didn't want to be seen at a political meeting and risk losing everything.

Shortly after we had heard the bus stop in front of the house and then the excited voices of the people on board, the three women came into the yard. They could not contain themselves as they came through the gate. In the excitement, the three tried to talk at the same time.

"Wait," Grandmother said, holding up her hand. "Three jack asses can't bray at the same time and make sense. If anything, I got to say that the three of you sound like you just got back from the Tower of Babel. Like Phillips really confused the three of you tonight."

"No, Ma," Alma said. "You would've had to be there to see how Sandra Ward stole the show. To see Phillips grinning like the cat that ate the butter and raising his hand in the air, I tell yuh, he was the boss-man tonight, totally in charge. Nobody could touch him."

I didn't see what they were so excited about. I could have told them about Sandra before, but I didn't think such news would have been that important. Besides, if I had told them what I knew, it would only get me into trouble with Grandmother. I would have had to admit that I still visited Mr. Bradshaw's and overheard some of the things discussed in the house.

"Everybody knows how much noise there is at a political meeting, especially at one like tonight with every man-jack from across the island there," Pretty continued. "But not this time. Everybody went real quiet all of a sudden. I couldn't believe these two eyes God gave me when I looked up at the platform with all the lights and banners to see this woman, the only white person, sitting up there and just smiling and waving. The only white face among the twenty-four candidates. To tell the truth, I had to ask myself if the Democratic Front for Independence is still a black people party. I heard plenty of people around me mumbling the same thing."

"I see," Grandmother said.

Alvin and Chester stopped playing draughts inside the house and came into the yard. I was sitting on the big rock beside Grandmother, with my head resting in her lap. All that was left of the fire were the dying coals and the only light in the yard was a solitary streak from the lamp through the door. Now they were home, we could at last go to sleep. I sat up and yawned.

"And when the time came for her to speak, the people started one loud clapping," Alma said, sounding just as excited as Pretty. "The clapping sounded like a big wave smashing against the shore. Then it was so quiet when she spoke. When she was finished, it sounded like the wave going back out again as the people started clapping and whistling again."

"Well, I must admit I was surprised tonight," Mavis said in a subdued tone. She was standing by the gate. "Who would believe something like this would happen? This turns the election upside down now. I can't wait to hear what Mr. Ward'll say."

"I don't like to comment on political matters," Grandmother said finally, "but hearing what you've just said about that Sandra Ward doesn't surprise me one bit."

She was speaking slowly and calmly, deliberately choosing her words. "I know the woman that raised her from a child. Her name was Mrs. Warner, Ernesta Warner, God bless her soul, and she always said Sandra was different from all the other Ward children."

"Can you imagine what Wardie must be thinking tonight?" Pretty crowed. "His own daughter! This should break up the Ward family for sure."

"I won't worry my head too much about that," Mavis said. "These white people real tricky when it comes to politics. I got a feeling that the Wards will come out of this one on top and look real good; they have now put themselves on both sides of this independence issue so that no matter who wins, they will still come out on top. It is we, the poor black people, that will always be at the bottom."

"I ain't saying you should trust no politician," Grandmother continued. "All I know is that Sandra is a peculiar bird. I remember hearing Mrs. Warner saying Sandra was like no other white child she looked after. That sometimes you would think Sandra had some black blood in her veins from the way she used to act. Mrs. Warner, may she rest in peace, used to say that the little girl would always want to come home with her to her little shack among the poor people in Water Street and that she always asked to eat from the same pot as the maids when they cooked a little something for themselves. She would steal into the kitchen and eat with the maids, eating real poor people food.''

"Maybe that's why she holding Bradshaw so tight," Mavis said. "Maybe she really likes the black blood in more ways than one. But all the same, I'll still bet my life she won't even be looking at Bradshaw if he wasn't a headmaster and making a good penny. I'm sure she'd be looking at one of her own people and that eventually, when she's had her fun, she'd go back where she belongs. Just look at the way the Wards treated the same Mrs. Warner when the poor soul died. They didn't even give her a decent funeral. She was like a mother to about three generations of the Wards' children, raising them from the day their real mother squeezed them out until they were big enough to go off to England. Still, she died a pauper. But I can't help feeling Mrs. Warner'd be real happy at the way Sandra turned out. 'Cause everybody knows Sandra is a born and bred politician. In fact, when her grandfather, Premier Jacob Ward, was on his death bed, the only person he would ask Mrs. Warner for was Sandra. The old man said that she was the only true Ward, the only true politician, in the family. The old man hung on until Sandra flew in from England so he could give her his blessing.''

"I don't understand," Pretty said to Mavis. "You mean to say Phillips shouldn't let Sandra run?"

"No. I'm not saying that at all," she replied emphatically. "All I'm saying is that Phillips got to be real careful with these people. The next thing he'll know white people will be running the DFI. Sandra will only be the first in the party and what would happen to poor black people then?"

"I don't know," Pretty said. "All I know is that I want to see the look on Mr. Toppin's face when he comes around here asking for votes. I want to hear what he'd say when people ask him why they should vote for him and Ward when Sandra Ward ain't. I won't want to have to explain that." With that, Pretty excused herself to look after Anderson.

"Toppin deserves what he gets," Mavis said. "I don't trust him one bit. Just because he was a headmaster, he thinks everybody has to bow down and worship him with their vote. That he's better than all of us, so good that he could be white. Well, not me. I'm too proud for that. In any case, I don't trust these brown-skinned people who think they're white and running for Ward. It's as simple as that and come independence we'll put them in their place."

"Well, I don't think Mr. Ward is all that bad," Grandmother said. "He still got some kindness in his heart even if he doesn't always show it. He's better than most white people. And Toppin, after all, he had enough brains to be a schoolmaster and without him a lot of people in this area won't be able to read and write today. We must remember that and give praise where praise is due."

"Not to vote for him though," Mavis Thorpe said, turning to leave through the gate. "Anyway, excuse me for the night. It's time I see how my piccaninnies are doing. Goodnight everybody."

"Good-night," Grandmother said for us. Now we could turn in for the night.

The highlight of the election campaign for the boys in the village was not the battle between Mr. Ward and Phillips or the independence issue that Mr. Bradshaw kept saying would decide what kind of world we would inherit, but Little Foot and the brand new red Zephyr car he was driving. Overnight, Little Foot had grown in our esteem. His car was new and bright and, socially, Little Foot was a cut above everyone, even the professional chauffeurs whose employers occasionally allowed them to bring the car home. Little Foot actually owned his car and did not need anyone's permission to park it in front of his house.

In the morning, the car would be positioned ostentatiously beside the new house, with a canvas from the previous night's rally covering it, leaving out just enough for passers-by to admire the big red lights and airplane-shaped fins. At nights, the car would be spotted wherever people congregated. Even the professional drivers shook their heads and lusted for the chance to sit behind the wheel. And like a good politician, Little Foot allowed a select few to drive the car, but laid down strict rules that nobody should drive out of view.

All day, Little Foot went around the villages, dropping off leaflets and posters and stopping to talk to people. As he talked, he would remain seated authoritatively behind the steering wheel with the engine running, occasionally pressing the accelerator; sometimes he got out and leaned against the hood. He would take a yellow cloth from his back pocket and, while talking, polish the car, taking care to wipe away the fingerprint smudges that dulled the gloss.

The fun began when he selected a group of children to help him deliver the brochures. It was an honor to be selected and to be seen by your friends driving around the village in Little Foot's car. After the few minutes of distribution work, Little Foot sent the children home with handfuls of brochures for their parents and neighbors.

"Remember to tell your mother and her man, if you ain't got a father at home, to vote Labour," he shouted after them, as he opened the doors for another group to climb in. When the car wasn't filled with children, it was filled with women going to and from work. By the second week of the campaign, every boy in my class had driven in the car. I decided not to be left out even if it meant sacrificing a few days of reading for the experience and was finally part of the gang that Little Foot had gathered for this particular run.

But if the car caught the people's attention, something else had a firmer grip on their political thoughts and imagination. Frustratingly, at every turn, Little Foot found that, after the initial admiration for the car had worn off, he was dealing with one issue that forced him to come up with more creative answers.

"I ain't paying too much attention to what you people are saying about Miss Ward," Little Foot was saying to a group of women who had posed the question. They had been anxiously waiting for the bus, which was already an hour late. As Little Foot's car approached, they saw the God-sent opportunity of getting to work a little late but still in time to prepare the supper, wait on the tables and to avoid any wage deductions or possible dismissal. The youngest woman in the group surprised the others by asking the question, setting the unhappy course for the conversation; the older heads tried valiantly but unsuccessfully to veer elsewhere.

As he parried with the women, apparently reluctant to open his car to them until he had firm proof of their voting intentions, the boys were busy playing with the horn and knobs on the dashboard. I was sitting in the front seat, waiting my turn at the horn and to flick on and off the car's interior lights. "In the end Sandra will be the one to trick Phillips when she turn her back on his party. You just watch my word. What girl you know won't vote for her father to become premier?"

"Yeah, but at the same time she's running for the other side," the inexperienced woman continued, settling the handles of her straw basket across her wrist. The others glanced up the road, still waiting for the bus. "She won't be going that far, getting up at DFI meetings and attacking Labour, if she didn't mean business. After all, we only have to remember that we're talking about the same Sandra Ward that moved the resolution at the DFI convention to ask England for independence."

"Yes, yes, I know that, too," Little Foot said impatiently. "But you can't take things as they look. You got to know the ins and outs first, what's below the surface. Like how them wicked people in the DFI say they'd blackmail Sandra if she didn't run for them. I keep telling you people"—he was wagging his finger in a stern warning, his eyes darting from face to face—"that them people in the DFI are Communists, pure and simple, and you can't trust them."

"What you mean?" the woman asked. Little Foot was showing some annoyance with the blowing of the horn and had slapped the boy ahead of me on the hand. As the woman spoke, Little Foot fanned his hand in a signal for us to stop tinkering with the gadgets.

"Cut it out now," he said abruptly. "And get out my car."

We opened the door to leave. The women took up their handbags and other tacklings, anticipating the invitation to replace us.

"Well, let me tell you a few secrets, 'cause nobody should make certain statements unless they know all the facts," Little Foot said, resuming the conversation. He switched off the engine. The women glanced at one another. We got out of the car. The invitation was still not extended. "Them brutes ganged up on poor Sandra and told her plain and simple: 'Look, you bloody well better run for us or we will destroy you and your family.' They said . . ."

"That's not true," I blurted out.

"Let big people talk in peace," Little Foot admonished sternly. "A little boy like you should be seen and not heard when big people're talking."

"Nothing like that ever happened," I said. No sooner were the words out of my mouth than I realized what big trouble I was in. The women exchanged glances again and smiled. Little Foot frowned and glared at the women, then at me.

"You see what I have to deal with," Little Foot said, his voice low and soft with anger. "I mean, here I am, a kind-hearted man letting every man, woman and child wear out the seats in my brand new motorcar and what thanks do I get? None. This little kiss-me-arse idiot here can look me straight in the face, a big man like me, and because he does be drawing up in Bradshaw's house every night, he feels he got to look me in the face and call me a liar in front my . . . my peers. Well, your arse will pay for your mouth some day soon, little boy."

"Look," one of the women finally said. "You're giving us the drop to work or not?"

Little Foot started the engine. He stared at the women as if giving them a final assessment.

"Yeah, what you say, man?" another woman asked. "It's getting late so make up your mind. We got to decide if to start walking real soon." Little Foot glanced up the road again. No bus was coming. He had made up his mind.

"Wait for the fucking government bus," he said. The wheels squealed and the car lurched forward awkwardly, leaving the women in a storm of dust and cussing at the top of their voices.

I walked away knowing Mr. Ward had a new problem on his hands, that his opponents would make sure that everyone across the island heard of how badly Little Foot had treated these women. I also knew that my name would be part of the gossip and that when it reached Grandmother, she would know that I was still visiting Mr. Bradshaw's house.

The next day, the DFI sent two similar Zephyr cars into the district to transport the people it claimed Mr. Ward and Little Foot were discriminating against. The buses began running on time, too.

Three days later, Mr. Toppin, the former headmaster, brought his campaign to Lodge Road and unexpectedly into Grandmother's back yard. All of us were at home when Mr. Toppin, Little Foot and about sixty people, including several boys from our school, showed up.

Grandmother invited them into the back yard, which was hard put to accommodate even half of the entourage. The others stayed outside, but within listening range. Alvin, Chester and I felt instantly elevated and elated that so many people had descended on our house, that this was the venue for what could be a political debate people would talk about for days.

"You're really looking good these days," Grandmother said, welcoming the former headmaster. "And from what I've heard, I can tell you the people really like what you're saying these days. You're only telling the truth and, as the Bible says, the truth shall set you free."

Mr. Toppin looked thin and fit as if he had gone into training. Mr. Burton, our deputy headmaster, was also in the party and moments later he came through the back gate with Little Foot. When I saw him, the pit of my stomach lurched: his eyes were fiery and wild, the corners of his mouth white with spittle. Mr. Burton looked just as he did the day he gave me the flogging in front of the school.

"You got to be careful with the people in this house," Mr. Burton declared loudly. "These are pure DFI people, Humphry Bradshaw's own people. He got them"—he twirled several times in the air above his head a folded fist with the first finger pointing out—"wrapped around his little finger good and proper."

"That can't be so." Little Foot feigned disdain, shaking his head. "I was right here in this house when Mr. Ward gave them the jobs, so they can't be so ungrateful. I mean, how can they take the jobs and then turn around and vote against the man? Don't forget it's three jobs in this house alone and nobody was working 'til Mr. Ward came along."

"You're watching the wrong people," Mr. Burton said, oblivious of the growing scowl on Grandmother's face. "Don't watch the old people; watch the young ones. Especially the one that takes free lessons from our friend Humphry Bradshaw; that does eat and sleep in his house almost every day and night. Them's the one to watch. Remember, little pigeons got wide ear holes."

"What you're talking 'bout, Mr. Burton?" Grandmother was almost whispering. "We don't support no political party that I know 'bout. In this house, I's still the head, the one that decides things. I'm the man in this house."

"If you must know directly, I mean little Howard right here," Mr. Burton said, not bothering to look in my direction, but continuing to stare at Grandmother. "You should hear him boasting about the things that go on in front his eyes when he's over at Bradshaw's."

"But Howard don't go over there anymore," Grand-mother said, raising her voice in righteous triumph. "I strictly forbade him. He hasn't been there since the election started."

"No, he hasn't, eh? Well, watch this." Mr. Burton turned to me and immediately I was encircled by all the people standing in the yard. I could not look at Grandmother. I knew what she was thinking: that I was embarrassing her in front of the growing group of party workers, some of whom she didn't even know, that I was making her look bad for having stuck out her neck to defend me, not knowing I had routinely disobeyed her. I had put three jobs on the line. Worse, this humiliation was happening in her back yard from which there was no escape.

Mr. Burton was staring at me, his arms still folded across his chest. As he spoke, he leaned back on his heels, looking like a policeman awaiting an immediate answer. "I hear that you were at Bradshaw's house the night Wardie's daughter, Sandra, was forced to run against her father. Is that true or not?"

"Well, I wasn't exactly there," I mumbled, digging my toe into the dust to avoid making eye contact with the teacher, Grandmother or anyone else. Grandmother was hearing me confess that I had disobeyed her. I would have preferred not to answer, but I couldn't. I had to answer truthfully. If I lied, and Grandmother found out, the punishment would be worse. The tears were brimming in my eyes and I tried not to look my inquisitor in the face.

"What you mean you weren't exactly there? Were you there or not?"

"I was in . . . um . . . um . . . the library," I said. When he did not immediately respond, I added: "Studying for the Common Entrance."

"Really," Mr. Burton said, scornfully. "The teachers at the school ain't good enough for you, eh?"

I didn't answer. What could I say? I wished he would just hurry up and end this torture and that he would let me explain the political discussions were usually held in Mr. Bradshaw's kitchen over beer. I wanted to tell him that often visitors didn't know I was in the library, which, I wanted to emphasize, was not beside the kitchen. But he didn't care for that. Around me, I could feel the circle closing in and I could hear the people breathing loudly.

"Even if you were in the library," he said, emphasizing the words, "you could still hear what was going on in the house, right?"

I nodded my head. "Don't shake you head like some mule, use the tongue God gave yuh. Now, answer my questions. Don't forget that you're still in one of my classes, that you fall under my supervision and I can cut your arse with my strap any time."

Desperately, I looked at Grandmother. She frowned and I knew she could not help me.

Under insistent questioning, I told them everything that I knew, jumbling the sparse information from several visits just to be rid of the inquisition. Mr. Toppin, Mr. Burton and Little Foot listened attentively, smiling among themselves.

Finally, Mr. Burton turned to the crowd and raised his hands in the air. "I hope you people heard every word, how Phillips and his people brainwashed that poor girl in the hope of cheap political gain. Now we really know why Sandra Ward would run against her father. Now we know what these people are capable of inflicting on us."

Mr. Toppin grimaced. "We'll deal with these swines. All this planning, scheming, and deceitfulness got to be exposed for the good of the people. And before the election."

"It's all because of that Humphry Bradshaw," Mr. Burton

said. "The sooner we get rid of him as headmaster, the better."

As they left, Mr. Toppin had a few last words for Grandmother. "I would advise you to stop this boy from going 'round with people like Mr. Bradshaw. You just heard for yourself how wicked these people are, how they could get a big woman like Sandra Ward to do things that even she wouldn't dream about. Just think what they can do to a little boy. And besides, a kind-hearted man like Mr. Ward can take only so much before—" he hesitated purposefully, "before he . . . well, you know what."

"All right, Mr. Toppin," Grandmother said. "Thanks for dropping by with Mr. Burton and pointing out these things to me. I'll have a good talk with Howard when you're gone. You's a man that I trust and respect. Mr. Ward too."

Mr. Toppin delivered his parting shot. "And another thing, I wouldn't be surprised if the little boy doesn't pass the examination. Don't feel too bad if he fails, 'cause some boys are born bright. Others—you know," he said waving his hand indecisively. "Special lessons ain't all you need."

Grandmother nodded that she understood. With the tears streaming down my face, I waited for the inevitable flogging. "Look at this trouble for me," Grandmother finally started. I braced myself for what was to come, for the "talking-to" she had promised Mr. Toppin she would administer. My only consolation was that the crowd and my friends, already preparing to taunt me at school in the coming days, were now several houses away and were unable to hear me screaming from the beating.

Perhaps Mavis heard Grandmother's voice, for she looked through the shed roof window, having returned to her house as the crowd dispersed. Alvin and Chester were standing in a corner of the yard with Alma. They looked desolate. Pretty was stooping in front of the fire, feeding wood into it with one hand and holding Anderson to her breast with the other. Everything was in place for my ultimate humiliation. I could not blame them for wanting to kill me.

"Who does that prissy Leroy Burton think he is?" Grand-mother continued. "Barging in here like that." This was going to be worse than I expected. Before the flogging would come the indignity of having to suffer through another of Grand-mother's scoldings, a punishment almost more painful than the beating to follow. "And that big-headed so-called head-master, Toppin. Who he thinks he's to come into my yard this evening, to bring a million people in my sanctuary, and then, in front of the world, to embarrass me—" she fiercely slapped her breast with an open palm as she addressed herself—"me, a God-fearing woman who never called either of them a fool, not once? How can he do something like that to me?"

"But these are the same people you were defending just the other night," Mavis reminded her. "You were the one saying Toppin can't be all that bad. That Ward is a decent gentleman. In fact, from the way you were talking I felt he done had your vote locked up for Toppin."

"But you can't expect two big grown men to come into the yard of a poor woman like me and pick on her grandson, can you?" Grandmother fenced back, her voice growing stronger. "Not even if they're politicians, you can't expect something like this."

I looked at her in disbelief. There was a special look on her face, the look of a warrior, of someone looking for a fight, a look I was more used to seeing on the faces of people like Ismay and other neighbors when they were ready to attack us. Grandmother was in a fighting mood such as I had never seen before. And it dawned on me—Grandmother wasn't angry with me; her anger at the politicians was simply her last-gasp attempt to fight back, to strike out, at all the people that had wronged us over the years.

Grandmother's contorted face was telling me she was too tired of everything. Just as noticeable was the defiance in her voice, a strain we had never heard, not even when Brutus Waite was stoning our house and harassing us when we walked the streets. Mavis Thorpe must have made the same observation. She was no match for Grandmother and quickly dropped out of the conversation.

"How could they come in here and do this to me? If they wanted to pick on somebody for what Sandra Ward is doing, why didn't they go and look for someone that is in politics like them, somebody who can defend themselves?" she roared. "But what can you expect of a big-headed fart like Toppin? Only goes to show that a big head doesn't mean a big brain."

Pretty had a blaze going and had placed the kettle on the fire to warm the water for Anderson's milk.

"We didn't tell Sandra Ward to do what she did. Because Howard was at Mr. Bradshaw's, trying to get an education, trying his levelest best to pass the examination, doesn't have one thing to do with Sandra Ward running in any campaign. So it ain't fair to come here and take out their feelings on me and my family. Them things ain't fair in the sight of God or man."

"You know what you're going to cook this evening?" Pretty asked, waiting for the opportune time as Grandmother caught her breath.

"Don't bother me with no cooking," Grandmother lashed back, startling Pretty. "Find something or other in the larder and everybody stop having to depend on me. I'm tired of having to fend, fend, fend. Tired of everybody passing and dumping on me and then I have to grin and bear and bite my tongue. I, like the fool, have to take all the shame and sorrow. Lord knows, I've tried my best to stay out of politics and out of harm's way. I won't even go to a political meeting so that nobody can say I like one party over another. But what more can I do when they bring the politics into my very house, into the very place where I seek shelter and refuge, the last place from which I cannot retreat and run away? What can I do? But you know something, if one of these three boys here was a man, if only one of you was big enough to stand on your own two feet and to flex a muscle or two, nobody would do what they're doing to me. That's the price I must pay for not having a man in this house. But time will tell. You all won't remain small forever."

"Ma," Pretty said quietly, perhaps hoping her voice wouldn't carry to Mavis Thorpe, "I ain't see nothing in the larder to cook. Only a few gills of rice."

"What?" Grandmother said. She sounded as if she had snapped awake from a frightening dream. "What you're saying?"

"Nothing in the larder," Pretty whispered again.

"I see," Grandmother said, also lowering her voice. "Give me the child to hold. Take the basket in there and go up to Babsie Bourne's shop and ask him to trust us some provisions until payday, Wednesday. Let's hope Burton and Toppin ain't over there in the damn shop buying so much rum that Babsie won't want my business no more."

"You're going to let the little boy go back to Mr. Bradshaw's," Mavis Thorpe said.

She had hit the crux of the matter. Whether she did it intentionally to egg Grandmother on, or out of concern for me, I don't know. But this was the question to truly test Grandmother's defiance and political smarts.

"He can go wherever the hell he wants to go," Grandmother said. She took Anderson from Pretty and sank down on the rock. She was still angry. The defiance was still in her voice. I could not believe my ears. She was not even scolding me for disobeying her. More than that, she had just given me full freedom.

"Take Alvin and Chester to help you with the basket," Grandmother said as Pretty was going through the gate. Alma followed them and Mavis disappeared inside her house. We were alone, I still standing on the spot where Mr. Burton had questioned me and Grandmother on the rock with Anderson on her lap.

"If you were a man, Leroy Burton wouldn't treat you so," Grandmother said softly. "But you'll be a man some day and all this foolishness will stop. Until then, we'll trust in God and keep praying for deliverance. I ain't give up yet on the good Lord making a way for you and your brothers to join your parents in England. I still have faith in the wondrous working power of my Lord. I got a plan that helped other people find their family in England and, by the help of God, it will work for me too. We'll keep praying about that one."

I went inside the house and remained there until Pretty called me for supper. At bedtime, I remembered what Grandmother said about praying and I thanked God for giving her the strength to stand up for me. But it was a prayer I didn't complete.

I couldn't bring myself to ask God to speedily work on our parents to send for us. I worried about what would happen to Grandmother if God granted my prayers. As she got older, I knew she would be more vulnerable in this hostile village. After all these years of struggling to raise and protect us, it would be unfair for the three of us to walk out on her just as we were reaching manhood and could defend her. Yet I still wanted to go to England, if only to satisfy the curiosity of knowing who my parents were. Perhaps I was too drained and sleepy, but I fell asleep without having resolved this problem.

Grandmother's anger and defiance was a passing phase. It turned out to be as brief and deceiving as a tropical downpour that lasts no longer than the time it takes to find shelter. In the morning, she was back to her old self, singing and praying loudly as she fed the fowl and made the morning cocoa and bakes.

"Howard," she said as I sat on the ground in front the rock. I was the last to arrive for breakfast as I had pissed the bed during a frightful night and had to spread out the rags on the rocks in the corner. "I was giving it some thought. I don't want you going to Mr. Bradshaw's house anymore, you understand what I am saying?"

"Yes, Grandmother."

"Absolutely, no more. You hear me?"

"Yes, Grandmother."

"We got to be careful in these last days," she said.

"The lesson . . ."

Not waiting for me to finish, she said abruptly, "No lesson either. We got to be careful, real careful. We're small fries and we can't afford to get caught in the big fish nets. We can't take no chances. So no lessons either. You hear me?"

I nodded. That wasn't good enough.

"Use the red flag in your mouth, the same one you couldn't control in front of Little Foot. Let me hear that you understand. No more going to Bradshaw's lessons on Saturday mornings; no more going to Bradshaw's house. That's clear?"

"Yes, Grand."

"You can borrow books from the library and let Pretty and Alma help you on nights. That would give them something useful to do instead of running to every political dogfight around this place. Or you can start back reading the Bible to me. But I want you and everybody else—you too, Alvin and Chester—at home on nights so I can keep an eye on yuh."

Pretty and Alma did not protest the prohibition extended to them, or the additional task of having to drill me with school work.

It was four weeks to the election and the Common Entrance and we couldn't wait for both of them to be out of the way and to escape from the prison that was our home. Without the lessons, everyone took it for granted that I would definitely fail the examination. I honestly wondered whether they were right.

24

In the distance we could hear the music from the political rally getting under way. Grandmother, feeling it was time to be seen at her employer's meeting and also to ensure his assistance in her new quest, had gone with Alma, Alvin and Chester to the gathering. I decided to stay at home, ostensibly to keep Pretty company, but mainly because I didn't want to be near Mr. Burton and Mr. Toppin. And I didn't want to run into Little Foot again. I was genuinely afraid of them. More than that, something new was bothering me.

As soon as the others left, I lit the lamp and took down from the shelf one of the books I had borrowed from the library. Pretty wasn't feeling well and after the long day working in the sun, she decided to rest for a while, to stretch out beside the baby on the grass bed. I tried to read but my mind could not focus. The house was too quiet.

Eventually, I closed the book and walked outside. The back yard was quiet. Even the turkeys and chickens were already asleep. I sat on the rock, looking through the paling gate into the darkness. My life had changed so much in the last while that I didn't know what was going on. One of my biggest worries was something Mr. Bradshaw had said one evening when I was still allowed to visit his house. Suddenly, that statement was making sense. At first, I didn't pay it much attention, but of late, and primarily because of Grandmother's surprise statement at breakfast, what Mr. Bradshaw said returned to me again and again. He had first told Sandra and repeated to the premier that I was one of the children who might never go overseas to join their parents. Whoever won the election, one of their biggest jobs after independence would be to help children like me adjust to this reality and to, indeed, create the favorable environment after nationhood that would make it so more people might not want to leave. Sandra had taken this remark in stride, but the premier had stared at me with a look that would bother me for some time.

At the time, I didn't know what he meant and even now the full implication still puzzled me. Later, when I asked Mr. Bradshaw for an explanation, he told me not to worry, that everything would reveal itself in due course. Nevertheless, I felt he was keeping something from me.

My mind skipped to the disagreement with Grandmother this morning, when out of the blue she said she planned contacting the chief welfare officer in Bridgetown to ask the government to locate our parents in England.

"Mildred White told me it worked for her," she said. "And as you know, her boy in England sent for his two girls a few weeks back. I know the chief welfare officer and I know he'd do a favor for me if I ask him. From what Mildred White told me, the government people here would contact the government people in England and quick, quick so, they could find where anybody is living and get them to look after their responsibilities."

This news confused me. But most surprising was the immediate effect it had on Alvin. He jumped to his feet, knocking over his tin cup of cocoa, and started crying. "I ain't going to no England," he shouted. I couldn't remember the last time I had seen him cry—not even when Grandmother flogged him. This refusal to cry convinced Grandmother more than anything else that it was a waste of time beating him. Even when he got into fights with the bigger boys, he didn't shed a tear. Alvin never cried, even when he should. He had to be strong and to always show how tough he was. That was why, even though I knew he loved and wanted to protect me, he got angry when the tears so effortlessly spilled down my cheeks as he accused me of having a head full of water.

Alvin was adamant he didn't want to go to England, not even if the welfare people pulled off the miracle for which Grandmother was hoping. He didn't know the people he would be going to live with and, if he was forced to go to England, as soon as he became a man he would turn right around and come back home, he said. Grandmother ate and drank in silence, her eyes never leaving Alvin's face.

"You don't know what you are saying, son," Grandmother said softly. "Listen to me. You got to make a life for yourself. I know better than you. And I know this ain't the best situation for you to be growing up in. Not with all of us being picked upon by somebody new almost every day and so many things you want to make right, so many people you'll want to get back at when you are a man. I can't let that happen to you, son. And not only to you, Alvin, but to your two brothers. I just can't. Otherwise, I may as well send you straight to prison. That's what those grudges in your heart would do for you. All that anger in your chest could turn your mind foolish and make you go off the top of your head the first time somebody says something stupid to you. I would rather send you to England and give you a chance."

The last words came in a hoarse whisper. She washed her tin cup at the barrel, returned to the fireside, picked up Alvin's cup, and poured the cocoa dregs into it. As she extended the tin cup to him, Alvin bolted through the back-yard gate. Later, I saw him at school. He wasn't crying anymore and appeared to be his own self. But when nobody was looking, he would lean against the school wall and gaze at his feet or into the distance.

Chester did not show his feelings. We talked on the way to school and he said that he wouldn't mind going to England. Alvin, he was sure, would change his mind and the three of us would sit together on the plane. When we got to England, we could have a big color picture of the three of us in our sweaters taken and framed and sent home for Grandmother. It would make her proud when people visited the house. Eventually, we could send money for her when we worked or let her come to live with us.

"Alvin will change his mind," Chester assured me. "It's just that he's tired of boasting he was going to England and having people laugh at him. But he'll change his mind."

I wasn't sure what I wanted. I supposed a lot of it depended on what happened in the weeks coming up. My certainty at wanting to leave was eroding. And I knew if I had a choice that I might even look favorably at Alvin's position. I didn't tell this to Chester.

In any case, Chester and I felt there was no rush to make up our minds. We knew how much Grandmother hated sharing her business with strangers, so we didn't really expect her to keep the promise to visit the chief welfare officer, or to visit him too soon. We were wrong. When I came home from school, she was showing Pretty and Alma the letter she had received from the welfare officer. "All I got to do now is to go to Mr. Ward at the vestry and get him to give me a letter of support," she said. "Then I can take them over to the Home Office for the British Government in Bridgetown and get things rolling."

Because of the haste she had shown, we knew how determined Grandmother was. Any hopes I had that she might have held off were quashed when Grandmother set out for the despised rally, giving Mr. Ward no reason for not putting his signature on the letter.

While I was sitting on the rock, turning these thoughts over in my mind, I heard a weak whimpering sound that seemed to be coming from underneath the house. I looked over my shoulder, but the sound stopped instantly. I returned to my thoughts, but the sound started again. Maybe it was Pretty saying something. I called to her, but she replied she hadn't said anything.

The light from the house was beginning to brighten up parts of the back yard. I turned to face the light and almost jumped off the rock. Slowly, through the rays of the light, a brown dog was walking toward me on wobbly legs. It looked wasted, its ribs were showing, the rounded tops of its hind legs that joined the main frame were jutting out into the skin. It was whining weakly. A brown spot of what looked like dried blood was on its face. The dog looked unsure whether to trust me, but was advancing slowly and cautiously, its tail between its legs.

It was Tupper.

I jumped off the rock and ran to him. The dog fell on its front paws and crouched, as if expecting to be hit again. I grabbed and hugged him. He smelled musty and the blood was fresh. His body was warmer than I had ever felt it. He kept on whining, pleading. In a moment, I had a bowl of food in front of him. It was leftover soup that I was planning to eat before going to bed. The dog lapped it up slowly, as if he didn't have the strength to eat. When the bowl was empty, I filled it with water. Tupper drank that too. He looked a bit stronger.

"I thought he was dead," Pretty said from behind me. I hadn't heard her approaching.

"I thought so, too. But I guess not. I'm glad he's back."

She smiled and put her hand on my shoulder. "You did miss him, didn't you," she said. I shook my head. We sat on the rock and I told her what had really happened: how I didn't want the dog to starve to death and had tried to kill it myself; that it must have recovered and gradually found its way back home. After that, we sat staring into the darkness, listening to the voices in the distance. Neither of us said anything.

"You think Dad'll still send for us?" I asked her eventually, still thinking of Mr. Bradshaw's comment, and hoping she would give me something to help me make up my mind.

"I think so. That would be good, wouldn't it?" she said thoughtfully. Then as if she had been reading my mind she added, "Don't listen to what people're saying. They would say anything. The same way people are saying Henry ain't going to send for me and Anderson to live with him in New York. But I know it ain't true. I know him too good. At least, I hope so."

She paused and sat rubbing the sides of her face with her hands. She kicked the earth with the old pair of shoes she wore whenever she was outside. Grandmother claimed they would prevent her from catching a lining cold in her womb that would kill her.

"Don't mind that Burton or Toppin. Don't let them upset you. Them's only political yard fowls for Mr. Ward. The people'll deal with them good and proper on election day. The people got more sense than they think they got. Burton and them are the old generation. If you study hard and do the best you can, you might still pass the exam. I'll help you with your work on nights. You could make something of your life, help your poor Grandmother. You would like that, wouldn't you?"

"Yes."

"Then, let's do it. Don't stop dreaming. 'Cause without a dream we ain't nothing. That's why I'm worried about Ma. I mean, things around here are so tough it looks to me like Ma's finding it too hard to dream anymore and I don't like it. She was always the one encouraging us to dream: to hope and pray things would get better. But now, she doesn't even buy a bingo card anymore. She doesn't even trust her luck anymore; she doesn't even bother with church no more."

We lapsed into silence again. I felt Pretty was thinking of her own dreams so I didn't intrude on her thoughts. Tupper curled up at our feet. I wasn't sure what Grandmother would do when she saw him, but I was sure of one thing: I would never let him go again.

It seemed I had just gone off to sleep when I felt a hand gently shaking my shoulder, not hard enough to disturb Alvin and Chester but strong enough to waken me.

"Come, Howard," Grandmother said, whispering. She was in her white nightgown and her head was still tied with her night scarf. That meant we weren't going outside. "Come and see how the good Lord does bring 'bout his retribution if you wait long enough."

The house was in near darkness. I could hear Alma and Pretty snoring. Grandmother stepped carefully around my brothers, as she pulled my hand. Stricken with sleep, I was clumsy and stepped on Chester, but he was so deeply asleep, he didn't notice. We couldn't have been in bed for more than a few hours.

"Keep quiet and come with me," Grandmother said, leading me to the front window. We peered through the closed flaps. At first I saw nothing.

"What's out there?" I asked. "What you want me to see?"

"Look good and don't talk too much. Look good. You'll see Brown Sugar and Brutus Waite. It looks like Anson Pinder caught the two of them together and they're in nothing but trouble now."

I looked again and made out the figures of three people standing on the other side of the road. Their voices, which I could now hear, gave away their positions.

"So that is what the two of you've been doing when I'm away," a voice that sounded like Anson Pinder's was saying. "Be Christ, I'm working hard, hard when the day comes, working overtime every night in the people's factory, trying to make a little money and to keep myself out of trouble and prison, and all this time the two o' you carrying on behind my back. You don't know, I got five minds to beat up the two of you right now."

Grandmother was listening carefully. "I hope you remember this even when you and your brothers are in England," she whispered. "Try not to move too much, so they won't know we're listening. I want you to think of this: that's why I woke you up; so you can see and hear for yuhself. Why is it that of all the places in the world Anson Pinder had to catch the two o' them right here in front my house? You don't think this is the work of God?"

"How?" I whispered back, baffled by the mysterious

workings of our Lord and Savior, who from all appearances was going to condone a murder right in front of our house. I could not understand why Grandmother should be so happy to see this kind of retribution; it was a strange attitude for a woman who had spent so many years teaching us to forgive and warning us not to prey on the weak and defenseless. I remembered what Pretty had said about Grandmother and it occurred to me that Grandmother had not only lost the power to dream but because of her despair and frustrations, she had become just like the people around us, the very ones she had spoken about so scornfully in the past.

"Remember when you went to the pipe for the skillet o' water the other day and you didn't trouble nobody! Not a soul. But that Brown Sugar doused you with a whole bucket o' water. And you remember how that Brutus stoned this very house and then stole my turkey? Well, this is retribution and it is right in front of this little old shack we have for a house. That is what happens when you leave things in God's hand." She paused and I strained to make out the figures in the darkness.

The two men were pulling Brown Sugar between them. Suddenly, Anson Pinder spun around and slapped the woman and pushed her heavily into the cluster of khus khus grass beside the road, the sound of the slap echoing in the early morning silence. Brutus let go of the other hand.

"Oh God, my head, my head," she bawled to no one in particular. "I ain't even done nothin'; I's just walking the public road peacefully with Everick here, not troubling a soul, and he started beating me like I'm some dog or something."

"He shouldn't hit her, though," I whispered.

"Sssh. You ain't see nothing yet, yuh brute," Grandmother whispered. Suddenly, she wasn't talking to me anymore, but to the prostrated Brown Sugar. "Defend yourself now. Let me see how bad you are. You see what I mean, Howard. The good Lord letting this happen right here for a purpose and that is why he won't send 'long anybody to help them with Anson Pinder. 'Cause all this time I have been praying to the Lord to help me with the two o' them and I have been waiting patiently. Who would think the Lord would send a jailbird like Anson Pinder to give me satisfaction?"

The arguments continued outside. There was a loud rip in the otherwise silent night and I saw Anson throw Brown Sugar's dress away. It had come off in one pull.

"Everick, you'll stand there and let him kill me or something?" she pleaded to Brutus. "You ain't know he's a jailbird. That he tasted prison already and that he could kill me this way."

"So I'm a jailbird now, eh?" Anson said, getting angrier and punching her. "All of a sudden I'm a jailbird. I ain't like your outside man here, eh? At least I don't thief Miss Howell's fowls and bring them to you to cook. I might steal from the white people that got money, but not poor-arse people like myself."

"You hear that, Howard." Grandmother was almost beside herself. "Pure vindication, sweet revenge. Lord, you work in wondrous ways. Still, all my chicken and turkeys they ate ain't do them no good, ain't give them the strength to beat one good man. So I don't feel too bad."

The three of them were scuffling, pushing one another ineffectually until Anson Pinder drove a right hand into Brutus's belly. He sank to his knees, holding his guts. "Oh, Lord. Oh, Lord," he groaned. "Oh, Lord."

"See that," Grandmother said. "Why his sisters don't come out and defend him now? Where are Mavis Thorpe and Ismay? You tell me that."

With Brutus on his knees, Anson planted a stiff kick to his chest with a loud thud. Brutus fell on his face, then struggled back to his knees. Anson found a thick piece of wood in the grass. He broke it over Brutus's head, and he fell to the ground like a stone, not moving.

"Oh. My God," Grandmother gasped, frightened and recoiling. "Come away from the window quick before anybody knows we're looking. I ain't got no time for going to court and taking no false-oath witness for anybody. If the police come around asking questions in the morning, you didn't see nor hear anything, you hear me."

Brown Sugar thought Brutus was dead. "Oh Lord, you killed him. You killed him. Just like that, you killed him." She started to run away but Anson cut off her escape. Brown Sugar spun out of his hands and ran toward our house, ducking between the trees and waking the turkeys and chickens. We could hear the birds fluttering awake in a panic.

Anson threw some stones in her direction. The first brought a loud scream, the second the shattering of bottles. He was now at the side of our house running on the rocks.

We saw Brutus get up from the ground, realize the coast was clear, and disappear into the darkness of the pasture where we played cricket.

"Lord, I never see one man run so fast," Grandmother said, laughing, but putting her hand to her mouth to smother it. "Look at the dead come back alive and run. Lord have mercy. From now on I'll have to start calling him Lazarus, not Brutus."

Just then we heard the familiar sound of Ma dragging her cane behind her. When she came into view, Brown Sugar dashed in front of the old woman. A stone hit on the road, between them.

Ma swore loud and long, slurring her words. "When it ain't that damn dog Miss Howell got trying to bite off me foot, it is somebody in her house pelting at me. I don't know what I do these people 'round here. I don't know what I got for her." I froze. Once offended, Ma might pull her gun and start shooting recklessly at the house, at us in the darkness. Grandmother said nothing. I kept quiet and listened to her deep breathing.

Suddenly the tension dissipated. Brown Sugar melted into the night, Anson turned disgustedly away from Ma and Ma stumbled on down the road.

Grandmother felt thoroughly vindicated, even if it took an extra effort to conceal what she knew when she talked with Mavis across the palings. I worried about how much Grandmother had enjoyed what had happened and knew that there was a time when she would have recklessly opened her window and let Anson Pinder know she was a witness; she might have even risked endangering everyone by opening the door to offer Brown Sugar refuge. Grandmother had really changed.

25

The bus was quickly gathering speed as it encountered the first long stretch of road. In the back, by the last window, I tried to look as inconspicuous as possible and not to show my fear. Why I was on the bus headed from Bridgetown, I didn't know. All I knew was that I wanted to run away, to get as far away from Lodge Road as possible; from Grandmother and her problems; from the Common Entrance Examination; and from Grandmother forcing us to go to England. I simply wanted to clear my head of all those conflicting thoughts.

When the bus had pulled up at the stop by the corner shop, getting on board seemed to be the only thing I could safely do. It had found me frozen at the crossroads: one artery led back to Lodge Road and home; another to Water Street and Christ Church Boys' Elementary School; and the third to Gall Hill and Oistins Library. In my heart, I wanted to defiantly walk down Water Street and into Mr. Bradshaw's final class before the examination on Monday. But on this Saturday, the last day for legal electioneering before the Monday vote, I dared not venture near the school.

So I climbed on board the bus, not knowing where I was going. I knew that at such a late stage, it would be a waste of time trying to tutor myself; in any case, my mind could not be confined to the library and books. So it was no use going into Oistins right away. I could return the books at the end of the day, before the library closed.

"Watch your foot up there on the gas, Mr. Driver," a short man sitting in the middle of the bus shouted. His voice rose clearly over the din from the people and the bus. "Not so fast. You might put us in a ditch. Remember, you got a lot of votes in this bus for Mr. Ward. So you better be careful with them."

"Votes for who?" the woman sitting across the aisle from him countered. "Look, you better let the man drive in peace. He's driving on freshly paved roads, that this government's been good enough to provide for the people, and in a brand new bus, too. So let him drive as fast as he likes."

"You mean a newly painted bus with new seats," the short man shot back. "How come your government that is so good to the people had to wait until it called an election to start paving roads?"

"Better late than never," the woman retorted angrily, turning so swiftly the heavy basket fell off her lap onto the foot of a boy standing in the aisle. The accident caused the passengers to break into loud laughter as the boy grimaced and fought to hold back the tears.

"Beg pardon, son. I didn't do it on purpose," she said. Almost as quickly, she returned to the issue at hand. "Don't laugh. All you supporters of the CLM and Ward are the same: you like to travel too slow. That's why when the changing times fly past, you don't even know. That's why you all so frightened, so timid as my man Phillips says, to take a drive down the independence road. So, Mr. Driver," she raised her voice to a scream, "press on the gas as hard as you like!"

The smooth road marked the farthest I had ever gone from Lodge Road on my own. The only times I had traveled this road were when Grandmother took me to the quarterly meeting in Bridgetown. But since she had been read out of the church, she had stopped going to those gatherings. There was no longer a need for me to accompany her to the city.

Now, I was on my own, knowing that when I got back home Grandmother would be demanding a full accounting of my time and the money I spent on the trip. But those were problems to be dealt with later. For the moment, there were too many things on my mind for me to wonder about what

Grandmother would do at the end of the day.

The thought occurred to me that I might not even return home. What was the use of returning, to face an examination that I most surely would fail, and the uncertain future that was bound to follow such a performance? Nobody had to tell me that when I failed the test, my life would be no better than that of most of the very people on this bus; or that I would have to be contented to do all types of menial work. Nobody had to tell me there was no future in such a life or that it could be different if I passed the examination and attended one of the grammar schools. A pass might even rescue me from having to go to England.

The houses in the villages along the highway had suddenly given way to endless fields of sugar cane. I felt I had passed the point of no return, that I had to continue with the trip until the end. I didn't want to be caught alone in such a desolate, frightening part of the island. The fear and the sound of the noisy engine changing into high gear held me transfixed to my seat as I surrendered to being transported to a part of the country I didn't know, to a part of myself that I didn't fully understand. I no longer knew the villages through which we were passing.

Around me the men and women continued to argue noisily, at times shouting one another down and acting as if they were about to come to blows. Almost everyone was wearing a T-shirt or a head band supporting the CLM or DFI. The women sat with big bamboo baskets on their laps, making it impossible for anyone to move. The men, as usual, traveled with bags over their shoulders or empty-handed. Listening to the conversation, I understood why Grandmother enjoyed being on board the bus. Now I knew why it caused her so much pain to give up the weekly rides into town and the friendly bantering.

Lulled by the noise and motion of the bus, I thought back over my day. I had returned early from Top Rock after selling the basket of papayas and eggs at the hotels to find the house empty. The entire village was deserted, except for those standing by the bus stop. Grandmother had always told me not to leave money unguarded around the house, so I kept the dollar and seventy-five cents from the morning sales in my pocket.

With nobody at home to talk to, I decided to return my books to the library and to take along in my canvas bag the last of the special homework from Mr. Allen. He must have realized I was the only boy up for the Common Entrance not attending the headmaster's classes. So he had taken it upon himself to prepare special homework for me. One evening as I was getting ready to leave for home, he had come over to my desk with a brown manila folder in his hand.

"Prescod, here is some work to help you with the Common Entrance," he said. "Do as much of it as you can. If you have any problems, ask me for help. Try to do as much as you can."

Mr. Allen never asked why I was not attending Mr. Bradshaw's lessons but he must have known. Everyone had heard of my encounter with Mr. Burton and Mr. Toppin. As Grandmother had prohibited me from leaving the house at nights, I had plenty of time for the homework. After supper every night, Pretty and I sat by the lamp and while I wrote in the exercise books, she read silently from a big *National Geographic* magazine about New York. When I encountered a difficult assignment, she helped me solve it. Otherwise, she sat quietly by my side until I was finished. Then she checked my work for errors.

Sometimes, we just talked, usually about things we wanted to happen for us, but mostly about how tough it was living in a village where the weak were so likely to be attacked by the strong; where there was no protection or caring for the defenseless. We never said it specifically, but we knew we were talking about Grandmother. Pretty said she hoped Phillips was right when he promised that independence would change the way people treated one another.

But this morning, I felt lonely at home. I knew Grandmother, Alma and even Pretty had gone to a rally Mr. Ward had organized as a last-minute show of strength for himself and Mr. Toppin. At the launch of the campaign, Mr. Ward said he planned to hold only three meetings in his constituency: the first to officially announce his candidacy; the second to explain his manifesto; and the final one to thank the people for having given him the privilege of representing them for the past twenty-five years. Grandmother and her daughters, like everyone remotely connected to the Wards, had no choice but to be in the final rally.

But I knew Grandmother didn't want to be spending the day marching in the hot sun. I did not think she should have been forced to attend, but I could not tell her how I felt. I had already created enough problems. Because of me, she had no choice but to attend the rally, for I had made her a marked woman in the eyes of the CLM supporters.

As we waited to hear from the chief welfare officer and the British representative, Grandmother kept encouraging me to write to my parents and to send the letter to the old address. Should it come back, I had lost nothing. If my parents received the letter, they might answer and say when we could join them. She suggested I might even send the letter to the welfare office to accompany the notices from the governments, so that my parents would understand why it was necessary to take this desperate, even if for them embarrassing, step as a reminder of their responsibilities.

That created my biggest problem. I was not sure if I wanted to leave Barbados. Not that I didn't want to see my parents, but I knew Grandmother needed someone around to help her as she got older. The way I saw it, Pretty might soon be going to New York to join Henry. Alma too would eventually find a man and go off to live with him. If they were lucky, they might even leave the island. If we were to go to England, Grandmother would be left alone. And she was getting older. I didn't want to rely on independence changing people so drastically that Grandmother in her old age wouldn't need protection at home.

At the same time, I wanted to be with my parents. There

was a hunger in me to know them and be with the people who were responsible for bringing me into this world. I felt there was so much they could do for me and that they could teach me. Every child should spend some time with his parents, if they are alive, I thought. Parents should be preparing a future for their children, trying to protect them. I wished I could be like Alvin or Chester who had made up their mind. Alvin was so adamant that he no longer wanted to go to England that he refused to discuss it with Chester and me. Chester, on the other hand, had given up the hope of things getting any better. The only solution was for us to be with our parents. I agreed with both of them. I wanted to be part of both worlds but I didn't want to give up anything. Most of all, I didn't want to give up Grandmother. I suppose I wanted my parents here, where they were supposed to be. I didn't feel I should have to make any choices.

"So what Wardie's going to do with his daughter after the election?" one of the women was asking. I was beginning to recognize some of the buildings at the sides of the road. The small board-and-shingle houses were now crammed closer together and more people were walking the streets. This meant the bus was nearing the city. Just about every building and pole along the way was covered with posters and slogans. As the bus approached the city, the mix of people on board seemed to swing in favor of the DFI, as were the posters and signs along the way.

"Probably he'd send her back to England where she belongs," someone said. "Didn't you hear that Ward won't even let her darken the inside of his house? That he has cut her out of his will?"

"Well, if he'd do such a thing to his own flesh and blood, what'd he do to poor people like me and you?" someone asked. "That's why we got to keep hard-hearted people like the Wards out of power. 'Cause what I hear, it ain't Wardie alone that rejected Sandra, it is all the white people on this island. She's in one sad state whether the party wins or not."

"Do you think Sandra will take Braddie back to England with her?" the first voice was asking.

"He might not have any choice. When this election's over and we've got a new government in place, I can't see him hanging around as headmaster anymore. I think Leroy Burton will get the job."

I cringed at the thought of Mr. Burton in absolute authority. Maybe my best bet after all was for my parents to send for me. If I failed the examination, I would have Mr. Burton for another three years. I could not bear the thought.

"In any case, I hear that people expect the results from the screening test to be so bad that Humphry Bradshaw will have to resign," the voice continued.

"So he'll have to follow Sandra to England?"

"If she wants him. I won't bet my life on that. I'm a strong DFI supporter, but I can tell you I don't like the way he and Sandra are behaving. And I think she's just using him."

As the bus drove slowly through the city, there was unanimity for the first time. Up ahead was the noisy Bridgetown bus stand, with people crowding around and arguing loudly, many of them women balancing large baskets on their heads, and hawkers with trays laden with confectionery and fruits. The bus swung sharply into the parking lot. In a sudden rush, everyone tried to get off at the same time, causing a bottleneck at the door. I congratulated myself for having kept my tongue in cheek, but I was no closer to a reconciliation of my thoughts. I decided to get off the bus as well.

The bus had hardly driven off before I became aware that Mr. Bradshaw was standing on the other side of the street. With the bus gone, there was nowhere to hide.

"How are you doing, Howard?" Mr. Bradshaw called from across the street. Sandra and a small group of supporters were three doors away campaigning. She was walking up to the front doors, knocking and then waiting for a response. De-

spite her enthusiasm, she was having little success. The home-
owners seldom answered the doors themselves, simply sending their domestic workers with dismissive excuses. Sandra
left some of her literature on the door steps or put it into the
receiving black hand through the door or window. In the
distance, I could hear the loud carnival music from Mr.
Ward's rally.

Now that he had called out to me, there was no choice but
to cross the road to Mr. Bradshaw's side. I could have kicked
myself for getting off the bus in Top Rock, instead of going
straight to Oistins and the library. Why did I choose to walk
the two miles from Top Rock to the library? I had no answer.
Maybe I was delaying returning home for as long as possible.

"You weren't at the lessons again this morning," Mr.
Bradshaw said. He wasn't as angry as I expected. He looked
physically exhausted and resigned, as if even to talk demanded
too much effort. Obviously, he was out campaigning simply to
give Sandra moral support. From the look on his face and the
unfamiliar low pitch of his voice, it seemed clear he had already given up hope of victory.

"Why haven't you been coming around the house?" Sandra asked, joining us at the side of the road. Beads of sweat
were on her forehead and her hair was bunched on the top of
her head like a ball. She reached into the bag at Mr. Bradshaw's feet and took out another handful of political pamphlets.

"The school work's been keeping you busy?" she continued. I hunched my shoulders. She didn't press for an answer. I glanced down the road, unable to look them in the face.
Sandra was, perhaps unconsciously, holding Mr. Bradshaw's
hand. The four young men out canvassing with Sandra were
standing on the other side of the street. From the dejected
looks on their faces, it was obvious they'd rather be elsewhere.
They must have been accompanying Sandra on orders from
the party headquarters. My eyes lingered on Mr. Bradshaw
and Sandra holding hands so casually in the one part of the

country where this was not supposed to happen. The conversations on the bus returned poignantly to me.

"Are you ready for Monday, Howard?" Mr. Bradshaw finally asked.

"I think so." What else could I have told him? I was sure he didn't want to hear I was not confident of passing. And I didn't want to explain to him why I had stopped attending the lessons. I suspected he already knew.

"Did you have any problems with the homework I've been asking Mr. Allen to give you?" he asked.

"Was it you that . . ." This revelation caught me totally by surprise.

"Yes. When I noticed you weren't coming to the lessons or to the house. Were you getting any help with the homework?"

"My aunt, Pretty. She helped me."

"The good thing for you is that your work has been fairly strong of late. The extra reading helped tremendously. I'm not so worried about the reading and English comprehension part of the test. It's the arithmetic you have to worry about. You're more fortunate than some of the boys who still have to be drilled for both papers. For you, it's mainly the arithmetic. That's your weakness."

I shuffled my feet. Maybe he was preparing me for the inevitable, for certain failure. When the results returned, we could always blame my failure on the arithmetic.

"I think we should run along now," Sandra said. "Look how the rain clouds are building out over the seas. We've still got a lot more houses to hit before calling it a day. Then there's tonight's meeting by the corner shop. We've got to go, Humphry." She unclasped their hands and walked away. The heavy rain clouds had fully blanketed the island in a big shadow.

Mr. Bradshaw was rummaging through the bag with the campaign literature. He stood up with two envelopes in his hand.

"Take these," he said, thrusting one of them at me. He kept the sealed one. "These are two hundred arithmetic problems I prepared for the class this morning. Do as many of them as you can. Give this to your aunt." He handed me the sealed envelope. "The answers are in there. She can check them off for you."

"Thanks," I said, putting the envelopes—I noticed my name on them—in the canvas bag with the library books.

"I was going to drop them off for you later," he explained. "Remember to concentrate on the arithmetic. But also make sure you get a good night's sleep on Sunday; and leave home early the morning of the examination. Don't arrive late and sweaty and have to spend valuable time calming your nerves."

"Thanks, Mr. Bradshaw."

He crossed the street. Sandra was walking up the driveway to another house. I noticed the curtains moved as if the wind had suddenly blown through the closed house. Nobody answered the door. Sandra left her pieces of paper and moved on, with Mr. Bradshaw and the four workers trailing her. Before heading up another walkway, she waved at me. I felt sorry for her. It was obvious Sandra wasn't aware of what the people were saying on the buses, in their houses and under the street lamps. It was clear she didn't realize that we were both headed for defeat and that, whether we liked it or not, England might turn out to be our only escape and refuge.

I lifted the canvas bag over my shoulder and started toward the library, walking away from the canvassers. The bag felt painfully heavy and my feet seemed to be made of lead. The music from Mr. Ward's rally was getting stronger. It had already swept through Top Rock and was headed toward Lodge Road and, ultimately, all of the island.

Two hours later, I was walking up Water Street thinking of what I should tell my parents and Grandmother now that my mind was made up.

Before I saw it, I heard the parade of people dancing and singing as if it were a small carnival, led by a loud bass drum and a piccolo. Hundreds of people were marching up the street with Mr. Toppin, Little Foot, and Herbert Ward in the lead. They were all happy, optimistic, tasting the victory. I hated them for being so happy, for robbing us of our joy and dreams.

Mr. Toppin, so certain of victory, was calling out to people as he passed in front of the homes, reminding them to join Superintendent Cox at his bonfire the next night. "Mrs. Jones, bring along your husband Bertie to the bonfire," he shouted to a woman standing in the front door of a newly painted house, a paint job, like so many on the street, that had been completed in the last week before the poll. "Come and throw a few sticks in the fire and see how things looking for you and Bertie. If the stick burns, then you know you're good and proper. If it doesn't, you'll have to deal with that, the same way that we'll have to deal with this question of whether we want independence or not."

They seemed in a rush to complete the street parade before the threatening clouds building in the east broke. Some young boys were running ahead, handing out pamphlets and enquiring if the residents wanted rides to the polling stations. Pastor Allsop had finally thrown his support behind Mr. Ward publicly and so had Evangelist Cox and Rector Weekes of the Anglican parish church. Everyone of note from the village was there in the parade.

The bass drum pounded nauseously, beating out a steady rhythm. Boom. Boom. Pip-peep! Boom. Boom. Peep-peep! Boom. Boom. Boom. Pee-eee-eeppp. I felt sorry for Sandra and Mr. Bradshaw, for Phillips and all those people that had fought so hard. Contrary to Sandra's optimistic view, I couldn't think of one person in Lodge Road—other than me and Mavis Thorpe—that still supported the independence forces. And I couldn't vote. I could only study hard for the Common Entrance Exam.

When I got home, Grandmother, Pretty and Alma weren't there. They were in the parade but it was so crowded I hadn't seen them. They too had angrily made up their minds on independence, as did many of the people who had been forced to join the march. They had not bothered leaving anything for me to eat before they joined the celebration. By the time they got home, a steady drizzle had started and the firewood in the back yard was soaked.

26

The morning of the election and the Common Entrance Examination broke to bright sunshine, with hardly a cloud in the sky. By eight o'clock in the morning, the sun was beating down fiercely on the land, lapping up the water from two nights and a day of continuous rain that brought virtually everything on the island to a standstill, everything except for the politicians making their final rounds, oblivious of the drenching and laden down surreptitiously with gifts of money and food.

In the bright sunshine, people said little, but went about their business with resoluteness, whether it was to work, or in my case, to the examination, and marvelled at how the dark clouds that blanketed us all weekend had unexpectedly given way at the first crack of dawn. For me it was a good omen that I hadn't pissed my bed.

As I was leaving, Grandmother, Pretty and Alma were getting ready for work. Taking me aside, Grandmother told me to do my best in the examination and to trust in God.

"That is all anybody can ask of you; that you do your best today," she said. "I remembered you in my prayers this morning by asking the Lord above to guide your hand and to give you wisdom and understanding to know what is required of you. So try your best. The Lord will take care of the rest, if it's His will that you should pass."

"Okay." I was at a loss for words. This was the first time she had told me she wanted me to pass. At times, I had had my doubts that she cared, feeling that her sole concern was to reunite me with my parents. But on reflection, I knew she wanted the best for me and that she would always guide me in the right direction. Some day, I hoped to repay her kindness.

"We still haven't heard from the government people about your father. I don't know if he's living or dead, if he's sick or not, or if he's still planning to send for you and your brothers," she said, looking me straight in the face. "I hope so, but," and this was also the first time she expressed such doubts, "—and I ain't saying it is so—but just in case you don't go to England, you got to try and make something of yourself by passing the exam."

Alvin and Chester didn't say anything about the examination. They simply looked at me and told me they would see me later. Their task for the day was to look after Anderson while the women worked. Pretty stood to save twenty-five cents by not sending the baby to the government daycare center. Throughout the day, my brothers' thoughts were with me, as were the hopes and prayers of Pretty and Alma. The entire family was rallying around me. I wanted to ask them not to expect too much, but I couldn't dampen their hopes. They might interpret that as an indication I did not plan to give my best. Of all the people in the world that mattered, only my mother and father did not know how big a day this was for me.

Walking to the school, past the rum shops closed by the government during the actual vote, I reflected on all that had happened since Mr. Bradshaw had come to the school. Because of his kindness to me, I simply had to pass the examination, to show him I was grateful and that his trust wasn't misplaced. Sandra would be happy, too, if I passed. It would be a consolation for them for the pending election defeat and the expected loss of Mr. Bradshaw's job.

When I passed in front of Mr. Bradshaw's house, I found myself looking for Sandra's red Triumph in the driveway. It wasn't there, although I noticed several other cars and a police van. A large group of official-looking men were standing by the side door. I wondered what strategy they were planning for the election and if they would use the vehicles to transport the voters to the polling stations. Standing alone to one side was Mr. Bradshaw. His clothes looked unusually rumpled and his hair was uncombed. He was not talking and he had a faraway look about him. I passed on quickly, waving to him. Mr. Bradshaw didn't seem to recognize me although he was looking in my direction. He didn't wave back.

We took the examination in the small schoolhouse by the plum tree behind the main building. The first exam of the day was arithmetic. It lasted one and a half hours, before a half-hour break for milk and soda biscuits supplied by the Ministry of Education. Nobody was allowed to go home for lunch as everyone had to be back at his desk on time. The first part of the English paper on reading and comprehension was handed out at exactly noon. The essay topics were distributed forty-five minutes later.

Throughout the day, people filed into the main school building to vote. Five minutes later, they came out. The Friday before the election, some men had arrived with buckets of white paint, brushes and measuring tapes. They marked off one hundred yards on both sides of the road from the main entrance to the school and drew two big bold lines across the road. Mr. Bradshaw had explained to the school that on election day people were not to talk or assemble in crowds between the two lines. It would be illegal, he said.

Occasionally, when stuck for a thought or needing inspiration, I looked through the window and saw the people dutifully obeying the law even though the rains had washed away most of the white paint and the earth was still soft from the rains. Those coming in groups stopped talking as soon as they crossed the line and would not resume their conversations until they had once again crossed the lines on the way out. Beyond the line, the conversation looked extremely animated.

On the resumption after lunch, I was feeling happier and more confident about the English paper—even looking forward to it. We had settled into our seats and the invigilator from the Ministry of Education began handing out the final part of the test. Mr. Burton came into the room and motioned to the invigilator. He had about him an air of importance and seriousness. We were all able to hear the conversation. We heard him say: "I'm afraid there's been some real bad news. Mr. Bradshaw won't be coming to the school at all today— Sandra Ward has been found dead in the quarry." He went on to say the police were investigating and that Mr. Ward had confirmed the tragic news.

I immediately went numb. My first reaction was to think Mr. Burton was playing some nasty trick. It simply could not be true. Sandra was still alive. Outside, I could see the voters entering and leaving the school; I could see the Wards' house on the hill, its galvanized tin roof gleaming in the sun. No matter how I tried, I couldn't stop thinking about Sandra. Chills of disbelief ran down my spine and I felt slightly dizzy.

I looked at the list of essay topics and my mind went blank. I remembered the conversation with Sandra and Mr. Bradshaw only two days earlier. I knew that she had always wanted me to write that letter to my parents. And I knew that Sandra wanted me to make the sacrifice to help my Grandmother, the same way she had sacrificed everything to help the poor and unfortunate.

Eventually, I settled on my topic: The Future Is in Our Hands. I didn't know why this appealed to me. It must have been the effect of the scenes from the voting, the sight of the tattered posters on the sides of the school and electrical poles across the street or the sudden news from Mr. Burton. But suddenly, I felt rebellious, just as Alvin must have when he raised his voice at Grandmother and risked being punished for arguing with her over something he believed in so strongly. Like him, I felt I didn't have anything to lose. The time had come for me to stand up and say what I really felt and, if necessary, to suffer the consequences. Unexpectedly, I began writing about independence and putting in my own words the thoughts and dreams of Mr. Bradshaw. I also borrowed heavily from some of Sandra's conversations with me. Then I added my own opinion, about what independence could mean for everybody on the island, and even to those abroad. Suddenly, as if someone had opened a window to a musty room to let in fresh air and bright sunshine, I felt capable of reconciling most of the problems that had torn my insides all this time. The answers were so simple. The words seemed to be flowing out of the tip of my fingers as if my hand was unconnected to my brain, as if I had no control over the limb, except to pause once in a while to wipe the sweat of my hand on my pants. When I was hitting full stride, the invigilator tapped me on my shoulder and asked for the paper.

"Come now, Prescod," she said. "Time's up and you're the last one in the room. Finish the sentence and hand in the paper." I looked around the room and saw it was empty; everybody was gone. In fact, nobody was even waiting on the outside. I had lost trace of all time. I scribbled the good-bye and handed the paper to her, wishing that I had had a chance to re-read and to look for spelling and grammatical errors, as Mr. Bradshaw had always instructed us to. I felt utterly deflated.

I left the room, depressed for choosing such a topic and for not finishing it the way I wanted.

Grandmother was at home when I returned. She must have seen the dejected look on my face.

"How did you do?" she asked.

"I don't know," I said truthfully. The arithmetic paper wasn't as difficult as I expected, although when I reflected on the way home, I thought I had made some stupid mistakes. Each time I thought of an error, my belly dropped. I felt even worse about the English paper and kept replaying in my mind the conversations in the room, how they had affected me and wondering if any of it could be true. As I sat on the rock in the back yard and recalled the exam, I understood how unful-filled Sandra and Mr. Bradshaw must have felt when failure became so obvious—for they were the ones who had worked on implementing this dream and they weren't going to be able to finish it. Now it appeared that because of my poor choice, I had ruined my chances. I thought of Trevor, the little white boy I had met in Top Rock, and wondered how he had fared in this exercise. I fancied his chances better than mine, for I suspected that even if he had chosen the same topic as I, he would have treated it as a straight essay. He wouldn't give one damn about the dream of independence or trying to communi-cate his thoughts with people he didn't even know or who didn't care about him. He would not have run the risk of getting bogged down in trying to write about something he had not fully thought through. He wouldn't have to worry, either, about defending Grandmother. Most of all, he did not have to try to blank pictures of Sandra from his mind.

I didn't bother explaining these details to Grandmother. I wanted to leave her with the impression that I had tried my best, that I had been cautious and took no rash chances.

"That's all we can ask of you, that you gave it your best shot," Grandmother was saying. She, too, seemed resigned to something that she wasn't ready to talk about. "You're hun-gry? I got some corned beef and biscuits waiting there for you. The others eat already."

Then Grandmother destroyed the tenuous hope still alive in my heart. "You heard about Miss Ward." It wasn't really a question, more a statement of fact. Hearing, as she put it, about Sandra meant only one thing. But I still wasn't ready to concede. I stared at her, making sure that I didn't even nod in acknowledgment. I wanted to hear the confirmation from her mouth.

"Poor thing," she said. "They dragged her body out of the quarry up by Ma's house. Somebody saw it floating and called the police. They haven't brought out the car yet. People say they might have to wait until the quarry's drained before lifting it out."

So it was true. This was the confirmation. The tears rolled down my cheeks. Grandmother continued talking.

"You should have seen the people gathered around that quarry. The people are even more divided on this than on independence. One group saying that Phillips and his people murdered Sandra and drove the car into the quarry to get sympathy votes. The DFI supporters say Ward and his people could never forgive Sandra for turning her back on the white people, on her family, and that they had always promised to get even with her. Many of the people don't know who to believe, who to vote for. Everybody on all sides agree about one thing, that the headmaster was involved one way or the other because recently you couldn't see one of them without the other."

"What you think, Grand?"

"I don't know, son," she answered thoughtfully. "There's a lot of talk that on Saturday night Sandra and Bradshaw had a big fight when he told her that she could not defeat her father, that it didn't make sense still going out in the rain to campaign. But she still went ahead. He didn't even report to the police that she was missing when she didn't come back from the campaigning and to me that says a lot."

"Do you think Mr. Bradsh . . ."

"I don't know," she quickly cut me off. "Judgment is mine saith the Lord. All I know is that independence was supposed to bring us together, but it's only driving us apart. It has only destroyed people. There are so many wounds that have to be healed. So many wounds. Even this family has not been spared. But people shouldn't give up hope."

Grandmother went into the kitchen and took a plate of food from under an enamel bowl that served as a cover. My thoughts were flitting back and forth between Sandra and Mr. Bradshaw and the morning scene of the police van and the men at the house. They were obviously detectives, not party officials planning how to get out the vote. No wonder Mr. Bradshaw had looked so distracted.

"But life goes on and the good Lord will reveal his intentions in the fullness of time," Grandmother said. "As the good book says: truth shall set you free. What is done in the dead of night must come to light some day."

"You voted yet?" I asked.

"Uh huh. Pretty's voting now. Alma's gone with her, but she's too young to vote."

"How you voted?" I didn't really care. I simply wanted to keep her talking, to fill the void.

"My business," Grandmother snapped. "You're a real politician now, just like that damn Little Foot asking everybody the same question all the time. All I'll tell you is exactly the same thing I told him: I voted the right way. 'Cause Little Foot, he doesn't know a few cans of corned beef and biscuits delivered in the dead of the night can't swing the head of a hard-back woman like me."

With difficulty, I ate the food she had placed on the table. My appetite was gone. Then I told her my head was hurting and I went to lie down. I was still numb and listless from the news and from thinking so hard and long on the composition. The only escape, albeit temporary, was sleep.

27

By the time we took up Mavis Thorpe's offer to join her listening to the election results, a trend had already been established. Mr. Toppin was among the first to be declared a winner and he made a short victory speech on the steps of Christ Church Boys' Elementary School. Then a noisy motorcade roared up the street, stopping briefly in front of Mr. Bradshaw's house, where Mr. Toppin took a small microphone and addressed his followers through a loudspeaker mounted on the roof of a car. From our homes, we could hear the speech.

"One of the first things that I will see changed is the way we administer and run our schools," he declared to loud applause. "We will not have anyone teaching politics in the classroom anymore. I'm an old-fashioned headmaster and I know how a school should be run. I'll see to that as soon as Mr. Ward tells the governor he is appointing me minister of education in Her Majesty's new government. And the first thing I'll do as minister is to make Mr. Burton the new headmaster of this school."

Within an hour of the polls closing, ten of the twenty-four constituencies were declared with an unmistakable trend. The CLM had won seven, gaining three in the process.

"At least we still have another fourteen to go and they haven't announced any of the seats from around the city," Mavis said. Nobody bothered responding. It would have been impolite to point out the obvious while inside her house.

Mr. Ward was on the radio, tempering his sense of great loss with jubilant talk of what he intended to do when he was sworn in. He was calling it one of the biggest rejections of any government in history. Sensing it was all over, we went home. We could hear the cars driving up and down Lodge Road loudly blowing their horns. "Babsie Bourne doing a licking business, tonight," Grandmother said. The celebration seemed to be centered on his shop. Some of the voices were coming across clearly on the brisk night winds. It seemed the majority of people in Lodge Road had received their wish with the fall of the government and the vote for the true and tried system.

Just as Grandmother told me to turn down the wick in the lamp in preparation for us to turn in, Mavis flung open her window and bellowed. "He did it; he just did it!"

"Did what?" Grandmother asked, not bothering to open her window. Chester stood rigid in the center of the house. He held suspended in the air one of the crocus bags he was spreading as the lining for our bed. Alvin and Alma exchanged glances.

"He just won the last constituency." Mavis was beside herself with joy. I did not believe that she, of all people, could change her mood so drastically and quickly and that she could be so happy over Mr. Ward's victory. "He's now saying on the radio that next week he's going to London to ask the Queen to hand over something he called sovereignty. You don't hear they ain't celebrating up by Babsie Bourne's shop no more?"

We were baffled, but not for long. Gradually, it sunk in. Phillips had won the election fourteen seats to Ward's ten. Mavis was right. The winds had gone quiet; no longer were the loud screams and singing coming to us from the rum shop. The calm of the night was quite noticeable. Even the crickets in the grass had ceased to chirp. Chester spread the bag on the floor. Then suddenly, we could hear the voices. Louder and stronger, as if someone had simply changed a record on a gramophone. Cars were parading on the main road. Neighbors who had been quiet all evening flung open their front windows and started to confess that deep in their hearts they never once doubted Phillips would pull off the victory.

"I knew he would win," Mavis was saying. "I knew because he got the women and the young people in town behind him. But it was the women of this island. They know things just got to change for the better, that we can't go on like this forever."

As if with one mind, Pretty, Alma, Alvin and Chester bolted through the door and disappeared into the darkness, headed for Babsie Bourne's shop and the real celebration. I scrambled after them but Grandmother was in the way.

"Not you," she commanded. "You stay right here."

"But they're going . . ."

"You stay in this house. Tomorrow, I still have to show up for Mr. Ward's work. I just hope Pretty and Alma remember that too, particularly Pretty. I mean, just look at how she ran out of here without even looking back at her child. What can you say to the young people of this world?"

I finished making the bed. By the time I fell off to sleep, the women had not yet talked themselves out and the others had not returned home to tell what had happened.

There was no celebrating in our house the day after the election even though the re-elected government declared it a public holiday and kept the schools closed for the rest of the week. Early on Tuesday morning, Mr. Ward sent word that the make-work program by the vestry had been terminated. No reasons were given—none were needed.

Grandmother was back to square one, without a paycheck of any kind. The question of finding work—and of hearing from the chief welfare officer—became more of an immediate concern.

Without us, the celebration continued for several more days. In the fuss, nobody seemed to remember Sandra or care about the Common Entrance Examination. Mr. Bradshaw dropped out of sight, except for his headmaster's duties. As the police had difficulty reconstructing the final moments of

Sandra Ward's life, he was never charged with anything, but neither was he absolved of suspicion. The only person who might have known what happened was Ma, but she steadfastly refused to discuss the matter with anyone, even when she was drunk.

Gradually, life around us returned to normal. People went about their lives as usual. Soon the only signs of the bitter election campaign were the tattered pieces of the posters still clinging to the roadside poles. The difference was that independence was now inevitable and at school we started to learn a new national anthem and motto, to copy a new flag and coat of arms, and to wait for the results of the screening test.

Every evening in the time between the election and the end of the school term, Grandmother watched the postman passing through the village without even pausing in front of our house. Every time, her hopes fell further. The burden of being the sole provider was making her tense and had led to painful shouting matches with her daughters. Alma often resorted to tears. One night when she could take it no more, she simply packed a few clothes in a plastic bag and walked out of the house. None of us had seen her since her departure. Grandmother talked about her younger daughter every night. But talking did not ease the pain of not knowing where she was sleeping.

"I feel like it's me alone against the world," she said one evening when the two of us were at home. Pretty had left home early in the morning in search of work and, although it was getting late, had not yet come back. Grandmother hoped that when she returned she would not only have news about a job but that at least that she had run across Alma. She suspected that Alma and Pretty communicated but that they kept her out of the picture. That provided Grandmother with the slim hope that if something really bad had happened to Alma, Pretty would forget their differences and tell her. As usual,

Alvin and Chester were under the street lamp with the men, their way of avoiding the pressures in the house. I had thought of joining them but decided to stay at home and keep Grand-mother company.

"It's me alone battling against the world," she said as she sat in the dark back yard with millions of stars twinkling far above her head, "without a mother or father to run to for help, not even a friend, a pastor or elder in the church to commiserate with. Alone in this big universe."

Grandmother had fallen back to talking to me on evenings but this time there was a difference in the tone of her voice and the frankness. For a while, I took this as a sign she thought I was big enough to help her shoulder the family problems, but it also occurred to me that usually I was the only one around to listen and she just had to talk to somebody.

I could understand why relations in the house became so testy that Alma had to flee and why our family was unraveling. Pretty was having her own problems. Every discussion with Grandmother ended with Pretty promising to get her own house as soon as she found a job. Anderson had begun creep-ing and was proving too much for his mother. Someone had to be watching him all the time. Pretty could not be looking for work and at the same time keeping a watch over Anderson. Instead, she spent most of her time sleeping, to blank her mind to the fact that after six months Henry had not written. Neither had she heard from the company that took him over-seas.

Pretty and, more so, Grandmother also knew these facts had not escaped the women of the village. Continuously, when the women walked in front of the house, their voices rose automatically and the women could be heard joking about how the man with the motor car blew her up and then went overseas, never to look back. Mavis Thorpe was no exception and, having turned against us one more time, was also "dropping remarks" at Pretty.

Grandmother knew how her daughter was feeling and she

suffered with her too. Unable to even talk to Pretty, she ended up unburdening herself to me in long monologues broken by periods of silence and thought and mumbling to herself.

"If I raise my voice a little too often, it's only to get rid of the frustration," she explained from her usual position in front of the fire. "It's only to get her to do something, anything to keep her mind occupied. It's not because I want anybody to just pick up themselves and leave and not even sending one word where you can reach them. That's not what I want. How do you think I feel as a mother going to sleep every night that God sends and not knowing where my last child is, not knowing who is feeding her or if some worthless man is taking advantage of her?"

Grandmother wanted Pretty out of the house working, so she would not have time to reflect on the gossip or on what Henry might or might not do. "If her mind was occupied, she wouldn't have time for idle talk and speculation, she'd be too tired to think," Grandmother reasoned.

In addition, there were the daily problems of scraping together enough money to buy food. "I alone am responsible for every bit of food that passes through the house. That was why I had to go back to buying the damn stale bread, and the bakery has the guts to increase the price," she said. To raise a few more dollars, she had taken to washing and ironing clothes for the white people in Top Rock. When everyone had gone to sleep, she would still be ironing the clothes, with the irons heating on the coal pot.

When she awoke in the morning, she was as tired as when she fell into bed. Her eyes were always red and her face drawn. More of her hair was turning white.

As soon as she was up, she would begin working, as if taking her own advice that this was the cure for thinking. She would neatly fold and pack in large bamboo baskets the clothes she had ironed the night before. I delivered them and collected the money and the new bundle. Then I went to the shop and bought groceries from a list Grandmother had made for me. At no time could we buy everything on the list, so it fell on me to juggle the items and to make sure we never ran out of the essentials. In a literal sense, I was responsible for bringing the food into the house.

Although I wanted to do more, the reality was that I could only be available to listen to Grandmother and to occasionally read the Bible for her. I knew Grandmother needed me, so I didn't mind when she again prohibited me from going to Mr. Bradshaw's house. This time it wasn't because she was afraid of what people might say; it was because she needed someone for conversation.

28

Mr. Bradshaw dragged himself onto the platform like a man carrying a heavy weight. This was one of the few times we had seen him in the six weeks since Sandra's death. He always looked somber and lethargic. In fact, we had wondered if he would show up for this assembly on the last day of the school year.

The headmaster seemed sapped of energy, uncertain and insecure. As he stiffly walked across the platform, he bowed his head in silent acknowledgment to Mr. Ward; his predecessor and the new parliamentarian, Mr. Toppin; his rector, Reverend Weekes of the Christ Church parish church; and finally to the Englishman, the educational officer, who was retiring.

This was the day when Mr. Bradshaw, like so many of us, was to be judged for his efforts. This was the day when we would hear if any of us had passed the Common Entrance Examination, if his gamble to personally tutor us, to change the school's teaching methods, had paid off. Undoubtedly, his actions would be closely watched and his remarks examined for any hint of responsibility for Sandra's death. The gossip remained just as strong.

Only moments earlier, the educational officer had handed him the envelope with the results of the examinations. Mr. Bradshaw took a brief look at the sheets of paper. A smile flashed over his face but was quickly replaced by the now familiar mask he wore. I didn't know what to make of the smile; it was like nothing I had seen.

Mr. Bradshaw's main job was to read aloud the names of

the successful boys, the last act before dismissing the school for eight weeks of vacation. According to the school clock above his head, he had only ten minutes for this task if he were to dismiss us promptly at three o'clock. That wasn't much time at all—perhaps the clearest sign that there were few successes. I sat on the bench beside Ollie and prayed that my name was on the list, or that if it wasn't that God would be kind enough to keep Theo and Ollie off as well.

"Good afternoon, boys," Mr. Bradshaw said. His voice boomed through the crowded and hot hall, reverberated off the rafters in the ceiling. Mr. Bradshaw stepped back from the edge of the platform and unintentionally positioned himself under the big red, white and blue Union Jack. Between him and the flag were the pictures of Her Majesty Queen Elizabeth and her husband Philip, the one with the nose so pointed that Grandmother said it could pick chigoes from your feet. All eyes were focused on the short headmaster, standing with the tip of the listless flag a foot above his head.

I thought of the fight Ollie and I had had in the schoolyard over the nasty things people were still whispering about Mr. Bradshaw and Sandra. I had not been able to let these things go unchallenged, even though I could not disprove them. I felt I had to defend Mr. Bradshaw and Sandra. I owed them that much. So I had challenged Ollie to a fight, a daring move that surprised even me. Mr. Allen separated us, and under his breath Ollie promised that after school and in the days to come, we would pick up where we left off. I didn't care about that. I was so angry I didn't cry either, something that appeared to surprise Mr. Allen as much as it did me and the boys in the line. Deep in my heart, I suspected Ollie was telling the truth. The absence of Mr. Bradshaw from the school had only fed the rumors.

"Good afternoon, sir," we bellowed in unison.

With a nod of his head, Mr. Bradshaw signaled Mr. Burton, the deputy headmaster, to start the ceremony. The elder teacher rose slowly from his chair and walked up the four steps to the raised platform. At the same time, he took the tuning fork from his breast pocket and listlessly slapped it in the palm of his hand. Mr. Burton stopped in front of the headmaster, whom he had hoped so dearly to replace, whom he had fought so furiously in the classroom, in the staff quarters, in private meetings and on political platforms. And he had lost every fight, except—for as far as we knew—the one on the Common Entrance Examination.

They exchanged words, not loud enough for the rest of us to hear, and smiled politely. The music master searched his pockets frantically. Unexpectedly, the small thin strap fell from his breast pocket and, grinning sheepishly, he stooped to pick it up, recoiled it and put it in his jacket pocket. There he found the small music book he was looking for, the much thumbed leather black book he had used for two decades.

The symbols of the strap and the music book must have had some effect on him, for when he spoke his voice was softer and sadder, almost as if he were defeated and too tired to fight anymore.

"Shall we stand and sing 'The Day Thou Gaveth Lord Is Ended.' " He banged the tuning fork on the side of the chair and held it to his ear. He didn't repeat the scale as he usually did. There wasn't the usual doh-doh-doh, each an octave higher, until he found the right range and pitch. "On the count of three: one, two, three."

"The day thou gaveth, Lord, is ended
Darkness falls . . ."

When the hymn was finished, Mr. Bradshaw invited the rector to say a short prayer. He asked the Lord to bless us and to let our lives be shining lights as we went from this place. Blessings were invoked on our political leaders as well.

"Amen," we responded.

When the prayer had finished, I opened my eyes to see Ollie looking at me. I scowled just to show him that no prayer was going to make me forgive him that easily. He shook his fist at me, his hand not leaving his side, and I sucked my teeth so loud and long that the sound carried through most of the room. The teachers must have heard it; they all looked our way, searching for the cause. Ollie, seeing their eyes focused in our direction, dropped his fist and stood erect, pretending he didn't know what had happened. I laughed to myself. He had blinked first. He wasn't as tough as I thought.

The retiring education officer, the old Englishman in the short white pants, gave one of his briefest speeches. There was no joy in his words. He said he was resigning to give someone else, possibly a national, a chance. He had enjoyed his work and he wished us all well in the future. Then he sat down and remained silent, almost transfixed to the spot, for the rest of the ceremony.

From the tension among the dignitaries, it was obvious something was wrong. Even Mr. Ward and Mr. Toppin didn't have much to say. They congratulated the boys for working hard for another year. "Finally, I would like to say well done to all those deserving boys who have passed this year's Common Entrance Examination," Mr. Ward said. "Well done and keep up the good work when you move on to a higher place of learning."

This was the first hint there had been some successes. At these words, there was a rustling as if a great breath had been released. My heart started racing. But why did Mr. Bradshaw look so serious? Then the thought hit me—he was sad because I had failed. Now it was a question of who the lucky boys were. I hoped for the sake of Mr. Bradshaw and Grandmother that my name was on the list. Putting my hand in the desk so nobody would see, I crossed my fingers and wished for the best or for instant death.

Mr. Bradshaw was back at center stage. Now, he was smiling broadly, his white teeth gleaming in his black face. "You may sit," he said. I could see the flap of the envelope was open. He waited until we sat and were quiet. Three o'clock had come and gone.

"This has been a fantastic year for all of us. For the teachers, for the government that spends millions of dollars every year educating our children, for the board of governors of the school that is represented here today by Mr. Ward, Mr. Toppin, our education officer, the rector, and, of course," he paused, throwing his hands out like one of the fishermen in Oistins casting a net, "you, the students. Each and every one of you sitting out there. I am very, very proud of you all." He looked up at the clock.

"This year," he said, bending over and picking up a brown envelope from a chair, "we had one hundred and sixty boys sitting the Common Entrance Examination." He opened the envelope and took out several sheets of paper. "In my hand are the names of all those boys that have done us proud," he said, flapping the sheets in the air, above his head. "The ninety boys that have done us proud by passing outright."

There was a loud sigh in the room. We looked at one another and smiled. Ninety! Unbelievable. The teachers, sitting in the front row, smiled at one another too, exchanged a few words, and then turned to look at the boys behind them. "We have never had an achievement like this. That is why I have had a special graduation certificate drawn up to present to each of the boys that has done us proud."

"Hear, hear," Mr. Ward interrupted, getting to his feet. "I think that deserves a special round of applause."

Mr. Toppin looked at him in disbelief, but stiltedly joined the clapping. Mr. Ward sat down, ignoring his political colleague.

"What's more, I have a very special announcement to make about these examination results and about what the government feels about one performance in particular. I will get back to that later, but I want you to bear that in mind as I call out the names of those students that passed. Now, as I call out your names, would each of you file out and receive your certificates from Mr. Ward. Adams Mark," he started, pausing a moment between the names, "Anderson Sylvester, Austin Frank, Austin Henry . . ."

The names continued to roll off his tongue, each time warming the heart of some boy and, in a few minutes, his parents. When they heard their names the boys jumped up, smiled at the rest of the class, pushed their shirt tails into their pants and almost ran to the platform. The rest of us waited patiently, biding our time, hoping our names would be on the list. I closed my eyes and silently prayed once again to God that I would be on the list. For all practical purposes, we had forgotten Mr. Bradshaw's statement about a special announcement, which we expected to be no more than maybe an extra week's vacation to mark independence. Passing was the only thing that mattered.

The numbers were thinning out and I kept my eyes shut. As Mr. Bradshaw got closer to the P's, I virtually stopped breathing. Ollie was already standing in the line with his certificate. "O'Neal James, Pinder John, Pine Albert, Raines Gerry, Reid Thomas, Thorpe Theo . . ."

I almost fainted. He had skipped my name. There was no Prescod. How could Mr. Bradshaw do this to me: skip over my name without even a momentary pause to indicate his disappointment, or to question if there had been a typing error? I tried not to turn my head, but from the corner of my eye, I could see Alvin and Chester with their heads bowed. The disappointment wasn't mine alone. Everybody realized what had happened and through half-opened eyes I could see Theo looking directly at me, smiling, daring me to find some way to join him on the platform. What would Grandmother say? Did she really mean it when she said that trying my best was good enough, especially now that Mavis Thorpe's son had passed?

"Those boys that didn't pass shouldn't feel left out," Mr. Bradshaw said, having come to the end of the list and giving what I felt was the usual empty platitudes reserved for those who were too stupid to pass a simple examination. What he was saying only made me feel worse; the professed kindness felt like salt being poured into a wound by a misguided person thinking it would ease the pain. Then he made what we thought was the government announcement he had promised.

"This year, for the first time, the government is awarding bursaries to those boys across this island of ours who showed promise in the examination, but just failed to make the grade. With these bursaries, they will be able to go to any of the independent secondary schools that the government doesn't run itself and the ministry will pay their fees. This is the ministry's way of marking our attainment of independence in four months' time." Mr. Ward seemed surprised at this news. He glanced quickly at Mr. Toppin and finally led a short applause, perhaps indicating his approval of this gesture.

"Will the following boys please come and collect the letters for their parents or guardians as I call their names," Mr. Bradshaw said. "Allan Errol, Andrews Dennis . . ."

By the time he finished, I was the only one sitting in the four Class Threes. The one hundred and fifty-nine boys were lined up in front of the platform and had spilled into the aisles, forcing the teachers to give ground and to eventually sit in the vacated area left by the boys. Everybody was looking at me. I wished God would open the earth and let it swallow me. Better yet, I wished I had the strength of Samson so I could pull down this cursed place, so that I would get killed and I wouldn't have to go home and face Grandmother.

"This has been an outstanding achievement by our school," Mr. Bradshaw was saying, reveling in his victory, not even sparing a thought for me. I wondered if he would have done this to me if Sandra were still alive. "I don't think there is another school on this island that can boast a record like this. Just look at them. I present to you a crop of fine young men that someday might produce the leaders of our fragile young country. Give them a hand."

He spread his hands over the students. Pride was bursting his chest.

"But there's more good news. I said earlier that I had a special announcement to make," he said, returning to the brown envelope. "Right here at Christ Church Boys' we have produced the top student of the examination. The top student," he repeated slowly for emphasis, "in both the boys and girls. One of our boys has written such an outstanding composition that it is being read in every school across this island today. This same student scored nine hundred and eighty marks out of one thousand to be the top student. I will now call on him to read his essay for us."

I was scarcely listening to what Mr. Bradshaw was saying. I was too busy reviewing in my mind the reasons for my failure. It had to be the arithmetic that had caused my downfall, although it seemed the English paper was harder than I thought. And if Sandra had not died, if the news had not broken just before the test, I would have spent more time writing instead of thinking about Sandra and I would have chosen an easier topic. The tears were rolling down my cheeks. It was worse than the beating from Ollie.

"Howard Prescod," Mr. Bradshaw shouted. "Come up here and read your composition, my son."

I did not move. It did not sink into my brain. I sat numb, unable to move. I heard someone calling my name but I wasn't sure whether it was the boys already taunting me or my mind playing tricks.

"Howard." The headmaster recovered that informality that we used to lapse into in earlier times, particularly before his reticence since Sandra's death. My feet refused to move, I was paralysed, stuck to the bench. Through the tears, I saw Mr. Allen approaching me. He put an arm around me and softly whispered, "Come, big boy, you come along. See what I told you about working hard. See what I told you, man. Straight to Harrison College for you."

He was beside himself with excitement. I leaned on him and he led me slowly to the platform, up the four steps. Mr. Burton was smiling; I was crying. Mr. Ward, Mr. Toppin, the rector and the education officer were standing waiting for me. Alvin and Chester were clapping their hands and hugging each other. The boys close by were talking to them and laughing. I thought of Grandmother and how she won't have to worry too much about facing Mavis Thorpe, about Pastor Allsop having read her out of the church. Maybe the news would reach my father in England and he'd write.

Mr. Bradshaw held out a hand and helped me to the platform. My legs buckled, and he held me, with a strong firm hand, so that hardly anyone noticed. The school erupted in applause. When the essay was handed to me, my hands were shaking so badly that the leaves slipped through my fingers, fluttering down from the platform on a draft of air to land—of all places—at Ollie's feet. He bent over, gathered them up and handed them to me. As I took them, he held the papers for a moment and smiled. We smiled together, as friends.

I started to read, the voice coming from somewhere else: "Dear Mum and Dad, How are you? I have been trying to write this letter for the longest time but I couldn't bring myself to put pen to paper. Something has been bothering me for the longest time. . . ."

I found myself racing through the letter so I slowed my pace. I was at the point where I was telling my parents how I had reconciled the difficult problem facing so many young Bajans who wanted to be with their parents living overseas but who still wanted to be part of the independence experiment.

The room was silent and I felt my words were falling on deaf ears. There wasn't even a murmur, nobody shuffled his feet and none of the words came back empty to me.

"Making my decision has not been easy, but I have spent a lot of time just thinking about it and I think I have the solution," I continued. Then for my reasons, I paraphrased Sandra's speeches and the reasons she gave for returning home and why she felt more expatriates should follow her example.

My voice was stronger. No longer was I crying. The mention of Sandra's name had caused my voice to break temporarily, but I quickly regained my composure. I looked at Mr. Bradshaw and he was smiling. He nodded so imperceptibly that only I noticed. I was coming to the point where the invigilator had interrupted.

"Come home and join us. It would solve the problem for me of having my cake and eating it too; or being with you and still being at home," I had scribbled quickly.

Everyone applauded again and the dignitaries on the platform nodded. I folded the sheets of paper and put them in my pocket.

After the reading, we sang "God Save Our Gracious Queen" for the last time. The next time there was a school gathering, the national anthem would be "In Plenty and In Time of Need," the words of which we were learning in time for Independence Day. But all of us were so emotionally drained, there was no spirit in the singing, just the ritual. I was walking on air as we left the school.

"I'm glad you feel that strongly about my daughter," Mr. Ward said as I stepped off the platform. I looked into his eyes and could see the loss was genuine. "It's a good letter, too."

"Thank you, sir."

"Howard," Mr. Bradshaw said, coming over to join us. "You have to give back the essay; we need the original for the school's records." Mr. Bradshaw and Mr. Ward were finally face to face for the first time since Sandra's death.

"Congratulations, Mr. Bradshaw," the politician said.

"Thank you, Mr. Ward."

An awkward silence followed.

"I heard the premier has asked you to reconsider your decision to resign?" This was the first time I was hearing this. Not even the rumor mills had picked up on any resignation.

"He has. . . ."

"And . . . ?"

"And my mind is unchanged."

"I wish you wouldn't," Mr. Ward said. "The school needs you. You have proven you can produce results."

"That's flattering, but they'll get by without me. I am satisfied that this school, this island, is firmly on a road to change. There's no choice but to continue unless we want to be out of step with the rest of world." He was talking calmly, but forcefully, with no hint of animosity. "I mean, we only have to look around the world at what's happening in Africa; in America where Martin Luther King is organizing and people are rising up for their rights; in other Caribbean islands around us. The winds of change are blowing."

"What are you going to do?" Mr. Ward asked.

Mr. Bradshaw hunched his shoulders. "Certainly not go back to England. Not after this letter." They looked at me and laughed. The two men shook hands.

Mr. Bradshaw walked out of the school into the sunshine, with me trailing him.

29

When we told her the news, Grandmother looked dismayed, as if we had caught her at the wrong time and in some illegal act. Her frightened eyes flitted from Alvin's face, to Chester's, to mine, as if we had given her the first words about some dreadful plague sweeping the island. Seldom had I seen Grandmother so dumfounded.

Unconsciously, she put her hands behind her back and with some difficulty finally produced a smile—a quick pull at the corners of her mouth that was gone from her strained face as quickly as a drop of water on the parched earth.

"So you did pass," she said, her eyes rolling in her head and finally settling on the tree beside the house. "The top student, eh? That's good. Real good. I guess we should all give to the Lord the thanks and the glory." Enthusiasm was distinctly lacking from her words, as if her thoughts were somewhere else and could only be expressed in monotones.

"And when Mr. Bradshaw asked Howard to come up on the platform and read his essay," Alvin was saying, looking closely for signs of a true response from Grandmother, "the whole school started clapping, loud, loud, loud. Like thunder itself. You should've been there to hear it, Grand."

"Thunder, eh?" she said, moving away from us and over to the rocks in the corner of the yard, where we had found her with the washing under the trees. "Thunder, eh? That's good. Real good."

With an effort, she leaned over the half-barrel that served as a washing tub and picked up a white dress soaking in the soapy water. Her long black fingers wrapped around the cloth and with great strength she rubbed the soiled piece of clothing against the jucking-board. Both the board and the tub were as old as me, Grandmother had said several times. My father, just before he left, had brought home the old wooden molasses barrel and sawed it in half. On opposite sides he had left pieces of the barrel for lifting, protrusions that were also used as a prop for the serrated jucking-board against which she rubbed the clothes. This board, too, was made by my father. In a slab of pine, he had chiseled the rivets and rough ridges, some of which were quite smooth now from the friction.

The tub and the jucking-board were the inseparable parts of the washing ritual. Grandmother took an end of the off-white dress and spread it on the jucking-board. Then she fished the cake of blue Bomber soap out of the water with her free hand and rubbed it against the dress on the board. No matter how hard she tried, the soap would not produce a lather, only a bleachy smell and a white oily film on the water and around the board. From the constant bending and splashing, there was a wet patch on the front of her dress.

"I don't know what this means," Grandmother resumed, still focusing on the washing. As yet, she had not looked me straight in the eyes. "Your passing the examination like that, I don't know what it means. I had this plan all worked out in my head, how the three of you were going to help us get some food when the day comes. Now, I don't know what all this means."

She paused for a moment, apparently reviewing her options.

"Just before the three of you came through the gate, Basil, the postman, dropped by this afternoon with a special letter, special delivery he said, from the chief welfare officer. My heart started such a pounding in my chest that I almost ripped up the letter on the inside trying to tear open the envelope. Maybe I should've. The same old thing all over. Nobody can tell where your mother and father're living. Even the government can't find them. Like they just disappeared off the face of God's earth. And now, you passed the screening test. The top student."

The three of us looked at her. We knew how much she was hoping that the British government would find our father. Apart from wanting us to join him, she wanted to know about his welfare, if he was still alive, so she could stop worrying about him too.

She gave the dress a half-hearted rub. "With the letter, all my hopes just collapsed. As I stand here washing these clothes, my back aching from all this bending and jucking on this damn board, I keep thinking of a way to tell the three of you boys what I was thinking. That the three of you'll have to start helping out, by looking for jobs. That I can't keep on doing this washing no more, the money ain't worth the effort, and when it comes it doesn't go far enough. Now, you come home and tell me you've passed the exam. The brightest boy. I don't know what that means to things anymore."

"It means Howard'll grow up to be a big-time lawyer or doctor," Chester said. "Mr. Allen said so when we were leaving school. I heard him say Howard could now do anything he wants; that in all his born days he's never seen one boy learn so much in such a short time."

"I don't mean it that way when I say I don't know what all this means," Grandmother replied, still talking in a soft voice, slowly and unrushed. She continued to concentrate on the water, on the meager suds swirling around her fingers. "What I mean is, who'll send him to school when the school doors open in a couple of months? Going to high school takes a lot of money: books, uniform, shoes for his feet, bus fare, lunch money, all them things got to be provided for. You need more than brains to do well in high school. You need to have a good breakfast in your stomach every morning and along with the books you need a good lunch in your school bag every day. And you need somewhere proper to rest your head at night in case you have to bring home one of your high-falutin friends. I don't know. Thing's real tough 'round here."

She turned away from the tub and inspected her fingers, looking at them cautiously. They were sore from the rubbing and the palms were white and withered from the constant soaking in the water. It was understandable she wanted to give up the washing. "I can't do no more than I'm already doing right now," she said thoughtfully, still examining her fingers. "The Lord knows that I would like to do more. But the truth is, I'm tired, real tired, weary to death. At the same time I just can't stop to rest, not even if I wanted to. I got to press on 'til deliverance come. But I'm getting old, I ain't the young yam I used to be."

She wiped her sore hands in her dress, near the spot that was wet from the splashing. Then, as soon as she had dried them, she submerged them into the water again, defeating the purpose of drying them.

"I would like to help you, Howard, the Lord knows, 'cause he's the only one I can cry out to. I would like to help you, not only you, but Alvin and Chester standing there. They need help too. But we got to get food to eat when the day comes; and then I got Pretty on my hands. And Alma . . . I just wish somebody would tell me where that little girl is."

Feeling thoroughly deflated, we stood in silence watching her wash. Taking the white shirts and underwear, which she had painstakingly separated from the coloreds, she rubbed them with her hands in the water, wrung out the excess water and dumped the clothes in a large bucket. Later, she would rinse the clothes in fresh water.

Grandmother looked at her hands again and flexed the fingers. They were paining her with what she said might be the first signs of arthritis or rheumatism. She believed she had caught a cold in them, from alternating between the hot coal pot and ironing at nights and the washing in the day. By rubbing her hands in the dress, she hoped to put some heat in them, to ease the nagging dull pain.

"I don't know," she said. "We's all the family we got and we'll survive somehow; but we got to pull together, help one another during the really rough spots. It ain't going to be like this always. But as to your passing . . . I don't know. I really don't know."

On her face was concern such as I had never seen. She must have wrestled with this problem for some time, perhaps feeling guilty for wishing I would fail the examination so she wouldn't have to make so painful a decision, but still wondering if it was fair to deny me the chance at a new life.

"I just don't feel that I got the energy to fight any more battles. I just can't," she said, pushing down with all her strength on the piece of cloth.

Alvin and Chester walked away in silence, as deflated as I. I remained standing near her. Tupper came from under the cellar and rubbed his head against my shin.

"Maybe your father will write soon," she said with no confidence in her voice, but grasping at the last possible straw. "He might remember he got three growing children here. Even if he doesn't send for the three of you, he might still decide to support you."

She paused for a moment and thought for a while, going through the motions at the tub almost mechanically. "Maybe Henry'll write soon too."

She bent over the tub and swirled the water with her hand, looking for another piece of cloth.

"Miss Howell, Miss Howell," a voice from behind the paling called. "Hold on to that damn dog of yours and don't let him bite me, you hear."

"Who's that?" Grandmother asked, drying her hands on her apron.

"It's me. Ma," the voice said. Ma came through the gate. She walked in, firm and sober, as if she was a regular friend. She had presumptuously cut through all the formalities and was standing inside the yard.

"Well, well, Ma," Grandmother said. "What brings you here? I mean . . ."

"Ah, mean what?" Ma said. "Who you think you talking

to? I know you when you was a child, before you had these boys' father and the two girls and I always know that you're a trier. I was walking down the road and I heard all the people talking about what a great job you've done with these three boys. No father to look after them, only you alone, just like me when I was raising my two girls, and you never once had to resort to a drink like me. Now you have here in this yard the brightest boy in all this damn land, and you should be proud of yourself. You prove that a woman can do it even if there's no man in the house; you once again proved what all women throughout these West Indies have been doing since Adam was a lad, that a woman can be a father too. You will find a way out. Women always find a way, we know how to cut the corners, we will be the ones to take the lead building this country."

Grandmother was at a loss for words. She stood over the washing unconsciously wringing her hands. I could not look at her face for the conflicting emotions etched on it. Nobody had ever said such warm words to her, had bothered to lavish such badly needed praise on her. It had to fall to Ma, the least expected person on the island. As she listened, Grandmother blew her nose in the wet apron.

"And you never took a drop o' grog. I don't know how you do it. Anyway, I'm on my way to Babsie Bourne's shop and, as an old woman nearing the grave, I'll fire back a drink or two to celebrate for your grandson. That's my blessing to him. I'll even fire down an extra grog for you, too, Miss Howell."

Then she was gone, through the paling door. We stood listening to the departing footsteps and the sound of the trailing cane. We had never seen Ma that sober and in such a mood. With her looking so approachable, I wanted to run after her and ask if she knew what had happened the night Sandra died, if she had heard or seen anything. I rushed through the gate with Tupper bounding after me.

Then I stopped. What difference would it make to find out about Sandra's last moments? Why shouldn't I just be as happy with the memories and the inspiration she had given me?

Tupper ran ahead of me. Ma must have heard the dog or expected me to come running after her. She stopped and waited until I caught up. "Miss Ward would be very proud of you, as if you were her son. She talked so much about you. She was so confident you'd pass." I waited for her to continue but she brusquely turned and moved on. Tupper rushed forward and rubbed his head against her leg, as if she were an old friend. She looked down at the dog.

"I had to nurse him back to health after you almost kill him; he doesn't look too bad now. I saw everything you did that evening by the well." She gave me a sharp look. "But we won't talk about that. Today is your day for celebrating. And when today is gone, and everything is back to normal, if you don't tell anybody about what happened by the well, I won't either." She walked away, dragging the stick.

I watched her heading down the road. Ma, of all people, was proud of me. If she was typical, I knew I would have a long summer vacation, maybe a lifetime, adjusting to the expectations of others. It was a frightening prospect.

"Ma home?" a familiar voice said from behind

I turned around. Alma was standing in front of me. She looked thin and taller. Her hair was cut short, like a boy's. In her hands were two bags.

"Yeah. She's waiting for you," I said.

"But she'd be mad and she'll start quarreling and shouting again and we'll end up fighting. I don't know if I should. . . ."

"Come," I said, taking one of the bags from her hand. "I'll take you home. Leave it up to me."

She followed me, still hesitant.

"I was hoping to meet Pretty so she can . . ."

"Pretty's taken Anderson to the clinic for his vaccine," I said. "But this will be the best news we can give Grandmother. She'll be happy to see you. Just don't say anything to her. Just let me explain everything."

We walked into the yard and Alma went quickly into the

house. Grandmother looked at her and then at me. We smiled. There was nothing to say. I turned around and headed back through the gate with Tupper at my side. It was time to start my vacation; time for Tupper and me to be alone, away from everybody.

Tupper and I headed down the road contented to enjoy the triumphs of this day and to worry about tomorrow, and possibly finding a job, another time.

ABOUT THE AUTHOR

Cecil Foster emigrated to Canada from Barbados in 1979. He is Senior Editor at *The Financial Post* and lives in Toronto with his wife and two sons.